Praise for Villimey Mist'

"In many ways, the new w
and we often mourn the lo
Mist's stories will make you reconsider. In her world, the
dangers of myth are all too real. Gods seek vengeance,
mythical beasts roil beneath the waves, and the undead
stalk the living. But the real threat lies in a parent's
desperation, a brother's mocking, a friend's betrayal.
This is a fascinating, unsettling selection of horrors."

—Brandon Applegate, author of
Those We Left Behind and Other Sacrifices

"Villimey must be magic. That's the only plausible
explanation. How else is it possible to produce such
varied short-form genre fiction covering so many
themes, each executed vividly and so well? From
Icelandic lore to mythical beasts, found footage to human
monsters, interwoven with a whole heap of revenge, this
collection will not only fuel your nightmares but also put
Villimey firmly on the map. As the Night Devours Us
delivers punch after punch and Villimey absolutely
(finger) nails it. "

—Janine Pipe, author of
Sausages: The Making of Dog Soldiers

AS THE NIGHT DEVOURS US

VILLIMEY MIST

Cover Design by Matt Wildasin
Interior Design and formatting by Platform House

Table of Contents

To my parents, Siggi and Silja,
For keeping a light in the dark when I explored
the shadows

AN INTRODUCTION:

THE DAUGHTER OF THE
MIDNIGHT SUN

In the frigid waters of the North Atlantic, just shy of the Arctic Circle, six-hundred miles west of Norway, there is an island. Barren, glaciated, volcanic, covered in waterfalls, cirques, and fjords, it lies at a point where the distant Viking age and the ultra-modern digital era meet, and has evolved into that rarest of things, unique unto itself, part of the Western World but a shade darker and glorious for it.

This is Iceland.

To the average couch potato tourist whose only familiarity with Iceland is through travel documentaries and random Google factoids (Hey! Did you know Icelanders drink more Coca-Cola *per capita* than any country on earth?), it is a quirky, enigmatic nation tucked away at the top of the world, out of sight and out of mind. Yet for those possessed with a willingness to explore, to observe and learn, Iceland, its people and history and culture, quickly becomes something altogether more captivating. My best friend Villimey Mist was born in Iceland, and lives there still, to the north of you and I and everyone else, to the north of everywhere, including the north. In the summer it is the upland of the Midnight Sun, bright, beautiful, ever illuminated. Yet darkness slowly creeps in, day after day until the dwindling light is devoured, and it's in those foreboding winter times of perpetual night that horror thrives. Villimey once told me all Icelanders share a pervasive gallows humor, and why not? Odin is the northern God of the Gallows, one-eyed and grim, picking at sacrificial corpses. In ancient days life was hard. Death came easy, and it fell upon a chosen few to conjure tales to warn the rest of us what sprites lurked in those eternal black hours. That tradition continues today, through authors like Villimey.

I first met Villimey Mist via that strange, sometimes turbulent Wonderland we call social media. Twitter can be, by turns, exhilarating and maddening, a never-ending upside-down disco funhouse party, and once I'd made the acquaintance of this darkly sweet and shy Icelander, I was curious to what her work would offer. We were both relative unknowns in the horror publishing field; I'd sold a dozen or so short stories and she'd released her debut novel only three months earlier. I made a promise to purchase a copy, and once fulfilled I was enthralled by the fast-paced tale of vampires *Nocturnal Blood* offered. As a reader it was everything I could've asked for: there were solid characters, a well-developed mythology, captivating villains, and blood, guts and gore galore. Yet it was Leia Walker, the novel's protagonist, who won my heart and my allegiance to Villimey's creative vision; her story was one of loneliness, of empowerment and subtle, quiet strength, and it struck a chord deeper within me than anything had in a long, long time. I identified with Leia, where she'd been, who she was. I'd walked in those shoes, and was, and still am, astounded someone else could articulate exactly how I'd felt treading that path.

When Villimey asked me some months later to provide interior illustrations for the subsequent sequels, I jumped at the chance to be included in the universe-expanding realms of *Nocturnal Farm* and *Nocturnal Salvation*, and I haven't been disappointed. The journey Leia has taken is twisting, surprising and, ironically for a series concerned primarily with the undead, full of life. That liveliness is a hallmark of Villimey's prose, and also comes through in her constant selfless support for others in the Writing Community, me included. Our creative collaborations are some of the most enjoyable I've had, and I look forward to many more.

Sometimes I worry terror in fiction has become toothless and stale, a zombified dead horse continually beaten. Few writers can rouse my imagination, and fewer still can inspire palpitating dread. That Villimey does so is testament to the formidable talent she wields. Her skill is careful, precise as a razor and twice as deadly to the horde of false horror pretenders who are content to dress up old ideas in new clothes and proclaim them innovation. To achieve this end, she always writes first by hand, in fine flowing script in hardback notebooks, and in the future, these will sell at auction for obscene amounts of money to frothing fans eager for a memento from their favorite best-selling author.

Being world-famous is her destiny. I truly believe this.

The volume you're holding is a collection of Villimey's short fiction, written over the course of a furiously fruitful year and a guidebook across the myriad highways of horror. But what gives her stories their heft isn't mere macabre candy splatter (though there is plenty of that for the faithful). What emerges foremost is the continual, complex importance she places on both the bonds of family and the value of friendship. In her *Nocturnal* novels, Leia Walker's inner power is epitomized in the close relationship she shares with her parents, her brother, and most of all, her friend Sophie, a connection so strong it extends *postmortem*. In Villimey's short stories, too, we see that ever-present theme: the sacrifice of the mother for her child in 'A Mother's Job', the demented actions a father in 'Hope' initiates in the name of his daughter. Villimey's reverence for the distinct mythology of her native isle appears in the chilling 'Taumur' and the found footage 'Skötumóðir', and the righting of wrongs provides much needed spiritual catharsis in 'The Thrill of the Hunt', 'Kokkuri-san' and especially 'The Banquet', a stark tale of torture more enthralling and emotionally resonant than a hundred Hollywood bloodbaths.

Each of Villimey's stories unfold like a movie in my head, except these films are more exciting, more original, more intense than celluloid. Her horror poetry lingers in the mind long after the last line is read. There's a fearlessness in her words, a willingness to tread where others don't, a tireless effort to push boundaries and unveil new dawns on a dark horizon.

She's the Daughter of the Midnight Sun and she's writing from the top of the world.

Listen to what she has to tell you.

Damascus Mincemeyer
October, 2021

Damascus Mincemeyer was exposed to the weird worlds of horror, sci-fi and comics as a boy and was ruined for life. Now a writer and artist of various strangeness, he's the author of a short story collection, Where The Last Light Dies, *and a novel,* By Invitation Only, *from TerrorTract publishing. He's provided interior illustrations for Villimey Mist's* Nocturnal Farm and Nocturnal Salvation, *and the two are currently collaborating on a horror-western novel called* The Brimstone Trail *that's best described as* True Grit *meets* The Evil Dead *with a whip-wielding female Icelandic bounty hunter as a protagonist.*

A
MOTHER'S
JOB

It is a mother's job to protect her child.

Skylar knew that. It was what echoed in her mind. It was rooted in her being. She had to keep Thea safe. It was all that mattered.

Heavy footsteps thundered across the house. Outside the house as well. They were being surrounded.

Guttural growls echoed in the narrow hallway. The stench of decay filled the air.

Clutching Thea tight in her arms, Skylar sprinted through the hall. She slipped in blood. Whose blood was it? Was it Isaac's? *Don't think about that*, her mind urged her. She cursed but kept going.

The panic room was at the top of the stairs. In there, she and Thea would be safe from… those creatures.

She knew she couldn't call them humans anymore. Not after what she had witnessed.

Thea whimpered in her embrace.

"Almost there, sweetie." Skylar cooed.

Noise came from the corner as she reached the stairs. Familiar noise. Something that used to fill her heart

1

with joy and warmth. It froze the blood in her veins now.

Her brain ushered her to keep moving, to run. But her heart kept her feet rooted on the floor.

Don't turn around, a thought hissed in her mind.

She chose to ignore it.

The ashen face of Isaac peeked from the corner. The infection from his wound had spread to his neck. Purple bruises spackled his skin. Bloodshot eyes. Bits of flesh hung around his bloody mouth that opened in an inhuman shriek.

Thea flinched and gripped Skylar's sleeve tighter at the sound.

In one quick motion, he lunged at them. His bloody hand clawed towards them.

As if on reflex, Skylar grabbed an ornament chair next to the stairs and threw it at him. It hit him in the chest. He tripped. Tangled in the chair, Isaac snarled at his wife, hand still reaching towards them.

Skylar struggled against her tears.

It's not your husband anymore, the thought pressed on, reaching down to pull the plug on her heart.

She sniffled, exhaled, and ran up the steps, leaving the only man she had ever loved.

The panic room was behind the wardrobe at the innermost guest room. Skylar hurried to slam the door shut and lock it while she prepared to move the ornate, oak wardrobe. She gently laid Thea down. The little girl didn't make a sound, just huddled against the wall, her face obscured by her honey-colored hair.

The wardrobe was heavier than she remembered. But then again, it had been Isaac that had placed it there. Or was it the movers? Skylar shook her head. Now was not the time for unnecessary contemplations. Her nails scratched the smooth surface as she slipped.

She cursed, then clapped a hand on her mouth, glancing at Thea in embarrassment. She shouldn't swear in front of her.

The door banged. Then came another. Like hands slamming on the wood.

Skylar resumed pulling the wardrobe to the side, her fear becoming fuel for her adrenaline. Her heart hammered against the rib cage. Her arms ached from the exertion and from holding Thea. She was tired, terrified, and hyperventilating.

Still, she pulled. The panic room was their only hope. Her child needed it.

The wardrobe gave a screech, leaving marks on the hardwood floor. But it revealed her salvation.

A steel door glinted in the ceiling light. Next to it, a pad with numbers.

Skylar picked up Thea, feeling how clammy she was in her arms. Did she have a fever? Or was she wet from her own sweat?

The bangs continued. More frenzied. The snarls nearly seeped into the room. The door bulged under the weight of possibly dozens of people, hungry for their flesh.

Skylar's hand shook as she punched in the access code. It was easy to remember. Thea's date of birth. It had been Isaac's idea. The pad glowed green. The steel door slowly slid open, revealing a small room with a cot bed, a toilet, a sink, and a shelf full of supplies.

She threw herself and Thea inside. Just as the door slid closed, the guest room was drowned with the walking dead.

Faint thumps pounded against the steel door.

Skylar paid it no mind. They were safe here. But for how long, she didn't know. She didn't *want* to know.

She put her child on the cot bed. "Let me take a look at your arm."

Thea had been cradling it ever since the attack. She had cried at first, but when the house had begun to be invaded by snarling maniacs, she had gone silent.

Skylar gently pulled Thea's arm to her. There was a nasty bite on her forearm. Purple and green bruises were already forming around it. A sickly scent of spoiled fruit wafted from the wound. The blood had already coagulated.

Skylar swallowed the bile building up in her throat. She couldn't let Thea know she was worried.

"Does it still hurt?"

Thea nodded; chin anchored at the chest.

Skylar stood up and got the first aid kit from the shelf. She doused a cotton swab with rubbing alcohol. "This is going to hurt a little bit." She said softly before dabbing Thea's arm with it.

Thea tensed, hitching in a breath. Still, she didn't cry. Not a tear in sight.

"You're such a brave girl," Skylar said with affection and admiration. She even envied her daughter a little bit as she was still battling her own anxiety and fear deep inside.

Thea gave her a small smile as Skylar bandaged her arm. It was the first smile since the incident. A good sign. She hadn't lost her innocence yet.

"Are you hungry?"

Skylar grabbed a bottle of water and a packet of cookies. Thea shook her head, tugging her arm closer to her chest. Skylar couldn't blame her for the loss of appetite. Not after their ordeal.

"I'll just leave them here in case you get hungry." She placed them nearby the cot, knowing full well that the sweet tooth in her daughter would rise from within and seize the packet.

"What about Daddy?"

Thea's worried voice went like a blade through Skylar's heart. How could she explain what had happened to her father, when even she couldn't comprehend it?

"Daddy will be fine, sunshine," Skylar avoided looking at her daughter. If she did, she might cry. She couldn't let Thea see the grief in her expression. "Why don't you lie down and get some rest? Mommy will be right next to you."

Skylar herself laid down in front of the door, hugging her knees. She listened to the steady rhythm of Thea's breath. It was soothing. Comforting. A form of daze threatened to overtake her mind. She washed it away with a sip of water. She needed to focus. She needed a sharp mind to think of a plan. What their next step was.

She didn't get her wish.

A blank canvas was all that was present in her mind. Soon, colors sprinkled the canvas. Huge blotches of memories crashed on it, forcing Skylar to relive the dreaded event.

It had been just a quiet Sunday morning.

The three of them had sat down in the kitchen for waffles and smoothies. They had been looking forward to a nice day out at the park. Thea in particular was excited for it. She had kept demanding that they gobble down their breakfast as fast as possible.

The TV had been on. Isaac never wanted to miss the morning news. The Sunday news usually brought nothing but sunshine and lollipops. But that day, it had been peppered with segments about unnerving attacks on people.

Skylar had frowned. "Do we need to listen to this while we eat?"

Isaac had shrugged at first, but upon seeing the looks of annoyance on both Skylar and Thea, he reluctantly turned off the TV.

The rest of the day had gone swimmingly. The visit to the park had been fun in the beginning. Thea had enjoyed the swings and had insisted that Skylar keep pushing her higher in the air. Thea's joy had been contagious. Isaac had laughed while taking photos to add to their collection of fond memories.

It had happened too fast. Too fast for Skylar to comprehend.

One minute, Isaac had gone to buy ice cream from the nearby vendor. A haggard looking teenager had shuffled close. Probably feeling sorry for the kid, Isaac had offered him his ice cream. Instead of accepting the nice gesture, the teenager had grabbed Isaac by the shoulder and took a chunk of flesh from his neck. Isaac's screams of pain resounded throughout the park.

It had taken both the ice cream vendor and a nearby policeman to get the crazy teenager off Isaac.

They had hurried away, Skylar holding Thea tight in her arms. The poor girl had cried in shock and fear. Skylar had turned her head to see the look of bloodlust on the boy's dirty face. His snarls had echoed in the park long after they were gone.

Isaac had had his wound treated at the hospital. Thankfully, the boy hadn't damaged Isaac's main artery, so he had only needed some stitching. Both Skylar and Thea had been relieved to hear that. The three of them had tried to end the day on lighter notes by taking Thea for burgers and fries for dinner.

The next day, Isaac had complained of feeling ill. He'd had a slight fever and his eyes felt dry. Skylar had insisted that he rest while she took care of Thea. He had brushed it off as side-effects from the painkillers. Isaac barely ate anything that night.

The following day, Isaac's condition had gotten worse. His fever had spiked, and he had occupied the bathroom most of the day. The stink of vomit had churned Skylar's stomach. Once again, she had pleaded with him to go back to the hospital.

Isaac would have none of it. He had insisted it was just a nasty case of the flu. Was he delusional? Had he failed to notice the yellow pus forming around the wound, like maggots? It had made Skylar's skin crawl at the sight of it.

Skylar was troubled. Isaac's parents and older brother were coming to dinner. They lived across the state and hadn't seen each other in a while. Should they cancel?

Isaac had shaken his head. His mother would only complain if they did that and he didn't want to hear her nagging, not when he was feeling so sick. He'd just rest for the day and then see them for a moment when they'd arrive.

Knowing how stubborn her husband was, Skylar had obliged and focused paying attention to Thea and preparing for what might be the most painful dinner party she'd experienced.

Thea had been by Skylar's side, wanting to help with the dinner. She had been a nice distraction from Skylar's worry over Isaac. Like her name, she always brought the sun everywhere she went. Thea had even stood next to her and greeted her grandparents and uncle with a toothy grin on her face. It had earned her a caramel hard candy from her doting grandfather.

Despite the mother-in-law's snide comments about the house being a mess (it wasn't), they'd had a nice dinner together.

They had all joined with Thea in the living room, where Thea had entertained them with the latest song she had learned in kindergarten when Isaac arrived.

He had stumbled into the room, deathly pale. His tongue had lolled out of his mouth, like a panting dog. His body had twitched, as if electric jolts were running through him.

An icy dread had coursed through Skylar and chilled her bones. His eyes had been so bloodshot, as if his tears had turned crimson.

Thea, in her ignorant bliss, had run to her father for a hug.

Skylar had extended her arm, but Thea was already in the embrace of her father.

To Skylar, it had felt like time had slowed down. She had waited with her heart lodged in her throat; her voice evaporated.

She had heard faintly her mother-in-law huff something about Isaac's poor condition. Had heard her father-in-law and brother-in-law chuckle at the sweet display.

Had heard her child's scream.

Wrenched forwards, as if her waist had been tied to a slingshot, Skylar sprinted to Thea and her husband.

Isaac had bitten Thea on the forearm. Smacking his lips as if Thea's blood and flesh had been a rare, delicious wine, Isaac let out a snarl and bowed his head for another treat.

Skylar had yanked Thea from his grasp. She had held her tight. She had felt the tremors, the shock, the fear all in one.

His brother and father had stridden to him, angrily jabbing him in the chest. A second later, Isaac had been on top of his father, ripping off a piece of his neck.

Screams from Skylar's mother-in-law had filled the living room. She had tried to pry her younger son off with the help of her older son.

The windows banged.

Skylar turned and blanched.

More people with the same faces, all contorted in rage, peered through them.

Skylar's father-in-law's gurgles for breath had been sickening. The smell of iron had made her queasy.

Skylar had heard cracks. Cobwebs of splinters appeared on the windows from the incessant slamming.

Isaac had been tearing into his own mother, his mouth colored in ghastly crimson, like a clown from hell.

Thea had ceased sobbing. That lack of sound had brought Skylar back from the shocked stupor.

Without hesitation, she had turned on her heels and had run as the glass had shattered and invited the ravaging humans into their home.

A cough pulled Skylar back from her horrid walk down memory lane.

"Are you all right?" She had her hand on the water bottle at once.

Thea nodded while covering the mouth with a small hand as she coughed once more.

"Have you had anything to eat?"

She knew the answer already. The packet of cookies remained untouched by her side. She opened it and placed a few in Thea's hands. "I know it's difficult, but you have to eat something to keep your strength."

Thea only looked at the sugary treats with a suspicious glare. As if thinking the cookies were the culprit behind turning her father into that...*thing*.

Skylar suppressed a sigh. She took the cookies and jammed two of them into her mouth. "Mmm...so yummy." She said, crumbs tumbling out of her full mouth.

Skylar waited patiently while she ate another cookie. If Thea saw that nothing bad happened to her, she would feel safe to try to eat it herself. She always used that tactic if Thea was being a picky eater.

After a moment, Thea reached out for the packet. Skylar smiled. The first smile since the incident.

"I'm cold," Thea mumbled.

Skylar grabbed an extra blanket from the shelf, crawled up into bed with her daughter and wrapped themselves in it. She felt how cold Thea's body was. However, her forehead was getting warm. She remembered how clammy she had felt. Was it a fever? A memory of Isaac, pale and feverish, scratched at her mind. It gave her goosebumps. She shook it off.

Whatever it was, she would take care of it. She had to. Thea only had her left.

The grief threatened to crash over Skylar.

She suppressed it by hugging her little girl tighter.

The coughs were getting worse.

Skylar and Thea barely got any rest that night. No matter how much water Thea drank, how many flu pills she took, she always regurgitated them in the form of a horrid, retching cough.

Thea's skin had turned pallid. Yellow pus was around the bite wound. If Skylar stared long enough, she could have sworn it wriggled like maggots. The sickly, putrid stench turned her stomach. Yet, Skylar continued to clean it. It was nothing. She had taken care of Thea whenever she got a stomach bug. It wasn't any different than that.

However, worry coiled her insides.

Thea had almost lost all appetite. She slept most of the time, except when she had to use the toilet for vomiting.

It's the same that happened to him, a treacherous thought knocked in her mind. *You know what happened to him.*

Skylar bit her bottom lip. If that's true, then they might not be safe here. *She,* Skylar, might be in danger.

12

She glanced down at the fragile girl in her lap. Is it possible that Thea could turn into one of those things? Her skin crawled with fear. Skylar's eyes searched the room. There was nothing in there that could be used as a weapon. Except, maybe the pillow. While Thea is sleeping, she could. . .

She looked down at her hands. Could she really do it? Could she muster the strength to pull the pillow over her daughter's face? Hold it there until she suffocated?

Revulsion filled her entire being. She almost threw up herself. How could she think of such things? Is it the brain's method of survival? Skylar glared at the door that kept them locked away. If only she had the guts to open it and find someone else to do the horrid job. But with the rampage beyond the panic room, was there any help for them to find?

Was civilization over? Were they the only ones left in their town that hadn't been affected? Perhaps in the entire world?

How ironic. There is nothing for us outside. Not anymore. And yet, there is nothing for us inside as well, Skylar thought as she stroked Thea's hair.

Despite knowing what nightmare lied behind their sanctuary as well as inside it, the faint thumps lulled Skylar to sleep.

Skylar awoke to tremors beside her.

Was it an earthquake?

She turned. Thea writhed violently in the bed.

Fear almost choked Skylar.

She sprang to her feet, removing her belt as she grabbed Thea by the shoulder. Thea's eyes were rolled back, the drool turned into white foam. Skylar thrust the belt into Thea's mouth and then secured her head between her thighs.

She could do it now. Grab the pillow and hold it down on Thea's face. The vicious thought entered her mind. *It would be mercy killing,* the thought prodded. *Thea is hurting more now. It would be kinder to end it.*

Skylar bit the inside of her cheek. Her heart was raging a battle with her mind. She looked down at her little girl, teeth clamped on the belt as she fought to stay conscious.

She couldn't do it. Not when Thea was being braver than her. She needed that strength. Shame enveloped her. How could she call herself a mother when thoughts like that invaded her mind? At a time when Thea needed her the most?

Her shoulders quaked with sobs as she held her child, not moving until the convulsions ended.

It wasn't long now. Skylar knew that. She just didn't want to accept it. She felt like she was standing at a cliff with grief rolling down from the mountain, pushing her into the sea of despair. If only she had cancelled that dinner party. Then maybe, none of this would have happened.

That night, as Thea slept in her arms, Skylar looked up at the ceiling. She decided to pray. If no one could hear her from beyond the door, then surely her Lord and Savior would listen. He always listened.

"Whatever is happening with the world right now, I pray that you'll ease my daughter's suffering. She's only a child. She doesn't deserve this cruelty."

She was met with silence, except for the thumps against the door. As if that was the answer from Him.

Angry tears burned behind her eyelids. All of this wasn't fair. Why hadn't Isaac bitten her instead? Why couldn't he have spared their child? Their sunshine?

Skylar wanted to scream. Grief had moved on to anger. She wanted to turn the panic room upside down in fury at the injustice. But that would only wake and frighten Thea. Skylar knew that she needed to stay calm. Thea needed all the rest. Even though Skylar knew it was soon time.

She wiped her eyes. Took a deep breath. And sang,

"You're my sunshine, my only sunshine. You make me happy when skies are gray. You'll never know dear, how much I love you. Please don't take my sunshine away,"

There was a scuffle around the shelf.

Skylar turned her sleepy eyes to the source of the noise. "Thea?"

She was crouched down in the corner. Skylar only saw her hunched back.

"What are you doing, sunshine? Are you hungry?"

Thea's ears perked up. She slowly turned her head. Bloodshot eyes met Skylar's. Thea held up her favorite teddy bear. "H-Hungry," Her voice came raspy, like she had inhaled a gallon of sand.

She stretched the fuzzy fabric of the teddy bear until the neck tore off. White fluff bulged out of it. Thea took one look at her once treasured toy and dropped it on the floor. Her eyes were devoid of that childlike innocence.

Skylar's blood froze in her veins. Dread squeezed her lungs. "H-Honey?" Her voice trembled.

Skylar refused to accept it. Her daughter wasn't gone. She didn't look like Isaac. She was still here with her. She just needed food. Wasn't it a mother's job to make sure its child was properly fed?

No matter what, she would stay by her daughter's side.

Skylar exhaled a long, shuddering breath. Then, with a heart full of love, she extended both her arms. "Come here, sunshine. I've got food."

Thea's fingers twitched and cracked at the mention of nourishment. She cocked her head to the side. The mere movement reminded Skylar, that in essence, her child was still there. Thea used to do that when she was being playful.

"M... Mommy," Thea rasped between gnashing of her teeth.

16

Skylar nodded tearfully. "I'm right here. I'm not going anywhere."

With a snarl, Thea leapt into the arms of her mother. Her small teeth plunged into the flesh of her neck.

Skylar embraced her daughter tightly. She would never let go. Until the end, she would be there for her.

That is a mother's job, after all.

THE
THRILL
OF THE
HUNT

That supple skin.

Smooth, beautiful.

I love how it feels against my big, callous fingers. How it tenses when I put more pressure.

Her eyes are widening. With shock. With fear.

Yes. Struggle more. Let me feel that despair.

Her nails don't hurt me. They only spur me on, urging me to squeeze harder. Her feeble strength is nothing compared to mine.

Those short bursts of breath that escape her lips are like a sweet serenade to my ears.

When she lets go of her last breath, I moan with pleasure.

The ecstasy is always so short, though.

I hate that.

I look down at the body. It's useless to me now. I need to feel the blood pumping into the veins as I squeeze the life out of her.

I drive to the nearest deserted highway and dump the body there. I don't bother with laying it down gently. It's just a heavy marionette. Absolutely useless.

Well, not quite. I have her necklace. It still feels warm to the touch.

It should quench my thirst for a couple of days.

The itch is back.

It's time for another prowl in the night.

I take my car and cruise downtown Portland.

I can't say there's slim pickings in Old Town. It's more like a smorgasbord, waiting for me to select the best of the best.

The women give me sensual looks, turning in circles to allow me to see the whole package.

None of them excite me, though.

I don't feel that rush bubbling beneath the surface.

I'm about to turn the car around, irritated that I can't scratch my itch tonight, when I spot her.

A bit younger than I usually pick. Sharp cheekbones, tanned skin, little braids on the side of her head, pulled into a thick ponytail. My fingers yearn to pull it.

She sees me. My heart gives a little jump.

Her eyes are big, almost doe-like.

So delicious.

I pull over next to her.

She gives me a coy smile while running her eyes up and down. Funny. It's as if she's appraising me.

"Good evening, stranger," she says when I let the window slide down and she leans over it. "What brings you here?"

I lightly lick my lips with the tip of my tongue. Her voice is like honey. I bet her gasps are like Turkish delights.

"I was hoping for a good time with someone special." I dip my chin down and give her my best, rehearsed smile.

She giggles. Her laugh is like a tinkling bell. "And I'm the lucky gal?"

I nod, gripping the steering wheel. "You bet. Hop in."

A tremor of pleasure runs through me as she jumps into the car with a triumphant smile. She waves to her "coworkers" while I take us to a more secluded place.

What a Godsend.

"What's your name?" I've never asked them their names. It never mattered to me, but I feel like I must burn that girl's name to memory. She doesn't seem to have anything on her that I can keep for later, anyway.

"Cynthia."

I glance from the road at her. She's got her eyes straight on the asphalt, a stoic calm about her. Something tingles within me. I've never felt that before. I shake it off by chuckling. "That's a pretty name."

She shrugs. "It's nothing special."

"You'd prefer something different?"

"I'd prefer a name that goes places. That people will remember."

Don't worry, baby. I won't forget yours. For some reason,

I feel compelled to take her further up into the mountains, where I did my first kill. That girl had been unremarkable. I barely remember how she looked, but she had satisfied my urges and that's a good enough memory. The place I killed her is secluded and quiet. I doubt even the animals there will bother us.

"Are we going hiking?" Cynthia giggles.

"I like a little privacy."

Cynthia's eyes glint. "So do I."

Once more, something creeps up at the back of my mind. It's like a tick, biting into my skin. Never felt that way before. I shake my head. It's probably nothing. It could be a new form of excitement. Besides, I have to be focused. My itch needs to be scratched.

The thought of running my fingers through that skin of hers is enough to make me hard.

Not long now.

"What are you expecting for tonight?" Cynthia asks as she twirls one of her tiny braids between her fingers.

I smirk. "Something of a thrill, perhaps?"

Cynthia nods, smiling. "I can give you that."

A surge of excitement courses through me. *I'll bet you can. You'll be my best kill yet.*

The road has become dark, with the moon the only beacon of light above us. Fir trees as tall as skyscrapers flank the car as we climb higher up the mountain. I couldn't be happier with the spot. I have to hurry. My hard-on is starting to hurt.

I park the car near a small rest area with a lonely bench almost shrouded by the trees. I better not dump the body there when I'm done. It'd be too easy to see.

"Well, we're here." I turn to Cynthia and graze her cheek with the back of my hand.

It's so warm, as if the whole sun radiated from her. I can't wait to squeeze it out of her, so nothing remains but the cold terror in her eyes.

"You really picked a great spot." Cynthia purrs as she sidles closer to me. Her hand snakes towards my thigh and caresses it. A greedy gleam in her doe eyes.

Not as greedy as mine.

My fingers drift down from her cheek, and I wrap them around her throat.

If she senses something, she's being coy about it. From what I feel, she's allowing me to take the reins.

The perfect victim.

I squeeze around the windpipe. My heart is jumping in my ribcage. My boner is raging. I look up to watch the terror unfold on her face.

Irritation clouds my excitement. Cynthia doesn't seem frightened. Her eyes aren't bulging. Her breath is stable. In fact, she seems mildly bored. Her hand has retreated to her side.

I throw pretense out the window. No more playing "Mr. Nice Guy".

I push her against the door, with such force that she bangs her head against the window. I clamp my other hand on her breast and dig my fingers deep into the flesh, as if ready to tear it apart from her body. That could be her memento.

She gasps, her eyes widening.

I smirk. There's the look I've been waiting for. The thrill rushes from within, giving strength to my arms.

Cynthia thrashes in the seat. She claws against my chest. The pain is bearable. It only makes me want to savor the moment longer.

However, my irritation remains. She's not giving me eyes of terror.

She's narrowed them. They shine with malice. I've never seen it on my victims before.

"Did you do this to Helena as well?"

Her question momentarily stuns me. My fingers freeze. How is she talking? I'm squeezing as hard as I possibly can.

Her smile is rueful. "Did you know that was her name? The woman you killed and left here in the woods?"

My own breath lodges in my throat. Cold sweat glides down my back. How does she know? Is she police? Are they already onto me?

Panic grips me. I clamp both hands once more on her throat and squeeze.

"Enough with the foreplay, I guess." She speaks calmly, even though I'm so close to crushing her windpipe.

She grabs my wrist and bends it. It hurts slightly. I grit my teeth. She smirks and bends it back more. My stomach drops. What is she doing? The ligament has begun burning. Her eyes glint with a dark purpose. She bends it back even further.

The crack of my bone penetrates my ears like a drill. I

stare at the crooked shape. Then blinding pain shoots up my brain, like venom. I scream.

"Did that hurt? I bet Helena was hurting more when you killed her." Cynthia cocks her head to the side, as if actually oblivious of her own action.

"Who the fuck are you?" I scream, clutching my broken hand.

She ignores me, instead opening the glove compartment and picking up the necklace that I had put there for safe keeping. "Another victim? Where's Helena's memento?"

"How do you know about her?" I spit angrily.

"Her sister, Lydia, prayed to me when Helena hadn't been found within a week. Given her line of work, Lydia knew she was dead. And Lydia wanted revenge."

Prayed? Is she a priest? She certainly doesn't look one with those ripped jeans and leather jacket.

A wolf howls in the distance. Cynthia smiles as she gently pockets the necklace.

"I thought I wouldn't find you. Portland's a big city. Lots of people. But I'm patient. As a hunter, you have to be."

My brow furrows. Hunter? What is she talking about?

She laughs. "You still haven't figured it out? Nah, you killers don't seem to have either the intellect or the patience. I go by many names. Cynthia after my birthplace on Mount Cynthus. Diana in Rome. I, however, prefer my true name. Artemis."

She slowly turns her head to me. Markings appear on her face and body, like stars popping up in the sky

24

outside. They look ancient, pagan even. Like Egyptian hieroglyphs and Greek letters melted into one. Black soot covers her eyes, yet they sparkle like diamonds.

My balls shrivel. I almost forget about the pain in my broken wrist.

"I promised you a thrill. You have twenty seconds to run. I wouldn't waste them. You saw what I did with your pathetic human hand."

I can't explain how she changed like that. Is she an illusionist? How can a girl her size be stronger than me? She said her name was Artemis. If I remember my high school mythology class correctly, she's said to be the Goddess of the Hunt. How is that possible? How can she even exist and inflict pain on someone like me? I want to stay and fight her, but my dominant hand is useless. I can't trust my own strength.

I do, however, trust my balls.

I scramble out of the car, and rush into the woods. I haven't run like that in ages, the searing pain in my side reminding me of that fact.

The moon is the only light in this maze of a forest. Trees everywhere. Nowhere to hide. Why can't I hear her running after me?

A wolf howls again. This time, it feels closer.

I don't like this. How my heart is almost exploding. Not with exhilaration, but with a fear that digs deep.

Something whistles in the air.

It plunges into my shoulder, nailing me to a Douglas fir. I scream. Wincing through the pain, I look down at the wound. Nothing. So, why do I feel like there's an arrow stuck in my bone? I grope for it in the dark. Again, nothing.

Another whistle.

I scream again. My other shoulder has been hit. I wheeze through the pain as it sends flames up and down my body.

A laugh echoes through the forest.

It sends chills down my spine. I've never felt fear like that.

She struts towards me, carrying a primitive bow. Her smirk is victorious. "Nothing beats the thrill of the hunt."

"All right, all right. You've got me. You've got your hunt. Now let me go." I demand.

She shakes her head, chuckling. "You're right that I've got my hunt. But I haven't avenged Helena's death yet."

Light footsteps pitter-patter on the soft ground. Too limber for a person.

A wolf strolls towards Artemis, its amber eyes gleaming in the dark.

Sweat beads down my temple. "Your pet?"

Artemis scratches the wolf behind its ear. "A companion. He usually gets what I hunt."

I struggle against the invisible arrows. The wolf growls as it approaches. I kick frantically, sweeping dirt into the air.

"Are you really feeding me to the wolf?" My voice comes out high-pitched in disbelief.

"Not just the wolf." Artemis' smile is sinister.

Heavier footsteps crush the ground. I feel slight tremors behind me.

I swivel my head. My breathing has become erratic, fearful. Not at all what I'm used to. What could she possibly have summoned from the dark?

A giant bear comes lumbering at my side. The scent of rotten leaves on its fur tickles my nose.

My legs go numb. Blood drains from my face.

"Please."

"Too late for pleas. You gave that up when you squeezed the life out of Helena. I'd wish you a good journey to the underworld, but I hear your kind isn't received well there."

She gives her head a jerk forward.

The bear stands up on its hind legs. It raises its clawed paw and strikes down in one, swift motion.

For a moment, I think it missed.

Something slithers with a squelch on the ground. My middle feels cold. I look down. My stomach has been ripped open. Innards leak in a mess down my pants. The grass below is painted in crimson. A part of my dick nestles between my feet.

Blood trickles down my mouth. My eyes shoot up when I sense movement.

The wolf's open maw is the last thing I see.

But it's not the last thing I feel.

I'm still alive as those beasts feast on my open stomach.

The last thing I hear is a girl's tinkling laugh.

TAUMUR

The warmth of the blazing knarr traveled across the ocean while Einar and Þórir watched in devastating silence as their once trusted ship fell victim to the fire.

The frigid air was alive with the stench of burning wood and the charred bodies of their fellow crew. Einar shivered as the maelstrom of events flashed through his mind. Things had been going fine. The winds had been fair and the waves still. Ketill's crew, himself included, had been celebrating the merchandise they had traded from a small island near Ireland. Those celebrations paled in comparison to what was waiting for them once they got back home to Iceland, a three-day journey at best. Like all Norse Gods, however, Þór was a fickle one. He had conjured a wicked storm which had kept them from the Icelandic shores. Tenacious, they had pressed home till they could almost feel the frozen ground beneath their feet.

It was a journey most of the crew never completed. They were all dead. The man responsible for that atrocity stood next to him in the narrow, long two-man rowboat that escaped the fire.

"Was this a part of your scheme, Þórir?" Einar's nails dug into his palms, drawing blood.

Þórir sighed. He wrenched water from his woolen tunic. "An act of desperation, not foolishness. Ketill had found my letter to King Canute. My confession of allegiance to his throne. I meant to kill only Ketill. He would not go silently."

Einar blew air into his freezing fingers. He glared at the dark-haired Viking. "Ketill was a fine leader and a great warrior. I'm glad he gave you a fight."

Þórir nodded. He winced as he gingerly touched his swollen eye. "That he did."

"Why did you spare me?"

Þórir sat down across from him. "This boat needs two pair of hands. Especially if we want to reach land within a day."

Einar slid out a dagger from his belt. The only thing he had salvaged from the knarr. "I could kill you right now. Avenge my comrades."

Þórir's raspy chuckle grated through the air. "Good luck rowing the boat by yourself, then."

"It's not impossible," Einar countered. He gripped the blade and took a cautious scoot forward. The boat swayed against his weight.

"True, but what about the cold? You'll freeze to death before you see a grain of sand on our black beaches. I propose a temporary truce. Once we make land, then take your revenge. Now, we need to start rowing." Þórir snagged one of the oars from the bottom of the boat and dunk the blade into the ocean with a splash.

Einar glowered at him. The heat of anger welling in his gut gusted away with the biting winter gale that swept through the air. Einar despised how calculating Þórir was. It manifested in the way he fought and how he traded with merchants. Always one step ahead. And now, he had known he would need one more person to survive the merciless sea. And Þórir had picked him. The runt. The least experienced. Unlikely to stand a chance against a seasoned Viking, and even less likely to harbor a desire to venture through the Atlantic Ocean all by himself.

Einar sheathed his dagger behind his back. He reluctantly took a seat beside Þórir. Tension stabbed at his neck and shoulders. As much as he hated the traitor, he loathed himself more for understanding his motivations. However, if roles reversed, he'd never do something similar. The Allfather wouldn't allow a treacherous spy into Valhalla.

The water nearby splashed.

Einar jumped. He scanned the sea like a hawk. Debris from the crumbling ship? Perhaps the friendly whales had decided to pay them a visit?

A head bobbed above the water's surface. A familiar one. A breathing one.

"Asgard's Allfather! It's my friend Trausti. He survived!" Einar grabbed one of the oars and leaned against the boat, balancing the oar with one of his hands. "Grab hold, Trausti. I'll pull you up."

30

Trausti's relieved smile heightened as he raised a burned hand toward the oar.

Þórir watched the young Viking's endeavor while cursing inwards at the same time. He thought he had been meticulous. No matter. Submersion in the frigid ocean that long wouldn't do him any good.

Under the uncertain light of the flaming ship, a wavering shadow approached beneath the waves. Þórir leaned over the bulkhead. He watched the shadow come closer to the wrecked knarr and the floundering survivor. A knot squeezed his insides.

Þórir grabbed Einar's shirt and yanked him to the center of the boat. "We must go. Quickly!"

Einar almost dropped the oar into the ocean. "Not until I've pulled Trausti to our boat." He groaned with exertion as he stretched further over the dark water.

Þórir shook his shaggy mane and began rowing. He turned the boat around, away from the burning wreckage.

"What are you doing? We're moving further away from him!" Einar shouted.

Trausti gave a weak cry of help.

"Leave him. He's dead, anyway," Þórir grunted.

"By the Allfather, I will not leave my friend behind. I'm not a monster like you," Einar spat and drove the oar into the ocean like a spear.

The shadow was directly beneath the drowning man. For a moment Trausti struggled, arms digging into the uncooperative water for purchase, when his head disappeared. Bubbles erupted in droves.

"Trausti!"

Þórir stopped rowing. He threw the oar to the deck. He fumbled under his tunic and pulled out a rune-carved bone on a leather string. He clasped it in his hands, praying to Njörður, Asgard's God of the sea.

Einar stretched over the railing, eyes squinting into the churning waters. No more bubbles. No Trausti. Nothing. "Þórir, hand me the other oar. Maybe Trausti can reach it if I put it under."

"You will do no such thing. You will doom us both," Þórir snapped as he held tight to the shaft.

A patch of brilliant crimson flowered in the expanse of cold gray ocean. A moment later Trausti bobbed to the surface.

What was left of him.

His entire lower body had been ripped away. Snaking threads of his pink intestines swirled through the waves, like earthworms after a night's rain.

Einar reeled, stumbling back, his mouth agape. The boat lurched. Einar tripped on the seat and tumbled backwards.

Into the ocean.

Þórir swore and kneeled in front of the railing. Several horrible seconds passed. Had the monster snatched the little runt as well? His fists gripped the wood as he scanned the frothy waves.

Einar emerged, gasping. Not missing a beat, Þórir grabbed the back of Einar's tunic and with a grunt, pulled his flailing body back into the rowboat. The waves played a dangerous dance to it as it swirled in circles. The old Viking's eyes never strayed from the ripped body.

Coughing and spluttering, Einar made to reach once more for the oar but Þórir slapped his hand.

"Sit in the center, boy. Don't make a sound," Þórir hissed. He threw his weight to the opposite side and exhaled as the boat righted.

"Wha-what happened to Trausti?" Einar's teeth chattered. He hugged himself for warmth but the tremors wouldn't dissipate.

Þórir shook his head, laying a silencing finger over his lips. His finger then drifted toward Trausti's remains.

Þórir leaned in close, his voice hardly above a whisper. "It never leaves leftovers."

Einar's brow furrowed. "What are you talking abo— "

An enormous wave rose in the air, followed by a huge, gaping maw. Rows of sharp, jagged teeth stained crimson shredded the remains of Trausti's body. The creature was enormous and thick, the size of the burning knarr in front of them. The smooth, obsidian hide glistened against the moonlight. The color of death. Only the white and pale pink streaking from the corners of its eyes and gnashing jaws insulted the ominous dark of its hide.

Einar stared, paralyzed. Hot urine mingled with seawater in his sodden trousers.

The black behemoth crushed Trausti's remaining bones between its powerful, shark-like jaws. The crunch echoed through the night. When near nothing was left of his friend except for bits and pieces of gnawed off flesh and cerebral fluid and brain matter tinging the dark sea, it sank back into the ocean.

A moment passed. The only sound? The hissing of the dying flames as they touched the water.

Þórir exhaled and dropped the oar. It clattered on the deck. "Perhaps Njörður heard my prayer."

Einar's teeth still chattered. He could still hear Trausti's bones breaking in his mind. "What was that?"

"That, my boy, is why we need to hurry back to shore." Þórir passed him the oar.

Einar grabbed Þórir's tunic and wrenched him close. His lip curled over gritted teeth. "What just ate my friend?"

Þórir chuckled at the young fool's sneer. "Every man fears something. Survivors? Survivors know just what to be afraid of." Þórir spat a wad of phlegm to the deck and leveled a baleful stare at the scrawny lad before him. "That nightmare has been a denizen of the ocean before we even sailed across it. Nasty temper. Impeccable memory. The sea is his domain and, as far as he's concerned, we've no place in it. If a boat or a ship nudges him in the slightest, he will stop at nothing to break it apart and tear everyone within it to shreds. Hardened sailors have called him 'Taumur' for the white streak that slithers around his fiendish eyes and trails across his massive body."

Einar slackened the grip on Þórir's tunic, his face white. "Such a beast exists?"

Þórir scoffed. "Wasn't Trausti's brutal murder proof enough? You should be lucky that I pulled you back before he wanted another taste of human flesh."

Einar glanced at the spot where Trausti had been obliterated. Nausea tinged his pale skin green. He bent low, holding his head in his hands. He's right. There would have been nothing left of his own body if Þórir hadn't saved him. He stared at the old Viking's boots, not daring to look up. His pride wouldn't allow it. Einar owed him a life debt. Even though Þórir was a traitor, he had risked his life to save his. The monster was likely not done with them and Einar yearned to go home to be with his wife. Þórir was a more experienced sailor than him. Perhaps Einar should give him a second chance. After taking a few deep breaths, he straightened. "Do we have a chance?"

Þórir's smiled crooked. "Together, we might."

Einar nodded and slipped the oar silently into the water. "Then, let's go."

Winter. An enemy no one could defeat. It brought forth cold northern winds, and the darkness stretched clutching fingers longer into the day. It could make a seasoned Viking stumble blindly in the snow as a blizzard raged. Many thought that Hel, Goddess of the Underworld, summoned winter with a whisper of her chapped lips and ordered it to stay until the Allfather noticed.

And stay it did.

Hot air crystallized out of Einar's breath as he heaved the oar up and rowed. His arms ached against the cold. Every muscle and nerve screamed with fatigue. Oh, how he wanted to take a break! To lie down and rest his weary body.

To do so would invoke a death sentence. His clothes hadn't dried at all through the journey. Hel's glacial fingers crawled up his legs.

To ward off the frost, Þórir suggested they sing the upbeat song the crew used to when they fought against terrible weather. It was quite simple. One would stomp the floor twice which was followed by a clap of the hands from the others and a raucous "HÚ!". It kept the blood pumping, the battle spirit soaring, and stoked the will to survive. Wanting to do anything to destroy the monotony of endless rowing, Einar agreed.

They exercised the song for a couple of hours. They weren't in sync and were birds around, they would have scattered off. But it didn't matter to Einar. They were having fun. Warmth had spread to their stiff limbs and Einar could feel hope peeping from the dark corner of his heart. He enjoyed the company of the old man and felt like they were back in the knarr, excitement building in their stomachs as they sailed for another adventure.

The boat bumped into a sudden rest in their tune.

Þórir immediately withdrew the oar and sat rigid.

"Was it Taumur?" Einar whispered as he clutched the other oar. Hope washed away with every slap of water against the hull.

Þórir said nothing. Only waited.

Einar's heart hammered. Dread squeezed his veins. The only music sounding now was the uneasy melody of lapping waves in counterpoint to Þórir's measured breathing. The big Viking's apparent calm boggled him.

"We should be fine. I don't see its shadow underneath the water," Þórir admitted after an interminable silence.

Einar glanced at him. Þórir had placed the oar back in the sea and kept rowing, his eyes darting up and then straight ahead, measuring the route from the stars. His energy seemed inexhaustible, though Einar's own flagged.

Einar tightened his grip on the shaft. He dug the oar blade into the black water with renewed vigor. He still had a duty. A duty to his fallen shipmates. *Survive the boat ride and then you can kill him.* The thought soothed his tired soul. Yet it also concerned him. With a life debt weighing his heart, would he find the strength to follow through? Would it be right? Would he be judged by Óðinn and not allowed access into Valhalla once he fell in battle? Einar bit his lower lip. Doubt snaked around his gut, spreading its venom. They both had survived the beast. They both deserved to live. *I'm sorry, my friends,* Einar thought, eyes drifting up to the stars. *I cannot go through with my pact. Life for a life. That's what Óðinn would have wanted.* He bowed his head in apology.

"Are we near the end?"

Þórir looked once again up at the sky, his lips moving as if he were counting the beacons. "Close. Look, you can see it up ahead."

Einar's gaze followed where he was pointing. Relief washed over him. Just a dot on the horizon, but land was surely up ahead.

"The Allfather wants us to live." Einar's words choked through the lump in his throat. They had escaped the monster. They had won this battle. Of course, they had. Vikings never gave into their fears. Einar would never let his toes touch the ocean again once they reached land. He would show that beast Einar had bested him. He let out a victorious scream and pumped his fist into the air.

He turned to Þórir—

An oar smacked him across the face.

Einar's vision blurred. He stumbled and fell to his side of the boat. Pain blossomed in his jaw, festering into his skull.

Þórir grunted as he grabbed a handful of Einar's hair and pulled him in a sitting position. "I'm sorry, Einar, but you chose the wrong thing to be afraid of."

Blood poured from Einar's broken jaw. It dripped from the railing where his head rested and into the ocean. "This…was…your…plan…" His words came out garbled through broken teeth.

Þórir's smile crept into his black eyes. "Of course, it was. I'm a survivor."

He slid his hands under Einar's armpits and heaved. The lift made Einar gag from nausea.

Þórir's second betrayal sparked a flame within Einar. He was dazed from the attack and his limbs cramped from the pain. Yet Einar held onto the flame. He envisioned Týr, the god of war, lending him his only arm for strength. It spread throughout his body, jolting his body into action. He spurted blood as he took a deep breath. He pulled the dagger from behind his back and plunged it deep into Þórir's side. "If I'm going to meet Hel, I'm dragging you with me," Einar snarled and twisted the dagger deeper into Þórir's wound.

Þórir growled as he fought the young Viking. The boat swayed dangerously from side to side, salty spray churning the gray water.

Blood splattered into the ocean. The icy abyss filled with grunts and heat.

Þórir's bulk gave him an advantage over the smaller Viking. He placed his foot in front of Einar's leg, tightened his grip on his arm and threw him over his shoulder. Þórir's manic glint faltered when he saw Einar's fingers wound into his belt.

Þórir's knees buckled with the weight. The wind burst from his lungs as his midriff slammed against the gunwale and Einar hit the water headfirst.

Cursing, Þórir tried prying Einar's fingers off, but the man held fast. Þórir looked down and spat at Einar's triumphant smirk bobbing through the waves.

The boat gave into the weight and tipped over, dumping Þórir into arctic hell.

Needles jabbed into every pore of Einar's skin. Ice clutched his heart as water seeped into his lungs. Þórir's heavy mass dragged the young Viking into the inky darkness. He knew there was no way out. His body had given up. He had succeeded, though. Succeeded in achieving revenge for his fallen comrades. Týr would be proud. Óðinn, the Allfather, would be proud. That was all that mattered. He was ready for his eternal stay at Hel's chambers.

Hel had other ideas.

Something monstrous moved closer through the murky water. The ocean swayed. The waves swirled and divided at the appearance of the accursed beast. As if the ocean itself bowed down in servitude to him.

The glow of angry red eyes made Einar's skin crawl. A jagged grin widened, ready to swallow Einar whole.

It's smiling at us, as if it knew we'd fall prey to it, Einar thought. Bubbles blew from his mouth as he let out a hollow laugh.

Þórir was right. Survivors knew what to be afraid of. We Vikings never conquered the oceans.

It had already been conquered and its king roamed the abyss, claiming its loot.

All hail Taumur.

THE
MOSS-COVERED
VOLCANO

F inn pressed his face against the tiny airplane window. He and the passengers hitched their breaths in unison.

Barren wasteland of rocks and moss greeted them as the plane descended. A single asphalt road crossed the middle from the small population of houses near the airport.

It really looked like entering a completely new world. Finn couldn't help but smile.

"Look, over there, further to the right." Tyler, one of his best friends since college, pushed his face aside to point downward.

Finn followed Tyler's finger. His smile split his face nearly in half.

Plumes of ashen smoke almost touched the plane as it circled around the newly erupted volcano. It wasn't big, not nearly as big as the one with the unpronounceable name that messed up everything a decade ago, but it looked magnificent, nonetheless. Hot magma bubbled over, spraying lava and ash around the crater. The orange color stood out like a wonderful sore thumb amid the depressing black.

It was the reason Finn and his friends from college had decided to vacation on that tiny island with the bizarre midnight sun.

"I can't wait to get closer to it," Bryce said, snapping a photo just before the magma disappeared into the chasm, biding its time.

Finn agreed. The anticipation was killing him. He dug out his phone and browsed the websites. He groaned. "We can't do it tonight. Road closes in an hour and the weather conditions there aren't good."

Jared glanced at the window. Murky clouds obscured the low sun and a few raindrops pitter-pattered against the fiberglass. "It looks fine to me."

Finn shook his head. "According to this blog, we should always be prepared for the weather to turn bad at a moment's notice."

Jared scowled. "Aw, man. If I wanted rain, we could have just gone to Portland."

"Then what should we do after we land?" Bryce asked.

Finn rolled his eyes. His friends grinned at his exasperation. Why couldn't they act like adults and make room for other plans? Finn fought the urge to snort loudly. Ever since college, his friends had been notoriously bad at planning their activities. If they saw something they liked, they did it without hesitation. That was their way of living. Which was infuriating at times.

"I think we should just go to the hotel and crash. It's been a long flight," Finn said.

Tyler imitated a buzzer right next to Finn's ear. "Wrong, idiot. The clubs are open all night. I don't know about you but I wanna bang some slutty Icelandic chicks."

Bryce whooped his agreement.

Jared's eyes shined with excitement. "Yeah, let's go. I've heard the night life in Iceland is crazy, even crazier during the summer, because you know—" he gestured to the brightness outside.

Finn pursed his lips, his eyes darting down at the itinerary he had saved on his phone. He sighed and stuffed it inside his jacket. "Yeah, sure, let's do this."

The three friends whooped and shouted in glee until a flight attendant came over and politely told them to be quiet. Despite himself, Finn grinned. He wouldn't ever tell them, but his friends knew how to make a weekend trip unforgettable.

A blinding headache pounded against Finn's skull when he woke up the next morning. Was it morning? It was really hard to tell with the bright light beaming through the windows.

Last night was every bit as crazy as Finn had suspected. He remembered bits and pieces, how Jared, Bryce and Tyler had laughed at the modern structures in downtown Reykjavík and its childish attempts to resemble city centers in Europe and the States. They had spluttered at the astronomically high alcohol prices, but their outrage soon melted away when the liquids filled their stomachs and their bodies moved in tune with the loud Euro-pop music. Finn had watched with an amused grimace as they had flirted with any Icelandic girl who had glanced at them with curiosity. Being the frat boys that they were, they had been completely clueless to the girls' disinterest and when one of them lucked out, they'd say she was just being a bitch.

Tyler groaned as he slid down the mattress, crawling to the bathroom. "Never mixing drinks again," he muttered before the door shut.

Bryce coughed. "Ugh, I can still taste the awful licorice shot." He fumbled for the water bottle on the nightstand, ignoring the plaque that reminded guests it was perfectly safe to drink from the tap.

Finn chuckled a little, glad he had stuck with a couple of beers, albeit strong ones. He grabbed his laptop and propped it on his knees, fingers clicking and clacking on the keyboard as he tried to assemble last night's fun into an enjoyable blog post.

Jared threw a pillow from the next bed, head buried underneath the sheets. "Stop that noise, you're killing me."

Finn smirked. "I don't care. I've got a deadline with my blog and I promised my readers to have a little bit of taste of our journey here. With that said—" he hit *publish* with a flourish and shut down his laptop. "Are we ready for some exploring?"

A collective grumble filled the room. Finn snickered. He had them played like a fiddle when he had given them that night in exchange for ruling the next day. A stupid deal they had agreed upon in their drunken mirth.

They settled for a guided walking tour that involved checking out buildings like Alþingi, the Prime Minister's Office and Hallgrímskirkja Church. Finn was fascinated with the street art, particularly one that featured the Huldufólk, elven-like beings that were known for protecting nature. They stopped at various restaurants to try out Icelandic cuisine. Tyler turned green as he caught a whiff of the putrefied shark and stayed outside. Jared and Bryce were more courageous tasting the whale and puffin meat, but their stomachs churned when it came to the shark.

Finn laughed the entire time, capturing their reactions on his phone to use for his blog. "This is gold," he said as he popped a cube of shark into his mouth.

Jared stared at him. "You actually *like* that stuff?"

Finn wagged a finger at the two. "I'm from San Franscisco. I was raised on eating weird fish."

Bryce rolled his eyes and chugged down the shot of Brennivín that was offered after consuming the shark. "Can we eat some normal food tonight?"

Finn muttered an apology to the chef and the tour guide before they left and assured them not all Americans were that rude.

"It's fine. We get all types here," said the chef with a grunt.

Jared huffed at Finn's apology. "It's not our fault their food is terrible."

Finn groaned. "You were just tasting a sample of Icelandic cuisine. Look, check out this Instagram account of one restaurant here. It looks delicious."

His friends ignored him and began chatting about Football and how Iceland was sorely missing out on that sport.

Finn gritted his teeth. They had been bitching and moaning all day, not at all satisfied with the wonders the country offered. He was beginning to regret taking them with him on this trip. But they had the volcano left. Surely that wouldn't be a disappointment.

Air squeezed out of their lungs.

The wind ripped at their clothes and faces, turning them red and raw. Finn's friends huddled together, wrapped their arms around their chest to preserve what little heat was left in their frigid bodies.

"How close are we?" Jared yelled at Finn who walked ahead of him.

Finn turned around, pushing the scarf down from his face. Unlike his friends, he had packed layers of warm clothes to prepare for the two-hour walk toward the volcano.

"About thirty minutes left," he shouted and chuckled when he heard Jared, Bryce and Tyler swear loudly.

He had warned them about the weather changes in Iceland, but did they listen? He had told them the hike to the volcano would be about four hours back and forth, so wearing good clothes and hiking shoes was essential. He glanced behind his shoulder at his three friends who shivered against the bitter cold in only light jackets and sneakers. He shook his head. They never listened to him.

A blend of grey and green colored the ground; ash sprinkled the top of the moss and sharp lava rocks that cluttered the desolate environment. The moss cushioned most of the rocks' edges, but Finn felt the jagged points pierce through each step.

It would have been a lonely place if not for the groups of fellow tourists and Icelanders marching in single lines up the mountain. He noticed none of them wandered off the path, keeping to the downtrodden earth, leaving the rest of the mossy desert pristine. It felt like walking on an unknown planet, not daring to explore further unless someone experienced did so first. Excitement bubbled within when the natives described the eruption and Finn had to resist the urge to pull out his phone and record their shining faces. He had to save it for the erupting beauty that was ever approaching.

Finn's legs ached when he reached the top of the mountain that was safe for viewing according to the Search and Rescue crew—SAR—that stood at various places along the path. Rope guarded the edge of the mountain to deter travelers from probing further than what was allowed.

The crater welcomed him a few miles away. Smoke billowed from the center and from the hardened stream. A sulfur stench filled the area, reminding Finn of the vague scent of rotten eggs that he smelled when he showered at the hotel for the first time.

"Wait, that's it?" Tyler wheezed when he stumbled next to Finn. Beads of sweat glided down his temple.

"Has it stopped erupting?" Jared asked, finishing his last sip of his water bottle.

Finn shook his head. "Be patient. It'll start erupting anytime soon."

He took out his phone and began recording, panning to each side to capture the surroundings. His friends fussed, stomping their feet to the ground for warmth. They waited a few minutes in silence until they felt it.

The earth rumbled. Tiny rocks jittered and danced on the moss. People gasped and pointed. Hundreds of phones shot up. Finn zoomed in, heart pounding in his chest.

Crimson, orange and yellow merged in a thick glob, bubbling out of the crater slowly at first in short bursts, but then it picked up speed and spewed magma high into the air.

Hot air blasted up the mountain. The Icelanders backed away, shielding their faces. Finn followed suit, careful not to back up against a fellow mesmerized tourist.

Once the geyser subsided, the lava streamed down lazily, following the hardened passage from earlier bursts. Finn felt blessed seeing the display, like he had ticked off an important event from his bucket list. He turned to his friends. An Asian couple smiled back at him. He frowned. Where were they?

He heard one of the Search and Rescue call something in Icelandic and point down the hill. Finn looked down and swore.

Tyler, Jared, and Bryce skated down the perilous trail toward the lava stream, cheering like idiots. They approached the lava as one would get near a quiet lake, high fiving each other and jeering at the audience safe up on the mountain.

"That's so irresponsible," a woman said, tutting.

Finn agreed. He wanted to go down there and drag them back up, but his scrawny body was no match to three big immature ones. He could only watch as Jared raised his leg and stepped onto the grey lava, the red-hot current a few feet away. Bryce and Tyler copied their friend, laughing with glee and jumping up and down. Orange ember flickered alive underneath them.

"Oh shit," Finn muttered. He shouted a warning to Jared, pointing frantically at his feet.

Jared, Tyler, and Bryce noticed a little too late as the steady heat melted their sneakers. They yelped in surprise, stomping on the lava as if dancing on hot coals. They clambered down onto the moss and tore large parts of it to use to soothe their aching feet, leaving unearthed patches of grey dirt around them.

The Icelanders gasped. One lady covered her mouth with her hand while others stared at them with scorn. The Search and Rescue crew descended upon them.

Finding his resolve, Finn slid down the hill, panting to join them. He could tell by the sudden grim atmosphere they had done something bad. Worse than risking their own lives.

He caught one of the SAR crew reprimanding his three friends as they sat on the ground, rubbing the moss on their feet.

"Not only were you irresponsible and reckless, but you tore our moss," he said, hands on his hips and glaring.

Bryce snorted. "So?"

The SAR guy's nostrils flared. "The moss around this area is over a hundred years old. It's very delicate and grows very slowly. Do you have any idea how long it will take to regrow?"

Tyler shrugged and threw the moss that had sticky shoe plastic over his shoulder.

"Decades. It grows very slowly because of our short, wet and cold Arctic summers and you ripping it apart is not helping."

Jared snickered. "Yeah, your summers suck."

"Jared," Finn moaned, rubbing his chin.

"That's it. I'm calling it in. You're getting a fine for this," the crew man said, pulling out his phone and dialing the police.

"Are you fucking kidding me? Over a patch of grass?" Jared sputtered, looking from one SAR to Finn who grimaced.

"Our nature is delicate, and we ask visitors to treat it with respect. That's what you all agreed when you took the pledge on arrival at Keflavík airport," an older looking crew man said, his weathered face sunburnt and wrinkled.

"That pledge is bullshit, and you know it," Bryce said angrily.

"Be that as it may, we take destroying our natural heritage very seriously," the first SAR man said. He gestured for the three to stand up and walk up the hill.

They cursed and winced the entire hike. Finn felt pity for them, so he helped Jared along the way, enduring his endless moans whenever his injured feet stepped on the rocky surface. But shame washed over him when they were met with disdainful stares from not only the Icelanders but the other tourists as well.

"What are you looking at?" Tyler spat at gawking children who hid shrieking behind their parents.

"It's just moss. You should be more concerned about my feet. That shit hurts," Jared said.

"The police are waiting for you at the parking area," The SAR man told them.

"You can't expect us to walk all the way back in our condition? My feet are all blistered," Jared said.

The SAR crew all glared at him. Finn could feel the animosity toward them, that they wanted to leave them there as punishment, but he knew they had duties to uphold. "No, we'll give you a lift."

Finn hated the smug delight his friends had in that moment. Like they had won an argument. He wanted to punch that arrogance when he watched them settle comfortably in the seats of the SAR jeep. He opened his mouth to speak, to tell them how sorry he was and that their behavior did not reflect every American, but something held him back. He didn't have the guts to meet their steely gaze.

Just as the SAR had promised, a police car waited at the designated parking area. A bus full of tourists pulled up near the road, curious eyes staring down at them.

The SAR and the police officers discussed the matter quietly between themselves. Finn used the unsettling stillness within the furious wind to round on his supposed friends.

"What the hell were you thinking?"

"What? I just wanted to get a closer look. The lava had turned to stone already, so it was fine," Jared said.

"There were ropes on the hill that clearly meant no one was allowed to cross it, and you guys just ignored it completely," Finn hissed.

"We didn't hurt anyone," Bryce countered. "Except our own feet."

"You made us look extremely bad. Do you know how many cameras were recording you?"

Tyler smirked. "Cool. Maybe we'll go viral."

Finn gave up. He threw up his hands. "What, for being idiots of the year? Good luck sleeping with a local with that record."

Tyler muttered something under his breath, but the gale swallowed it before Finn caught his words. He shook his head, pinching the bridge of his nose to combat the headache knocking on his skull.

Two policemen approached them. Finn straightened. He glared at Tyler, Bryce and Jared, a silent threat to comply to whatever they would ask of them. He was *not* spending his last night in Iceland in a jail cell.

"So according to Helgi here," the police officer jerked his head to where the SAR crew man stood. "You guys did a little vandalizing near the volcano."

"It wasn't on purpose, sir," Finn hastened to answer. "Their shoes almost caught on fire."

The policeman nodded, his mouth a thin line. "Because they ignored safety protocols, am I correct?"

Finn glanced at his friends and for once, they bowed their heads in shame.

"Yes, sir, we're sorry about that. We just wanted to get a closer look at the volcano," Jared said.

"We all would like to do that, but nature's unpredictable, especially here in Iceland. The lava could have changed course and then you wouldn't be standing here."

Tyler bit his lower lip. Finn saw the leer in his eyes and knew he was resisting the urge to chortle.

"Well, you will still need to pay for the damages as well as having the SAR help you." The policeman handed them a fine. "Make sure you pay it before you leave the country."

They gave a solemn nod, their mouths twitching. They watched the police car disappear from the horizon.

Jared burst out laughing. "Did you hear that? We don't have to pay it until we leave." He held out the fine in one hand, then released it. The wind caught it and carried it out of sight.

Finn gasped. "Why did you do that?"

"Don't you get it? We don't have to pay the fine if it's no longer there. Especially when we're out of here."

"But—"

"What are they going to do? Search for us in the States?" Jared keeled over, his shoulders quaking in mirth.

"I wouldn't celebrate just yet," the old SAR man said.

Jared froze. That man had seen him toss the fine. Bryce and Tyler flanked their friend, puffing out their chests. "What are you going to do about it, old man? You don't even know who we are, you can't report us."

The old man shrugged. "You've disrespected pretty much everything Iceland has to offer, and there's nothing I can do about it. But our nature has a way of punishing those who don't respect it."

"Are you threatening us?" Tyler asked.

The old man sent him a yellowed smile. "I'm just saying you should be careful from now on."

He gave Finn a somber nod before joining his fellow crew back up the mountain.

Finn sat hunched on a bar stool, sipping his last beer. No matter how many drinks he would guzzle down, he couldn't shake the day's event from his mind. His phone kept reminding him with notifications of videos taken by tourists and Icelanders. He couldn't read the Icelandic comments, but he imagined nothing positive was being said about him and his friends.

Friends? He glared over his shoulder, where they jovially played pools without a care in the world. Their shoes and dirty socks littered the floor. Finn scoffed. He now saw what they truly were, complete douchebags. They hadn't even apologized to him as they went to the small rural bar near the volcano for their last night. They had planned to go to the Blue Lagoon before their flight the next day, but Finn couldn't bear the looks of contempt from the Icelandic employees. He had to skip it. Once the trip was over, he would sever ties with them. They were still living their frat lives, not bothering to grow up and be responsible adults.

A pool cue clattered on the hardwood floor.

Finn turned around, almost sliding out of the stool. His soon-to-be former friends stood frozen together, jaws slacked.

"What's going on?" Finn rubbed the exhaustion from his eyes. If they were planning on destroying yet another Icelandic property, he would leave them to it. He leaned over to the side, craning his neck towards the entrance.

He had to rub his eyes again.

Right in the middle of the open door stood the most beautiful woman he had ever seen. White, wispy hair that seemed to float, despite no wind banging against the threshold. Blood red lips that curled into a coy smile. Slender fingers that beckoned them to come hither.

Finn clambered out of his seat, almost faceplanting the floor in his haste.

"Have you ever seen anyone like that?" Jared's voice was hushed, as if scared his normal octave would repel the woman.

"I hope she has friends," Bryce muttered as he smoothed his hair.

As if on cue, three women walked inside, joining the white-haired beauty with alluring smiles. They all shared the same charm that seemed so otherworldly yet so irresistible at the same time.

Finn and the others walked across the bar to meet with them. They were wearing old-fashioned clothes of long woolen skirts, starch-white shirts, and decorative vests. Finn remembered seeing clothes like that on an advertisement for the Árbær Open Air Museum.

"Evening, ladies. Are you looking for a good time?" Tyler asked.

The women giggled. The one who had appeared first inside wet her lips with the tip of her tongue. "We might be. Would you like to join us?" She spoke serenely, as if her voice fluttered in rhythm to the small raindrops that had fallen from the sky earlier.

The guys nodded eagerly, like dogs begging for a treat.

"Then follow us. We know of a great place where we can have fun."

The women turned around in unison and ventured outside. They began walking on a small path from behind the bar, that lead to the mountain and the pillar of smoke rising below it.

Jared, Tyler, and Bryce grinned like idiots and gave chase, barely reacting when their bare feet hit the hollow rocks scattered around the route.

Finn hesitated. It was the middle of the night. The next bar or hotel in the vicinity was nine miles away and they had a flight to catch the next afternoon. He should go to the town's hotel and get a good night's rest without worrying what kind of havoc his friends would wreak.

But there was something about those women. Something that launched his feet forward and soon he was jogging to keep up.

Deep in his heart, he knew he didn't want to miss this.

The walk turned out to be harder than the one they had done earlier that day. Their blistered soles left a bloody trail of breadcrumbs in their wake. Finn found it weird they weren't complaining, like they had when they had their shoes on. The women turning around at intervals and blowing them kisses might have soothed their aching limbs.

They never seemed to be able to catch up to the women. They marched ahead, giggling and singing an ethereal tune, occasionally glancing behind their shoulders to see if Finn and the others were following.

The stench of sulfur assaulted their nostrils as they drew nearer to the volcano. Finn noticed that they were not on the regular path that led them to the back of the mountain. They were on unknown territory that only the women seemed to recognize.

"Are you sure this path is safe?" he called.

The lead woman paused and looked him straight in the eye. He hadn't noticed the ice gleaming in her almond-shaped eyes at the bar.

"It's safe…for us," she said.

Finn furrowed his brow. They were about twenty feet away from him. Had they always been that far away?

A painful shout brought him back. He looked down and nearly lost his footing.

A huge crevice in the earth lay hidden among the dull grey dirt and moss. Three figures moaned inside the darkness. Jared, Bryce, and Tyler had stumbled feet first into the gaping mouth.

"Fuck, I think I twisted my ankle," Jared groaned.

"Hey, Finn, help us up," Bryce yelled.

Finn sighed and crouched down, ready to extend his arm.

A mixture of hot and cold touched his shoulder. The woman pulled him up and shook her head.

"What are you doing? They need our help," Finn said as he tried to shrug her off.

She gripped him tighter. "This is where they belong."

Finn stared at her. White hot fury swirled in her ice-cold eyes. Her features instantly turned from innocently playful to dangerous. He then noticed the slightly elongated ears poking from the wispy hair. The sharp teeth. The claws digging into his flesh. The moss tinging her temples. He remembered the street art depicting the elven-like beings, the protectors of nature in Iceland.

"You guys aren't real," he gasped.

She cocked her head to the side. "The natives know better than to disrupt our nature, our home. They've seen what we can do. Your friends will find out soon enough."

A bead of sweat pearled on Finn's forehead. Her grip felt like icicles stabbing him. A warm gust of wind smacked him in the face. "What are you going to do to them?"

The Huldukona chuckled. It made the hair on the back of his neck stand on end. "Earlier they robbed the volcano of a meal when they stood upon its ground. It's only fair it gets to eat now."

Finn stared ahead. Hot orange lava cascaded toward them. The approaching heat got so intense it seared Finn's eyes. He screamed in pain.

"Finn, what's going on?"

"What's that noise?"

Finn barely heard their questions through the rumbling and hissing of the lava scorching the earth, destroying everything in its path.

"You can't do this," Finn blinked back tears to soothe his stinging eyes.

The Huldukona gave him an indifferent look. "An eye for an eye."

"What about me, then?"

She surveyed him, her eyes piercing his very soul. "We'll let you live. You tried your best to educate them. I hope you'll do better next time."

The ground shook violently, rocks tumbling down the hole.

"Holy shit, the fucking *ground* opened!" Jared shouted.

"Get us the fuck outta here, Finn!" Tyler yelled.

Finn turned away when the oppressing heat almost smothered him, the crimson glare burning into his retinae. He covered his ears as the lava poured over his friends. He could imagine their skin blister, white liquid popping like zits, their bodies burning and turning into jelly as the volcano consumed them. The stink of scorched flesh invaded his nostrils and festered inside.

His friends had been right. He would never forget this trip.

NAILS

"Look how loose my tooth is!" Jimmy's little brother, Dennis opened his mouth, and with a stubby finger moved a tooth in his lower jaw from side to side.

Jimmy grimaced. It was Dennis' third loose tooth within the span of a few weeks, forcing him to listen to his brother's excitement once again.

"Good for you," he droned as he reached for his headphones.

Dennis danced around Jimmy's chair. "Yes, it is, because I get a visit from the tooth fairy. Soon I'll be a dollar richer."

Irritation prickled Jimmy's skin like a consistent itch. He shouldn't feel jealous of his little brother—he got more allowance than Dennis—but the way Dennis gloated about it every single time got on his nerves. He needed to find a way to shut him up. Jimmy glanced down at his hand that covered his computer mouse. The fingernail tapping on the clicker. He grinned. A wonderfully, nasty idea sprang into his mind.

"You're lucky it's the tooth fairy that will be paying you a visit."

Dennis' dance slowed in mid-swivel, head cocked to the side. "What do you mean?"

Jimmy stared at the computer screen, forcing himself to hold his face straight. "There's another being who visits people at night, but it doesn't collect teeth."

Dennis inched closer to Jimmy's desk, his eyes as wide as baseballs. "What does it collect?"

Jimmy's mouth twitched as he extended his hand toward his little brother and flexed his fingers. "Fingernails."

The cheerful blush vanished from Dennis' face. "Ew, why does it do that?"

Jimmy shrugged. "No one knows. But do you remember the old Norse myth stories that Great-Grandpa Björn used to tell us?"

"I guess," Dennis said, eyebrows scrunched together in an effort to remember.

"Remember Naglfari, the hellship that's made out of dead people's fingernails and toenails?"

Dennis swallowed. "I remember you dropped a toy ship on my head when I was in the bathtub and I peed in the water."

Jimmy's big brother heart warmed at the memory. One of his best pranks ever. "Well, some say this being or imp likes the taste of fingernails, but others say that it collects them to add to Naglfari. I've even heard that if it's particularly hungry, it'll go for the toenails for a bite."

Dennis' eyes darted to the floor, no doubt looking at his own toes.

Jimmy allowed himself the tiniest of smirks. His stomach swooped in pleasurable waves as he basked in his little brother's dread. Messing with him was too fun to pass up. "So, if I were you, I'd keep those hands underneath the blanket tonight. Just as a precaution."

Dennis instantly balled his chubby hands into fists, hiding his fingernails, and nodded vigorously.

"Good, now get out. I've got homework to do."

Dennis tottered off, but not before giving Jimmy a worried glance over his shoulders. "Do you think it'll visit me tonight?"

Jimmy shrugged. "Don't know. Maybe it struck a deal with the tooth fairy. Someone else's tooth for your fingernails."

Dennis blanched and disappeared from the doorway with a frightened whimper.

Jimmy let out a small scoff that transformed into a fit of giggles. He had to stuff his knuckles into his mouth to stop from bursting into laughter. That had been too easy. Better than the boogieman.

Jimmy's mom entered his room just before bedtime. Her arms crossed, lips pursed in a thin line and brow furrowed.

A stone plunged into Jimmy's stomach. That look on her face only meant one thing: He was in trouble.

"Dennis can't sleep," she said, her tone flat.

Jimmy avoided her piercing eyes and busied himself with changing into his pyjamas. "Oh?"

"Yes. Apparently, he's afraid that some imp-like creature will come into his room and steal his fingernails." His mom took a few more steps into Jimmy's room until she towered over him. She wasn't much taller than Jimmy, but her silent, white-hot fury stretched her body, so she almost reached the ceiling.

Jimmy gulped but continued to slide into his pyjama pants while trying to ignore the beads of sweat sliding down his back.

"I asked him where he'd heard such a story…" his mom's voice trailed off.

Jimmy couldn't hold off the inevitable any longer. He looked up. His mom's brow was still furrowed but the angry flash in her eyes had deflated to sullen disappointment.

She sighed as she stooped down to pick up the jeans he'd dropped on the floor. "I wish you would stop scaring him like that, James. You're fifteen already. Try to grow up. Or else you'll be keeping watch in his room while he sleeps."

Jimmy only felt a slight twinge of remorse. It was in his blood to tease his little brother. Siblings did that. It was harmless. But it'd be best to apologize to appease his mom.

"I'm sorry, mom. It was just a little joke. Won't happen again."

Jimmy's mom gave him a curt nod, handed him the folded jeans and made toward the door. "Oh by the way, and for that little 'joke' you're grounded for two days."

The stone in his stomach cemented everything it touched within his body. Jimmy wanted to throw the TV remote at the door, to scream at the injustice. Grounded? Just for telling a make-believe story? He punched his pillow. It was all Dennis' fault. That little shit had to go and tell on him. Jimmy wanted revenge. He opened his drawer and pulled out a blank sheet of paper. He grabbed his markers and began sketching the imp. Pale grey, huge black eyes, razor sharp teeth and four arms instead of two, to make it even scarier for his six-year-old brother.

He held up his masterwork with a smirk. So, Dennis couldn't sleep, huh? Well, Jimmy would give him something to enhance his nightmares. But not now, not when his little brother was still awake and would alert their mom of his prank. He'd pin it on his door in the morning. It'd be the first thing he'd see.

Jimmy shuffled into bed with a delightful snicker and hoped that his time being grounded would pass at the speed of light.

Sleep eluded Jimmy. Throughout the night, he tossed and turned, heat enveloping him tight like his own sheet. His once-pleasant dreams of shooting up bad guys in *Call*

of Duty evaporated until a void of darkness summoned him. There he saw nothing, heard nothing.

Then the skin around his fingertips prickled, as if minuscule pinpricks punctured the flesh hard enough that Jimmy groaned in his sleep. The void then filled with skittering and buzzing, in which flying insects and scorpions flitted around, taking turns at pinching Jimmy's fingers and toes.

One such stinger hurt so much Jimmy jerked awake, his pyjama shirt sticking to his slick back. He pushed hair from his face, panting. What the hell kind of dream was that? It had been so vivid. His fingers still tingled. He turned on the lamp on the nightstand and examined his hand under the warm light. Nothing. They were sweaty, but normal. It had just been a dream. A very uncomfortable one. It took Jimmy a while to settle back under his sheet and he kept the light on for the duration of the night.

Jimmy's mom noticed how sluggish he seemed the next morning.

"Rough night?" She raised a skeptical eyebrow as she laid down a bowl of cereal in front of him.

Jimmy yawned. "Had a weird dream."

"Me too!" Dennis piped up and looked wide-eyed at his brother. "I dreamed the imp was staring at me through the window."

Jimmy's spoon full of wheat pillows hovered before his mouth. He forgot to pin the drawing on Dennis' door. But it didn't seem like he needed it in the first place. His smirk vanished when he caught his mom's glare before she handed her younger son his breakfast.

"Oh, don't worry about that. It saw that you were a kid. It apparently only comes after *grown-ups*." He emphasized the last word, as if that alone would make his mom worry.

Dennis hitched in a breath and clutched his mom's arm. "Is mom in trouble, then?"

"Don't be silly, honey. Jimmy is only teasing you." She ruffled Dennis' hair affectionately.

Jimmy scowled while muttering "it was only a joke," into his cereal.

The other two soon engaged in a cheery chatter, with Dennis holding his loose tooth and yapping away on what he was going to spend that dollar he was expecting. As Dennis began listing the toys and candy, Jimmy rummaged in his pocket for the portable earphones to tune out the drivel. His eyes travelled across the table, at the open newspaper laid on it, and he noticed something.

His mom rested her fingers on the paper. One of her nails was chipped. It wasn't an obvious chip, just a missing piece in the corner of her nail.

Jimmy raised an eyebrow but thought nothing of it. His mother was prone to nail-biting when she read crime fiction. She probably started on a new book last night.

Jimmy had the same dream that night.

Tiny legs skittering across his fingers and toes. Wincing as the insects bit into his flesh.

He woke with a start, the window outside still pitch-black. This time, a slight stinging sensation buzzed his fingertips.

Jimmy jumped out of bed and threw the sheets on the floor, convinced that some bug had bit him.

He found nothing, even when he turned on the ceiling light, even when the bridge of his nose was less than an inch from the mattress, scanning it for invisible bed bugs.

Someone giggled.

It was low and fluttery. If Jimmy hadn't been already alert, he wouldn't have heard it.

His head whipped up and stared at the door, certain that his little brother had finally worked up the nerve to prank him.

"Dennis?"

He hated the caution in his voice, bordering on fear. Why was he afraid? There was nothing in his room. His mind was still jittery from the dream, still in the process of separating it from reality.

He shook his head, dragged the sheets back on the bed and climbed inside.

He was being silly, letting his imagination get the better of him.

The goosebumps on his arms took a long time to subside, though.

"Jimmy, it's time for you to wake up. Don't make me come up there and drag your ass downstairs," his mom hollered from the kitchen.

Crust covered Jimmy's eyes, more than usual. It took him a few moments to rub it all away. Was that normal? He wasn't sure, perhaps it happened when people didn't get enough rest. His brain was mush. Getting back to sleep had been a Herculean effort that succeeded only when sleeping over his superhero comic books. He knew he was only imagining it, but he still felt that weird tingle in his fingers.

Yawning with almost every step down the stairs, he lumbered to the seat in the kitchen.

"Did you stay up late last night too?" Jimmy's mom sighed as she placed his usual bowl of cereal in front of him.

"No, I had that weird dream again."

"Oh? What was it about?"

Jimmy glanced at his little brother who was licking his heated Pop-Tarts, jam smeared across his face. If he told his mom about the dream, Dennis might get affected by it and then his mom would blame *him* for it. He didn't want to risk getting grounded again. He bit the inside of his cheek and shrugged. "I don't remember it. It was just weird."

When his mom handed Jimmy his lunch, he noticed she had a Band-Aid on her middle finger, concealing her fingernail.

"Mom, what happened to your finger?"

"Oh, this? I must have pricked it on my earring or something before I went to sleep last night. It's nothing, barely hurts anymore."

Jimmy's brow furrowed. He stared at her hand. The chipped fingernail had been clipped off. "Were you reading the night before?"

His mom shook her head. "No, I had to fold the laundry, which you still haven't put in your closet." The sharpness in her voice was back, and Jimmy winced at his forgetfulness.

"Sorry, I'll go do it right now. Hold on."

He went for the stairs, but not before glancing back over his shoulder at his mom. Had she clipped her own fingernail last night?

The weird tingling had been the strongest in his middle finger. Right around his fingernail.

Jimmy spent the afternoon researching.

It was silly, he knew, but he just had to know. He didn't dare voice his concern out loud because it was ludicrous. But a tiny voice in the back of his mind whispered, *what if his little tall-tale was true?*

He scoured the internet, Reddit forums, Wikipedia pages and wound up with nothing. The only thing that came close to his make-believe imp had been the Duende, a gnome-like creature from Latin American and Filipino folklore.

He studied the art from various people who had claimed that they had been visited by the Duende. Long ears, tomato-shaped nose, a friendly smile and usually a hat that covered the stringy hair.

Jimmy frowned as he glanced at his drawing that laid sideways on the desk. It didn't look like the imp. His drawing, while crude looking and amateurish, sent off sinister vibes. The Duende wouldn't be able to scare his little brother, but Jimmy's drawing of the imp might. He also remembered that he hadn't described the imp to Dennis, only described its actions and motives.

Jimmy stared at the drawing. It didn't make any sense. He had to remind himself that he hadn't been dreaming of the imp, only of insects.

Maybe that's what he is. A lord of insects, his mind betrayed him.

A chill scurried down his back, almost like a beetle…

Jimmy smacked himself on the back. Such a stupid thing. That imp didn't even exist. He took down the browsers, not wanting to look at the smirk of the Duende. Almost as if it was mocking him. He tore the drawing into little pieces and shoved them into the waste-paper basket.

Jimmy wasn't afraid. He went for the pantry downstairs and grabbed a container of bug spray. He kept it behind the nightstand. Whether it'd be stinking bugs or the imp itself, Jimmy was going to be ready.

They plagued his dream again. Made a nest of it.

All Jimmy heard was tiny pitter-patter like raindrops on glass, only harder and faster. The noise of thousands of little feet crawling all over him, nibbling on his flesh, pulling on his fingernails…

Jimmy yelped awake. Without hesitation, he reached for the bug spray and cast a putrid mist of chemicals around him.

Eyes stinging, he coughed and swatted the air, hoping flies would drop dead on his sheets.

He heard no plops, no small thuds. No agonizing squeaks he imagined bugs would have if they had voices.

It was just him in his room that now stank of pesticide.

His heart quieted. Stomach acid rose to his throat in frustration. Silence seemed to swallow him whole.

Yet, in the back of his mind, that little imp cackled like a madman.

Jimmy glanced down at his hands.

A couple of his fingernails were chipped—

Wait, chipped? They looked like something had bit them.

"You don't look so good, honey." Jimmy's mom felt his forehead. "You're all pale. You don't seem to have a fever, though."

Jimmy mustered up a shrug. That movement alone felt like moving a boulder an inch or so. He was so tired. He had upended his room last night, pulling drawers out and dumping clothes and knick-knacks on the floor in search of the elusive imp. Of course he hadn't found it and had spent the rest of the night carefully folding everything back into the drawers so he wouldn't face his mother's wrath.

But he was certain the imp had been in his room. How else could he explain the chipped fingernails? The mere idea that someone had nibbled on his fingers, that someone's tongue had licked them, sent a nauseating chill down his spine. Jimmy shoved his hands under his thighs. He couldn't even think of looking at them at that moment.

"Maybe you'll perk up after you've had some breakfast." Jimmy's mom slid the usual bowl in front of him.

Jimmy looked down.

The bowl was full of fingernails. Clipped ones, yellowed ones, even whole ones filled the bowl. Blood tinged their ends, coloring the milk in Pepto pink.

If rouge remained on Jimmy's pale face, it instantly switched to the shade of green. A burning pinch in his gut flipped his stomach, sending his dinner on a backwards slide up his esophagus.

His mom leaned down, rubbing her hands on her pants. "Jimmy, are you—"

Steaming hot chunks of last night's half-digested meatloaf spewed out of Jimmy's mouth, splattering the corner of the table and landing with a wet *splat* on the floor.

"Jimmy!" His mom yelled and hurried over to him. "My goodness, you really might be sick."

Jimmy coughed and hacked, the stomach acid searing his throat. "Get that bowl away from me," he rasped.

"But it's your favorite," his mom said feebly, glancing at the kitchen table while rubbing his back. "It doesn't matter. Why don't you take the day off and go rest in bed? I'll call the school and tell them you're sick."

Jimmy didn't want to stay at home. That's where the imp hid. At school, he'd be safe. He'd be surrounded by friends and his mind would be occupied by schoolwork and gossip. He wouldn't have to look at all those fingernails.

"C'mon, let's get you cleaned up and into bed. Don't worry about the mess, I'll clean it up later." His mom gently pulled Jimmy from his seat and led him upstairs.

"I'm sorry, mom," he mumbled.

She offered him a sympathetic smile. "It's fine, honey."

Jimmy told himself not to, but his disturbed curiosity got the best of him. As they ascended the stairs, he looked in the kitchen. At the bowl. Wheat pillows had turned into beige mush within all the milk.

Jimmy blinked.

Wheat pillows? They hadn't been fingernails? Had he been imagining it all along? He pushed the heels of his palms deep into his eyes and groaned.

He was so tired.

"Is it a stomach bug?" Jimmy's mom wondered aloud as she fluffed his pillow and wrapped him even tighter in his sheet.

It was sweet of her. She used to do that when Jimmy was sick as a child. But he wasn't a little kid anymore and the coddling felt a bit uncomfortable. He stayed silent. He didn't want to seem ungrateful to his mother's kindness.

"Well, whatever it is, you'll feel better after a good rest. I'll bring you some chicken noodle soup later today." She brushed strands of hair away from his eyes.

"Don't you have to go to work?" Jimmy asked.

She shook her head. "Not when my baby is sick."

Jimmy groaned. "I'm not your baby, mom. I'm fifteen, remember? I'll be fine. You can go to work."

"But what if you get sick again?"

Jimmy pointed to the waste-paper basket underneath his desk. "Then I'll use that or go to the bathroom. It's not that far. Besides, I'm not that sick."

Jimmy's mom hesitated, her eyes darting between the door and Jimmy.

"Your boss will get annoyed if you take the day off, especially to look after your teenage son." Jimmy pointed out, remembering the times when his mom vented about her unreasonable boss during dinner.

She chewed on her thumbnail. More Band-Aids adorned her fingers. Some were moist with blood.

Jimmy stared. Had those Band-Aids been there this morning?

A drop of crimson trickled down her hand. "I suppose you're right," his mom muttered, unfazed by the increased stream of blood running from her injured fingers.

"Mom, are you okay?" Jimmy asked, dread numbing his limbs. "What happened to your hands?"

His mom's brow furrowed. "Nothing. They're fine. It's just a little scratch."

Jimmy blinked rapidly. Just a little scratch? Didn't she see the blood? It was running like a waterfall down her arms, drowning the carpeted floor with crimson.

He shut his eyes, breathing fast through his nose. He dug his fingernails deep into his clammy palms, registering the dull pain. He remembered what he had said to Dennis yesterday, about the imp attacking adults. That being was affecting his mom as well, yet she didn't notice it. Couldn't she feel what was happening to her?

"Just go, mom. I'll be fine," Jimmy urged her, waving her away with his hand.

She shouldn't be in the house. That's where the imp's effects were the worst.

"All right, if you say so. I'll call you later today to remind you of that soup, okay?"

"Yeah, fine. Just go, before it's too late." Jimmy's heart pounded, warmth seeping out of his pores and transforming into cold sweat.

"Mommy, is Jimmy going to be okay?" Dennis' concerned voice asked from the doorway.

Jimmy gritted his teeth, waiting for his little brother's shriek at the puddle of blood underneath their mom's feet.

It never came.

"Yes, sweetie. He's just a little under the weather. He'll be fine."

Jimmy opened one eye, just a slit.

The blood was gone. So were the Band-Aids, save for the one on her middle finger. What was going on? Was he still dreaming? He quickly pinched his thigh. The sharp pain coursed through his body. Not dreaming, he concluded, but it had been so vivid.

Jimmy's mom leaned over and kissed his forehead. "You're a little warm, honey. Remember to take one painkiller before you rest."

The kiss felt real. His mom was real. But he couldn't trust his mind anymore.

"Feel better, Jimmy," Dennis squeaked by the door before he and their mom left him alone.

Jimmy hid underneath the sheets.

It was childish of him, he knew, but he felt his mind clear within the stuffiness. He wasn't sure if the sheets gave him protection against the imp. He racked his mind. So far, the vile creature had only attacked him and his mom, because it only attacks adults. Why was that? Had he, Jimmy, thought of the reason for it? Was it too late to think of one?

It didn't matter because he was already affected.

But didn't that mean that his little brother was safe? Could that also mean that Dennis' room was safe? Maybe the imp was bound to attack in places that belonged to adults. Maybe Dennis' innocence protected from the imp. Perhaps some of that innocence still lingered in his room.

All of these were speculations. Jimmy had no real proof of this, but he had to give it a shot.

He threw the sheets off and climbed out of bed.

The soles of his feet stung and pinched.

He winced and looked down.

Fingernails and toenails covered the entire floor.

Broken ones, calcified ones, curved ones encrusted with dirt, nails that still had skin hanging off from them. All kinds filled the bottom of his room.

Jimmy covered his mouth, clenching his teeth to suppress his gag reflex. He reached for his shoes, only to find fingernails cascading from them like a waterfall from hell.

Sweat beaded down his brow and stung his eyes. Wild drums beat within his chest.

He knew the imp wanted him to walk to the door on his bare feet. Fat chance. He turned around and clasped his hand on the lock of his window. He'd open it and climb outside on the gutters. The lock wouldn't budge, no matter how hard he squeezed it and turned right and left. He balled his hands into fists. The imp had thought of everything. Going through his room was the only way to get to Dennis' room. He swallowed his bile and pressed his foot harder against the sea of fingernails and toenails.

They crunched, bristled and stung his feet like tiny, sharp, disfigured Legos. He gritted his teeth against the pain that shot up his body with each touch. His stomach rolled as with each crunch, the air filled with copper and the stench of old soil. Grave dirt, Jimmy was convinced of it.

After all, the imp took some of the nails to add to Naglfari.

Damn his twisted imagination.

He limped for the door, careful not to let any of the fingernails that clung to his soles dig into the flesh any deeper. He exhaled, unaware that he had been holding in his breath the last leg of the journey, as he slumped against the wall opposite the door. The hallway was thankfully fingernail-free.

Jimmy plucked the ones stuck to his feet one by one, wincing and recoiling at touching a dead person's body part. He shut his eyes closed for one second and opened them again. Nothing had changed. His room was still the center of human nails galore.

It wasn't an imagination. It was all very real.

Then he'd be safe in Dennis' room. He just had to be.

Jimmy limped to the end of the hall where his little brother's room almost seemed to beam with protective energy, beckoning him forward.

He shut the door and slouched in Dennis' small computer chair—way smaller than his own— and expelled a long sigh of relief. Plushies and toys covered every nook and cranny in the room. Toy cars and driving lanes made of cardboard littered the floor like trash at a landfill. Not a single fingernail could be seen. Jimmy smiled, his eyelids getting heavier with each passing second.

He was safe.

Jimmy heard giggles.

Was Dennis home from school? He had to get out of his room to avoid awkward questioning.

His eyelids were so heavy, almost as if glued shut. He grunted.

More giggling, this time nearer.

"Dennis, is that you?" he asked, his voice hoarse from sleep.

He felt a tug in his little finger. He flinched and realized that his arm hadn't flown up in defense like his brain had commanded. It stayed put on his lap.

He tried moving his arms again. They were cement blocks. Not budging.

He blew frantic air through his nose, his heart jackhammering against his ribcage.

This couldn't be right. He was in Dennis' room. He was supposed to be safe.

He put all his mental focus into opening his crusted eyes. They flickered and everything was blurry for a moment.

Something yanked at his ring fingernail painfully.

Jimmy yelped and blinked his bleary eyes downward. Dread ran through his veins as the stomach acid made a come-back up his throat.

An imp-like creature sat hunched on his knee. No bigger than a large Starbucks cup. It giggled as its huge, oval-shaped, completely dark nocturnal eyes leered at Jimmy. Its flaky skin stretched thin against its pointy skeleton. It had four gangly arms instead of two, with three needle-like fingers, reminding Jimmy strongly of the insects in his dreams. It wore nothing but a crude armor plate made of various fingernails, some of them old and brown with deadman's blood. Its mouth took most of the space of its tiny, misty pale grey, hairless head. It spread wide, revealing rows of long, sharp teeth, like box cutter blades.

Jimmy's own creation.

"You can't be real," Jimmy croaked, his bottom lip trembling. He tried to wiggle his knee, to throw that abomination off his leg and away from him.

His knee felt numb. No matter how much Jimmy grunted and groaned, his body was as still as the very chair he sat in. Rooted to the ground.

The imp let out an excited giggle that sounded like the trilling of a thousand insect wings. The hair at the back of Jimmy's neck stood on end.

"What are you going to do?"

The imp cocked its head to the side, as though contemplating its next move. Then it raised two of its four arms and jabbed the needle fingers into Jimmy's fingernail. The sensation felt like getting his finger jammed between the crack of a door.

Jimmy hurled curses at it, spittle dripping from his mouth. He tried to swat it away with his other hand. It hung limp and heavy by his side, like dead weight. Why couldn't he move?

The imp snickered, bent down over the fingernail, and nibbled on Jimmy's cuticle.

The tiny teeth sunk into Jimmy's flesh and shredded his skin like multiple deep papercuts.

Jimmy shrieked in pain. His muscles tightened and loosened with each cut, short bursts of electric jolts coursing through his body.

"No, stop! Please!" Jimmy begged, tears burning behind his eyes.

The imp didn't listen or chose to ignore Jimmy's pleas. When the flesh was shredded away, it used its four arms to pull the entire fingernail away from the finger. The needle-like fingers dug deep into his flesh.

Each nerve connected to the nail severed one by one. The pain felt like Jimmy was being whipped as the taut nerve slung back into the bloody, meaty pulp left in the middle.

It examined the fingernail like a jeweler would a precious ring, and then opened its maw and shoved it into its drooling mouth.

Minutes felt like hours as the imp meticulously removed the rest of Jimmy's fingernails, storing them in its bulging mouth.

Jimmy had succumbed to the pain with a faint at first, only to be brutally awakened when the imp got to work on his thumbnail, his biggest nail. A whimper or two escaped his lips now and again. His throat was raw from screaming and crying, his eyes were dry and stinging.

He would die here. He was certain of it. The imp wouldn't leave him alive. It was too cruel for that. He didn't want to think what kind of method the vile creature would use for execution. He didn't want to give it any kind of weapon.

Then he heard the front door open and close downstairs.

His mom had come back home. Hope soared in the air.

"Mom!" He bellowed. "Help me!"

He heard hurried footsteps clambering up the stairs.

"Guess you can't finish me off now, fucker! I beat you." Jimmy's elation flowed through every nerve, even the severed ones in his fingers, and he couldn't suppress his triumphant laugh.

The imp simply stared at him, dark eyes squinting. Then it smiled.

The door burst open, and Jimmy's mom rushed inside. She gasped and clutched the doorknob. "Jimmy!"

"Mom, help me get rid of the imp. Kick him off or something," Jimmy shouted.

His mom's eyes were wide with shock. "Jimmy, what in God's name are you doing?"

"What are you talking about? Can't you see the imp?" Jimmy nodded down at his lap.

His heart almost stopped.

The imp was gone. His blood was the only thing on his lap.

And his fingernails.

Jimmy's eyes trailed to his right hand. Dark crimson covered the tips of his fingers and the pliers he was holding.

"What were you doing?" His mom repeated, fear laced into her quaking voice.

Jimmy dropped the pliers. He could move his arms. He stared at his hands. "No, no, no, no. It wasn't me who did this. It was the imp. I swear, mom, it was the imp!"

His mom was already on the phone, speaking to the nine-one-one operator, pleading for help.

"No, I know it was the imp, he's here somewhere." Jimmy pushed the drawer from the wall with naked, raw fingertips, hoping it'd be hiding behind it. He swept the toys away with his legs, the toy trains and their inhabitants banging against the wall. He went on all fours and checked under the bed, his open-mouthed panting swirling up the dust beneath it, the blood dripping from his fingers painting a crude drawing across the floor.

But there was no sign of the elusive imp.

"It was here, I know it was. I have proof." Jimmy grabbed his mom and pulled her to his room where he had crossed the sea of nails.

His bedroom was spotless. Not a toenail in sight. Jimmy expelled a gasp of air, as though taking a punch to the stomach.

"No, no, no, no. It wasn't like that. It was full of fingernails and toenails. I had to walk on them and everything." Jimmy fumbled for his shoes next to his bed, turned them over to see if a single nail would fall out. Only a pebble dropped.

This couldn't be right. Did the imp erase everything before his mom came home? The trilling of thousand wings echoed in his ears, the imp's mocking giggles consuming his senses. He clamped a hand on one ear while chewing on the meaty pulp that was left of his thumb, his manic laughs syncing with the imp's.

His mom wouldn't listen to him, no matter how much he screamed. The EMTs didn't listen as they hauled him into their ambulance, bound on the gurney.

They soothed him with a sedative.

As the drug numbed Jimmy's senses and fraying mind, he felt himself relax. Maybe it was for the best. Perhaps all these sleepless nights had made him hallucinate the atrocity. Maybe he'd get the help he needed. Maybe the hospital would help him get rid of the imagery of the horrid imp.

His mom looked through the ambulance's window, teary-eyed but waving a hopeful hand. Jimmy nodded. He would get better, for his mom's sake. He settled into his temporary bed and waited for the drugs to take him to slumberland.

He heard taps.

Jimmy opened his eyes. The imp tapped its needle claws on the ambulance's window. It turned its pale grey head over its shoulder to look at Jimmy's mom. It smacked its huge lips at the sight of her juicy fingernails.

Jimmy's screams filled the ambulance as it drove him away from his mother.

HOPE

ope is what made life worth living for Barry.

It's what made him capable of finding Nicole. He didn't think rediscovering that spark of affection was possible for a guy like him.

But then again, hope doesn't work in mysterious ways.

It's intentional.

It has purpose.

Nicole's lips spread thin across her mouth as she gazed up the mountain that lied ahead of her. That was Barry's surprise? A hike?

Barry smiled as he took the hiking gear out of the trunk. "You don't look enthused."

Nicole hitched up a grin, helped him with the gear and gave him a peck on the cheek. "I'll admit, it's not what I expected but I'm willing to give it a shot."

Barry's eyes shone with excitement. "You'll love it. This is one of my favorite spots. I have only taken one other person up the mountain…"

A cloud drew over and Barry got silent. Nicole chewed her lip. That's the second time since this morning that a darkness seemed to possess him. She took his hand. "I'm sure you'll be able to take her here soon."

Barry squeezed her hand and let out a shuddering breath. "Yeah, I hope so. Come on, let's get a move on."

She nodded, tightened the straps of her backpack and followed him on the trail.

The Douglas firs and pine trees surrounded the pair, reaching high into the sky. Nicole craned her neck to get a proper look. Despite herself, she whistled her awe. "I always knew they were tall, but seeing them up close, *wow!*"

"You're more of a city girl, aren't you?" Barry asked.

Nicole giggled. "Guilty as charged. I like being outdoors, jogging and stuff but going this close to the mountains isn't something I'm used to."

The cloud that swirled within still darkened Barry's features. Nicole cursed inwardly. Now he probably thought she didn't want to be here. Which was true, but she would never tell him that.

"But I'm glad, you know, that you asked me to come. I'm happy we're spending more time together," she hurried to add.

A smile crept across Barry's lips. Nicole sighed in relief. She *was* glad that he asked her. They hadn't seen each other the last couple of days, but that was to be expected; His daughter was sick, something to do with her kidneys, and treatment was so far away from the horizon it blurred the lines. This hike up the mountain would hopefully lift his spirits and create happy memories. Or the very least distract him from his daughter's condition. Despite going out for a few weeks, Nicole felt something for Barry. Whether it was affection, pity or the big L, she wasn't sure. But she was keen to explore it further, even if it meant climbing up a steep mountain besieged by vast woods.

The autumn breeze rustled the remaining leaves. The golden fragments fluttered in circles until one landed on top of Barry's head.

"It fits your beard," Nicole said and picked it off. An aroma of crisp fall, of sour apples and campfires, overtook her senses.

"Beats the pumpkin spiced lattes any day, am I right?" Barry asked with a playful glint in his eyes.

She nodded. "Definitely."

He went to one of the Douglas firs—the young lean ones— and gave it a mighty shake. The leaves tumbled down in a flurry. Nicole gasped as colors of auburn, gold, amber and umber drifted around them in an autumn shower. She spread out her arms and spun in circles, her laugh echoing throughout the forest.

Barry joined her, clapping and smiling widely. His joy made Nicole's heart dance.

It was going to be a good day after all.

Higher and higher they climbed, Barry in the lead and Nicole trying her hardest to disguise her fatigue.

They had gone deeper into the forest as they ascended. The trees cluttered so close together, it was as if they had merged in a grotesque experiment. A branch snagged at Nicole's hair, and she yelped.

"You're not getting scared, are you?" Barry asked, chuckling.

Nicole straightened. "No," she huffed. "But we're going a little deep, aren't we? There aren't any bears around here?"

Barry shook his head. "They're hibernating. Don't worry, we'll be back to the car before sundown."

He continued onward, unperturbed by the reaching claws of the forest giants.

Nicole opened her mouth to say something but decided not to. He needed this distraction. It wasn't time to start nagging or asking to turn around to go home in the comforts of a warm house and cushy sofa. *Wait a few more days, Nicole, and then you can show him some of your true colors.*

Barry veered left, yet his head swiveled in both directions. His steps slowed, as if hesitant.

"What's wrong? Are we lost?" Nicole wiped sweat from her forehead.

Barry turned around. Nicole blinked. For a moment, the dark circles under his eyes, which Nicole found charming and understandable given the circumstances, seemed to have colored the whites of his eyes. Sudden dread crawled down her spine.

Then he smiled and the darkened woods lit up. "Nah, I'm just looking for the markers." He pointed to a neon yellow smudge just above his head on one of the pine trees. "I marked them the last time I came here."

The dread flushed down along with Nicole's sigh of relief. She shook her head while chuckling under her breath. Silly of her to immediately think of the worst. Her heart hadn't slowed down, though, and sweat drenched her cotton T-shirt underneath her fleece jacket.

"Mind if we took a little break?" she asked.

"Remember, I'm not much of a hiking person."

Barry glanced back at her, a slight curl of the lip. Worry creased his forehead. "Of course."

He guided her to a straight-looking tree which had been stripped of its bark. "Thank you," Nicole wheezed. She gratefully accepted a bottle from him and took a few swigs of water, waiting for her heartrate to ease up.

Barry crouched down. "May I?" he asked, pointing at her legs.

Nicole raised an eyebrow but nodded. Barry gently massaged her calves, fingers digging into her strained muscles. Heat traveled from her heart and spread down. Barry's eyes, however, darted further into the forest. Something was bothering him, Nicole sensed it. Was it her? Was he getting annoyed at her lack of hiking experience? Now *she* needed a distraction from her obtrusive thoughts.

"Tell me about your girl, Barry. How is she doing?"

Barry narrowed his eyes for a second before his features softened as his mind seemed to travel back home. "There are times when the kidneys are inflamed, the lights within her seem turned off but thankfully that doesn't happen often nowadays. She knows it kills me. When the lights are on, however, she brightens up the whole house, my entire being. After Sharon passed away, it was hard to get up in the morning, but Hope made it worth it. She's the sole reason I'm functional now. She's so *kind*, Nicole, just absolutely precious. Her smile is so infectious my cheeks hurt every day, but I don't care. Her wellbeing is more important than my pain."

His hands balled into fists. Nicole noticed the tremors before he got them under control.

"She puts on a brave façade even when her body is on the brink of shutting down because she doesn't want me to see it. But I always see. I always know. And it kills me there's nothing I can do."

Nicole's heart sank. Talking about Hope had had the opposite effect on him. She bent over and wrapped her arms around him. His muscles tensed.

"I'm sorry. I shouldn't have asked. I'm sorry," she whispered.

He sniffled, took a deep breath and shrugged her off. "It's okay. Let's just keep moving."

For the second time, Nicole wanted to say something. That they should turn back and go see Hope. Hiking had been a bad idea.

"Just a few more miles and then we can go back. C'mon, we've come this far." Barry held out a hand.

Nicole bit the inside of her cheek. She had been aware of Barry's baggage since they met on Tinder, and she felt bad calling Hope that, but she admired his strength. She wanted something of that strength for herself. At the beginning doubt's gnarly fingers had begun clawing at her heart. Now Nicole kicked it and locked it away. She took Barry's hand.

Jumping into the deep end never hurt anyone.

Nicole had lost track of time.

She gazed up at the haunting giants who obscured what little sunlight dared to peek through. Her side seared from the effort and her bottle of water was almost empty. Her stomach growled as she realized she hadn't had any food since breakfast. That was hours ago.

"How much further?" she asked, pressing her hand on her hip to ease the pain.

Barry didn't look back, just kept going, taking her further away from the car. "We're almost there. I've got a surprise waiting for you."

It had better be food, Nicole thought and pushed the little wormy dread out the door in the back of her mind. It had no business staying there when food was a priority.

The maze of grabby, stingy trees thinned until only one or two stood on their path. The big roots and pointy rocks drowned under luscious green moss. Midday rays broke out from the trees' clutches and bathed the clearing in warmth. Barry stood in the middle, eyes closed, absorbing the light. This place was beautiful. Peaceful and all for themselves.

"Oh, Barry," she gasped, stooping down to touch the petals of an Indian Paintbrush that grew near the roots of a lonesome tree. "This place is wonderful."

Barry thrust his chest out with a smirk. "I told you this place was worth it." He pointed to the checkered blanket spread on the moss. "Go get comfortable. Have something to eat."

Nicole blinked. "You prepared a picnic?"

He nodded, that playful gleam shining bright. "I sure did. I had a feeling you weren't going to dig a simple hike through the woods. I don't know, I just wanted you to have a happy memory here."

Butterflies fluttered in Nicole's stomach. No one had ever done such a thing for her. Not even her ex-boyfriends. She moistened her lips as she tugged at the hem of her jacket. "That's so sweet of you."

He shrugged in a it-wasn't-much kind of way.

Nicole marched up to him, a blaze ignited in her chest. She pressed her lips against his, the beard tickling her chin. "Thank you."

His smile made her blood surge to all the strange places. He gave her shoulders a squeeze before walking in the opposite direction, back into the thicket.

Nicole furrowed her brow. "Where are you going?"

"Gotta take a leak. Be right back."

Nicole snickered and plopped down on the woolen blanket. A picnic basket rested against a big rock. Sandwiches and a hot thermos full of cocoa beckoned her forward. She stuffed her mouth with Wonderbread and salami, throwing proper etiquette out the clearing. She was too hungry to care. She moaned with pleasure, already feeling her body getting energized. She poured herself a mug of cocoa. Her shoulder relaxed at the sweet aroma.

This place is just perfect.

Nicole stood up and wandered around the clearing, marveling at the wildflowers still in bloom. A squirrel clambered down a nearby tree and scampered toward an old, hollowed trunk.

"So cute," Nicole squealed. She tiptoed closer, smiling brighter as the furry forest dweller sniffed at something inside the trunk.

It took off as Nicole approached. She cursed herself for not capturing the moment on film. A big white rectangular shape stored in the trunk caught Nicole's eye. She bent down to get a closer look. It looked like a regular cooler but it had a detailed lock on the side. *Why wasn't it next to the picnic basket?* Wrinkling her nose, Nicole reached forth and opened it.

Cold air *whooshed* into Nicole's face. She coughed and blinked. Three clear Ziplock bags in three different sizes lied on a small bed of ice. The medium-sized bag had a "Celsior" label glued on while the other bags were marked with saline.

The hair on Nicole's arms stood on end.

Soft footsteps thumped behind her. Nicole turned around. Barry loomed above her, arms raised, clutching a shovel.

"Barry?"

He gave her a sad smile before slamming the smooth side of the spade against her head.

The brisk autumn air tickled Nicole's skin.

She didn't understand. Last thing she remembered was putting on clothes today. Her eyes fluttered open. She groaned. Her head felt like a cracked egg. Her left ear rang and something wet had congealed above it.

Tongue feeling like sandpaper, Nicole tried to speak. Her lips wouldn't move. Duct tape across her mouth shut her up.

Another breeze passed by. Gooseflesh prickled her back. Her heart pounded against squished breasts; she was lying on her stomach, but she didn't remember lying in that position to begin with. She tried getting to her feet but couldn't. Duct tape bound them as well as her wrists. A muffled whimper escaped her lips.

"Oh, damn. I was hoping I had knocked you out longer than that," Barry's voice said somewhere behind her.

His feet sunk into the moss as he squatted in front of her. Something long and small glinted in the twilight.

A scalpel.

A horrid realization dawned on Nicole. She squirmed on the blanket, shrieks muffled through the duct tape.

"Don't you see, you can save Hope's life."

Tears welled in Nicole's eyes. If he had only asked, she might have considered it. Saving a child's life wasn't on her bucket list, but she could have given it a shot, gotten tested and see if she's compatible. Maybe she wasn't. They have to share the same blood type, but Barry doesn't know that. She stared at him.

Barry smirked. "You're wondering if you two are a match. You are. Do you know how I figured it out?"

Against her better judgment, Nicole shook her head.

His eyes gleamed in suppressed euphoria. "Your Tinder profile."

Nicole's heart sank. She remembered now. Her friend, Izumi, had put her blood type on her profile to see if any Japanese guys would swipe right. In Japanese culture, having a certain blood type determined certain personality traits. Nicole had found it silly at the time, but she had forgotten to delete that part when she met Barry.

Barry's fingers touched her bare skin, just below her ribs. Nausea swept over her. Bile threatened to erupt from her stomach. She pleaded through sobs, her entire body trembling.

Barry held firm. "Stay still. I don't have any anesthesia equipment, only a numbing cream."

Each stroke of his fingers as he applied the cream caused ripples of terror within Nicole.

Barry gave her no time to mentally prepare herself as he slipped the scalpel into her flesh. She let out a scream when the blade cut into meat and muscle. White hot flames coursed through her, burning her from the inside.

In-between the thunderous heartbeat ringing in her ears and her own bloodcurdling shrieks, Barry's grunts carved through as he continued slicing her open. He pulled the muscles apart, tendons snapping like chords from a violin. Warm blood soaked the blanket, pouring like magma with each labored breath.

Electric jolts pulsated with a snip here and a cut there. The last separation of nerves lingered still in the back of her skull. Out of the corner of her eye, Nicole saw Barry extract a pink, wet lump the size of an avocado and slip it into the bag marked "Celsior".

He took her T-shirt lying next to the tree trunk and wiped his bloody hands clean. "Thank you again, Nicole. You don't know how much this means to me." He wiped a tear from his eye.

Nicole's consciousness faded quickly. She barely registered him as he placed the bag into the other bags and closed the ice box.

He waved his phone. "I'll call nine-one-one when I get to the car. The service here is crap."

Blood bubbled out of her mouth. Nicole's voice was but a hoarse whisper of a plea as she watched his retreating form move further and further away from her. The determination in his steps confirmed her fear and fueled her rage. Her eyes drifted up to the darkening sky, at the ascending moon, before they flickered shut.

Barry hummed a tune as he descended the mountain. He clutched the ice box, knuckles stark white. He had to be careful. After all, his daughter's last hope remained inside.

He couldn't believe his luck. To find a woman through Tinder of all places and she was Hope's savior. He knew that asking her to become an organ donor would be a hot mess because they had only been going out for a few weeks. He had planned on broaching the subject as time went on, but Hope's condition allowed no such thing.

So, he *had* to take action. He had to find a kidney, and really, what a find! So innocent and naïve, gawping at trees like she had never seen them before.

He paused for a moment and wondered if the sour taste in his mouth was some form of guilt. He shook his head. The stench of blood had probably gone through his nostrils and seeped into his tongue. He wasn't that sorry for Nicole. Hope mattered more to him. She was his light, his reason for walking on this godforsaken planet.

He glanced up. The sun had almost disappeared behind the opposite mountain, painting the sky in magenta and blue violet. Night was upon them. He had to hurry up and get the box to his contact in the hospital. Hope was there too, waiting for him.

He jogged down the path, occasionally looking up to find the neon yellow fluorescent markings on the trees.

The path gradually got steeper. He stumbled a bit but gained balance by thrusting his feet to the side. He chuckled. *Gotta be careful.* Pointy rocks jutted out from the ground. His jog turned into a run. He held the box in his arms, his stomach swooping in unease each time he heard Hope's kidney slide in the ice.

His foot sunk into a crevice. It was instant, not even a time to curse. Losing his footing, Barry tumbled down the path.

Rocks scratched his face. Each fall shoved dirt up his nostrils and mouth. The treacherous roots bent his fingers. Cracks resounded in his ears and he wasn't sure whether the fall was breaking his whole body or if brambles were snapping in half. He finally came to a stop a few miles off the marked path. His head swam, dark spots obscuring his sight. Mind-numbing pain surged through his body that started from his crooked foot. Coated in slick blood, the bone protruded out of his torn flesh. His heart hammered in his chest, causing blood to spurt in rapid successions, soaking the gravel.

He frantically searched his pockets, breathing fast through his mouth so he wouldn't throw up. His fingers scratched metal. He flinched, yanking his hand. Drops of blood bloomed on his fingertips. Stomach plummeting into the depths of his bowels, he withdrew his phone carefully from his back pocket.

Broken glass and a bent phone winked at him. He tried turning it on, but the cob-webbed screen remained black as the sky transformed, with the pale round moon his only source of light.

He cradled the box up to his chest, tears burning behind closed eyes. He wasn't giving up. If he had to, he would *crawl* his way back to his car.

A wolf howled nearby.

Barry froze. Another howl echoed through the forest, clearer and closer. A bead of sweat ran down Barry's temple. He reached for a broken branch on his right while tugging on the sleeve of his shirt. The seams on his shoulder tore at the same time a branch snapped in the darkness across from him.

Barry's breath quickened, and he fumbled with the torn sleeve, his eyes fixated on the darkness. He was *sure* he had heard growling inside the gloom.

A lean, hulking shadow silhouetted between the guard of trees. It snorted, a puff of air floating through. It took a step out.

Barry's gasp lodged deep in his throat.

A beast lumbered on its hind legs towards him. Blood, tissue, and torn skin matted its grey, bristled fur. Its snout wrinkled in a snarl, drool dripping from its elongated teeth. Locks of long hair—*human hair*—snaked around its muscled shoulders. Sharp claws, protruded from long arms, twitched, and flexed.

"Oh my god," Barry breathed at last, hot urine trickling down his pants. He flipped on his stomach, gritting his teeth in a silent scream as he put pressure on his broken foot.

The beast roared and jumped. It clamped its teeth on his healthy calf while its claws dug into the exposed flesh on his crippled one. Barry screamed yet he still held on to the ice box as the beast tossed him from side to side until it flung him across the path.

Both his legs were on fire, heart throbbing through his veins. Barry whimpered, but his perseverance trumped his fear. He continued to crawl, trying to ignore the heated breath that followed him.

A growl penetrated through his ear canals. Teeth pierced his flesh again. Barry's screams filled the forest, but he knew he was alone. His body took flight when the beast threw him against a cypress. His shoulder cracked, pushing his arm forward at an awkward angle. Nerves popped and he lost all sense in his right arm. It limped down and the ice box slipped out from his fingers. He coughed up blood. Something leaked into his eyes, whether it was crimson or clear, he wasn't sure.

Heavy footsteps in parallel to its growls approached Barry. He fell onto his disabled arm, but he pulled at the yellow grass, cursing when he split the roots. His abled fingers grazed the hard plastic of the ice box. *Almost there, Hope.*

The beast kicked his hip, flipping him on his back. A mixture of groan and sob escaped Barry's lips. The rocks pricked his back. He wiped the gore from his face, blinking up at his attacker.

The beast's eyes had a blue tint around the iris. A few strands of bloody hair plopped on Barry's chest as the beast bent over him. A wound on its side winked at him.

"Baaaarrrr," a guttural growl issued from its throat.

All color drained from Barry's face. "Nicole?"

The beast's bloodied lips curled into a grin before its jaw unhinged and tore Barry's face along with his upper jaw apart.

Hope had a purpose indeed.

THE
DOLL
MUSEUM

Nellie cursed as a flyer got stuck underneath her shoe. "God dammit, I hate it when people spread garbage like that."

Chloe, her friend, stopped walking and snickered. "What is it, another flyer for a lousy indie band?"

Frowning, Nellie straightened the purple paper. A caricature of dolls stacked in a row, as if posing for a class photo shoot, featured in the center. In bold white letters above and below the picture stood, "Come see Bomma's Traveling Doll Museum for a limited time only. $5 admission fee."

"Wow, never seen a traveling doll museum before. Do you want to check it out?" Chloe asked as she leaned over Nellie's shoulder to take a better look.

Nellie stared at the flyer. Her skin prickled. Uncomfortable sweat gathered in her armpits. Images of being locked in a room full of old, cracked porcelain dolls flashed in her mind.

"Nell?" Chloe's brow furrowed. "You okay?"

Nellie tossed the flyer away, as if it had burned her fingers. "No, gross. I'm not going there. Ever."

Chloe raised an eyebrow. "What, are you afraid of them or something?"

Nellie rubbed her hands on her jeans, trying to get rid of any excess dirt from the thin paper. "Yes, ever since my idiot brother locked me in my aunt's room for an entire night when I was little. Do you know how creepy dolls are in the dark?" She shuddered. "It was traumatizing."

Chloe's eyes goggled as she blew air out of her cheeks. "Yikes, I had no idea. Although, that explained why you wouldn't set foot in Mandy's room at her party a year ago."

Nellie gave Chloe's shoulder a push. "I'm not crazy. Everyone finds dolls creepy. Only clowns are creepier."

Chloe chuckled. "Yup, nothing beats them."

Nellie's stomach growled, just in time to cut the uncomfortable conversation of her horrid childhood memories short. "Time to get food before Chemistry starts."

Nellie awoke to the shrill shouts of her mom the next morning. She stumbled out of bed, her hair all a mess, and opened her bedroom door. "What?"

"Chloe's mom is on the phone. She's asking if you've heard from Chloe since yesterday?"

Nellie rubbed the crust of sleep from her eyes and blinked at the hallway. "No, not since our walk home after school."

Her mother paused before shouting from the base of the stairs. "You sure? You didn't hang out last night? Linda is saying that Chloe told her that she'd be with you."

Nellie rolled her eyes. "No, we didn't. I couldn't because you grounded me two days ago."

Concern layered her mom's voice when she spoke after another moment's pause. "Oh, right. I'll tell Linda then."

"Good." Nellie called before closing the door and shuffling back to the comforts of her bed.

She wanted to go back to sleep since today marked the weekend, but something gnawed at the back of her mind. Did Chloe go somewhere last night and failed to tell her? She usually kept her updated on what was happening if Nellie got grounded—which happened a lot— and vice versa. That's why she liked Chloe the best.

Nellie reached for her phone on the nightstand and scrolled through her social media. Nothing on Instagram or Twitter, but then again Chloe has family members that watch her feed there. She wouldn't post anything that would get her in trouble. That left Snapchat. Nellie fired up the app. Lo and behold; Chloe left Nellie a stream of short videos around midnight. Nellie had already crashed in bed that time, her belly full of cookie dough ice cream. Nellie pushed her hair out of her face, frowning. Had there been an impromptu party Chloe went to?

Nellie opened the videos.

A blurry, shaky view of a grey building sprung into view. Nellie squinted. Wasn't that the old, abandoned building by the town's limits? That mannequin warehouse?

Chloe's labored voice came through as she filmed while walking swiftly. "I know you don't like dolls, Nell, but I couldn't resist checking it out. I hope you won't get too freaked out by what's to come next."

Nellie scowled at Chloe's teased giggling and tapped on the screen for the next short video.

The next one showed a darkly lit room. Silhouettes of still human forms lined the walls. Sitting, lifeless dolls littered the floor, eyes dull and frozen arms outreached, as if begging for a hug.

Nellie's stomach churned. Unbidden memories threatened to spill out of her closed trauma box. She hastened to close the app. She took deep breaths, riding the hot wave of fear out.

So, Chloe went to the doll museum. By herself. Nellie found that unnerving, especially since she went there at *night*. She could have asked some of their friends to come with her, but Nellie knew that none of them found walking through a creepy doll museum an appealing activity.

But why didn't she go home afterwards? Was she trying to get grounded as well? Nellie quickly sent her a text, asking where she was and if she wanted to hang out today.

She only waited fifteen minutes until her friend replied. *That's odd. Chloe is more attached to her phone than a tick to a dog's skin.*

Chloe's text informed her that she just came home from a party next town but realized that she'd forgotten her wallet at the museum.

Nellie's stomach sank when she read the last part of the text: *Can you go there with me?*

Why did she need her to come, too? Hadn't Nellie been clear about her feelings about dolls?

Nellie sent back: *Can't u go there by urself?*

A twinge of guilt coiled around within as she waited for a response. Was she a bad friend for not wanting to go?

Her phone vibrated with Chloe's reply: *Pls. Something happened at the party. I can't tell you through text. Pls come. I need my friend today.*

Nellie chewed on her bottom lip. Chloe had to go and do that. Played the friend card. She couldn't say no. Chloe would probably tell everyone that Nellie ditched her in a time of need. *I'm not that kind of friend.* She groaned and got dressed, ignoring the slithering dread that seemed to have lodged itself in the pit of her stomach.

Nellie's feet dragged on the ground; they felt like lead. Sweat streamed down her back and made camp in the crevice of her butt. She kept clenching her fists, only to realize her nails dug too deep into her clammy palms. She must be insane. *Why am I going through all that trouble? Chloe could just get a new wallet. All of it was*

108

replaceable. Nellie sighed. While that may be true, she couldn't admit to herself that curiosity was pretty much the only thing that propelled her feet to the place of her nightmares. What on earth had happened to Chloe that couldn't be told through their usual means of communication? Dread wrapped itself more tightly as scenarios of Chloe being attacked or raped ran rampant through Nellie's mind.

She shook her head, banishing the thoughts away. *Chloe is a smart girl. Like me, she always carries a taser.*

Nellie rummaged in her bag for the fourth time, breathing a sigh of relief every time her fingers wrapped around the hard, plastic casing. She pulled it out and held down the button. Blue sparks danced between the two, thin rods. Nellie smirked. *Good. It works.* That helped loosen the knot in her gut.

The sun dipped behind the trees, welcoming the change of colors in the sky. Magenta kissed the horizon one last goodbye before indigo blanketed the heavens.

Nellie shivered. The wind that blew suddenly in her face felt chilly but not as cold as the continued apprehension clenching her sides. Why had she slept in this morning? Why didn't she go to the museum when the sun was up? *Why* did Chloe even think this was a great place to share something personal? These thoughts spun in her mind like a wicked carousel as she reluctantly approached the mannequin warehouse.

The place looked even worse than she remembered. Black garbage bags covered every shattered window. Cracks in the cement walls crawled in the corners. Ivy grew out of the cracks, its gnarly sentinels holding the ancient building in place. Nellie wished Mother Nature had been more aggressive in smothering it in vegetation, but beggars couldn't be choosers.

Nellie raised an eyebrow at the lack of advertisements pertaining to the doll museum. It seemed like the exhibit had already packed and gone. Nellie held on to that hope for dear life.

She stuffed her taser behind her jeans, took a deep, shuddering breath and marched toward the entrance.

To Nellie's dismay, the door stood intact. Faded letters belonging to the extinct warehouse loomed above Nellie. She puffed out her chest and rapped her knuckles twice on the wood.

The silence almost suffocated Nellie as her eyes darted in all directions. *Where was Chloe? Wasn't she already here? Weren't they supposed to be meeting up at this spot?*

"C'mon, don't make me enter this place all by myself," she muttered under her breath as she bounced on her heels, ready to sprint.

No one came to answer. Nellie scoffed and tried knocking again. *If no one comes, not even Chloe, then I'm done. I'd come here worried sick about Chloe, but then my so-called friend stood me up.*

Her phone vibrated in her pocket. A new message from Chloe: *Hey, where are u? I'm already inside. U gotta c this.*

Nellie's temple twitched. She worked her fingers furiously on the small keyboard; *I'm here. YOU come outside*

Nellie waited for a reply. It never came.

Nellie swore loudly and banged her fist on the door. "Stop screwing around, Chloe!"

The door creaked open.

The hair at the back of Nellie's neck stood on end. She rubbed her arms to get rid of the goosebumps. She put her toe on the threshold and leaned forward. "Hello? Chloe?" she called.

She's just messing with me. Trying to scare me, Nellie thought as she bit the inside of her cheek. Trying as Chloe might be at scaring her, she was actually doing a great job.

Nellie's brain screamed at her to turn around, that Chloe's crude exposure therapy wasn't the answer. Her stubbornness and sense of pride trumped logic and she stomped inside.

A pungent aroma of pine trees punched Nellie's nostrils. Her eyes watered and she stifled a cough. It smelled like someone had gone trigger happy with the Febreeze. Dozens of cans of it. Wrinkling her nose, Nellie squinted against the dim light. The interior had been transformed into an Ikea pathway. Thin walls that didn't reach up to the ceiling separated the rooms. Red copy paper with arrows printed on them stuck on the walls and indicated where the path started.

Nellie's mouth slid into a thin line as she slowly followed the arrows. Her hand already had a firm grasp on the taser.

She kept her eyes on the floor. In the video, she saw the dolls lined up on the floor and Nellie was going to be prepared for that.

A limb peeked out of the corner as she entered the first room. A bare leg outstretched on the floor. Nellie stopped dead in her tracks. Her stomach rolled. She squeezed her eyes shut and swallowed the sour taste in her mouth.

It's just a doll. It's just a doll. They won't do anything. They won't hurt me, she chanted in her head. She took another deep breath through her nose and fully entered the room.

She flashed back to her childhood. To her aunt's room. It felt distorted, as if watched through a magnifying lens. The pine stench grew stronger in the room. The small dolls sat there, sure, but she hadn't taken into account the large ones. Nellie vaguely remembered seeing them in Chloe's Snapchat video, but she must have blocked it out.

They lined up against the wall. Dead, hollow eyes stared back at Nellie, frozen in time like the wax statues at Madame Tussauds, but these wore frilly, doll-like clothing. All of them had ringlets of curls framing their faces. Even the male ones had ridiculously curly hair to match the female ones. Nellie wanted to laugh but couldn't. The absurdity was too horrifying.

With a trembling hand, she pulled out her phone and used the flashlight app to shine a light at them.

Two patches of dull rouge painted their cheeks, their lips a chapped crimson. However, unlike with wax or porcelain, the light didn't bounce off their skin.

Cold seeped through Nellie's veins. Her heart hammered wildly like a frenzied drummer. Her stomach felt rock hard, as if nursing a boulder within her.

Curiosity cruelly beat her fear. She approached one of the statues—a woman with her hands clasped together as in a prayer, her glazed eyes turned upwards. A chemical scent wafted through the air, the closer she got. Sand seemed to fill Nellie's mouth, yet her hands swam in sweat. She reached up with one finger aloft and poked the cheek.

Soft. Squishy.

Not at all hard like porcelain, or sticky and moldable like wax.

Nellie gulped as she moved her hands across the statute's arms. Soft, like the cheek. Her fingertips stroked strands of hair. *Dolls don't have that. Neither do wax statutes.* As her fingers traveled along the statute's arm, small bumps and coarse stitches made her freeze. Ignoring the ringing in her ears, Nellie rolled up the doll's sleeves. Long stitches lined the statute's arm like beginner's patchwork.

Nellie's legs turned into jelly as she backpedaled away. She hit her back against the wall with a gasp. *Those were bodies. Dead bodies made to look like horrific dolls.*

Nellie wanted to scream, but her voice disappeared somewhere between her chest and esophagus. She needed to find Chloe.

Now.

She backed away from the room of horrors, not daring to turn her back against those things, in case they'd start moving.

A big, calloused hand shot forward and covered Nellie's mouth. Her heart almost stopped. The rough hand pulled her backward while another grabbed her wrist and twisted it behind her back.

"I thought you'd never come," a raspy, foul-smelling voice muttered near her ear.

Nellie nearly gagged from the stench of rotting meat permeating from the man's mouth and body.

Black spots threatened to obscure Nellie's sight as dizziness from sheer terror engulfed her. Her eyes darted to the side where the mouth of that man breathed in her ear.

"You worried about your friend? Don't be, you'll soon join her in my little collection."

Nellie's veins pumped ice-cold blood into her heart. Her worst nightmare closed in on her. She whimpered as she dug her heels onto the floor, resisting as much as she could. The man didn't cackle like a horror-movie villain. He grunted as he dragged her into another room, filled with the sickly sweet aroma of roses and honeysuckle invaded Nellie's nostrils. She squeezed her eyes shut. She couldn't handle seeing more of those bodies and didn't want to let her mind comprehend the atrocities he had committed to those poor souls.

Her closed fist brushed up against cold, hard plastic.

Her eyes flew open. *It's not over yet*. She still had her weapon. A flush of adrenaline surged through her body. She grabbed the handle of the taser, flipped it and jammed it into the man's side.

"Fuck you!" Nellie's voice came out muffled through his hand, but she wanted him to hear it.

"Wha—" He went rigid as a board when the electricity entered his nervous system. His grip on her wrist slackened. Nellie spun on her heels and rammed the taser into his neck.

Nellie didn't stay and watch. Still clutching her weapon, she sprinted in the opposite direction. Her flight response rang in her ears, but she ignored it. She needed to find Chloe first.

Nellie burst through a double door and into a new room. She slipped on something wet and dark. Blood covered the floor in a deep puddle centered around a long, metallic, surgical table. Chloe laid there, plastic tubes in the crooks of her elbows, the ends in buckets filled with her blood. Her head hung on the edge of the table, her throat slit and matted with dried blood.

Bile rose in Nellie's throat. She covered her mouth to prevent herself from screaming in shock and grief.

My best friend…

Hurried footsteps stomped near. *Shit, Chloe's killer is coming. He probably knows where I am.*

115

Nellie frantically looked around the room. *Why are there no windows here? The only exit are the double doors where the stomps of doom echo behind them.*

Her mind raced as her head swiveled from left to right. She spotted a dozen plastic bottles on the counter across the room. She rushed to the counter, grabbing one of the bottles and examined the label. Formaldehyde. Nellie remembered seeing that liquid in biology class when they had to dissect a pig fetus.

A few empty syringes laid on a surgical tray nearby Chloe's body. Nellie grabbed one, plunged the needle into the bottle and withdrew the liquid into the syringe.

The doors flew open.

Nellie gasped and hid the syringe behind her back.

The man bared his teeth at her. His muscles still twitched and jerked from the taser attack. Nellie noticed he had a distinguishable tattoo on his right forearm; A thin circle was at the center while a thin, crescent moon hovered slightly within it. A vertical line slashed through them both. She had never seen a tattoo like it.

"Thanks, you bitch. Now I don't have to drag your dead body across the building. Like seeing your friend on the table? She'll be a beautiful doll."

Nellie squared her jaw. She slightly eased her grip on the syringe. It wouldn't do her any good if it broke in her hand.

"Now, be a good girl and become a part of my lovely collection. I promise I'll treat you like the princess you are." Without waiting for Nellie's answer, he flipped the table.

Chloe toppled down on the floor with the thump like a lifeless marionette.

He raised his arms, ready to grab her.

Nellie screamed and thrust her own arm forward. The needle entered through his fleshy part of his stomach. She squeezed her thumb down. The formaldehyde drained out of the syringe.

The man stiffened and gazed down at the protruding needle. "What did you do?" His raspy voice became slurred, as if his mouth had filled with soggy cotton.

"Gave you a piece of your own medicine. Don't you want to be a part of your own collection?" Nellie managed a shaky smirk before kicking him out of her way.

The man collapsed in the puddle of blood, clawing at his throat. Blotchy purple and crimson quickly peppered his skin. Blood trickled out of his eyes as he choked and writhed, painting his already gruesome body with more gore.

This time, Nellie didn't run. She watched in the corner, making sure he wouldn't move. If he twitched, she injected him with more formaldehyde. She reveled in his gasps, the way he pleaded for mercy with his bulging, blood-stained eyes.

He hadn't done that for Chloe. Why should she offer him that kindness? Nellie shook her head. "An eye for an eye, you sick bastard," she muttered and spat at his spasming body.

When he finally stilled, the last gurgles leaving his mouth, Nellie stood.

She heaved Chloe's body onto her shoulder. Doing that contaminated the crime scene, but she couldn't bear the thought of having her friend in the same room as her killer.

Nellie relished every drop of sweat that slipped down her back, every muscle strain as she carried Chloe out of the building of carnage. *I'm so sorry, Chloe. For not being there with you at your time of need.*

Nellie laid Chloe's body on the pristine green grass. Stars twinkled from Chloe's dull eyes. With a sniffle, Nellie swept her hand down and closed them.

She picked up her phone and dialed nine-one-one. "Hello? Yes, I'd like to report a murder. At the traveling doll museum in the mannequin warehouse."

A shadow watched Nellie from the cover of the forest to the left of the building. It caught the copper odor of blood as it drifted through the air from the body lying on the grassy ground and let out a sigh. It dug inside its pocket and dialed a number on its phone. The light of the screen illuminated a tattoo on its exposed wrist; A thin circle was at the center while a thin, crescent moon hovered slightly within it. A vertical line slashed through them both.

"Yes, Master. Bomma failed. The girl survived. We'll find another means to deliver you the blood. Don't worry, we'll take care of the girl. You can count on us."

The shadow turned off its phone, right before the screen's light caught two others emerging from the woods.

SPLIT

The setting sun painted a blend of orange and magenta across the Millers's white minimalistic décor. The toys scattered around the floor bathed in the rays. The sun matched the soulful saxophone tone that played throughout their house. The music masked the grinding buzz of a skin grafter slicing through Harry Miller's arm.

The cloth she tied around his mouth muffled his screams. As Katherine Miller gripped her husband's arm, she felt his muscles tense to the point of tearing in those few seconds the Dermatome device she wielded touched his flesh. She imagined the nerves splitting like guitar cords. How the veins pulsating underneath were on fire. She gritted her teeth. It was cruel but necessary.

She positioned herself in front of his limp form, kicking a plush elephant out of the way. Harry squeezed his eyes shut, tears streaking down his cheeks. His reaction left a small puncture wound in Katherine's heart. It made the situation all too real. Her thumb caressed the smooth skin on his arm, a sign of affection she thought she had abandoned in lieu of the mission.

She shook it off. She had no time for such luxuries. Not anymore. She gripped the skin grafter tighter.

"Look at me," she said.

He winced at the authoritative tone in her voice. It had been so long since Katherine's Russian accent had come out. How her presence alone dominated the area and everyone around her. She had missed it in that deep slumber of tranquility. It felt good to be working again.

"Look at me, Harry," she repeated.

Her husband was still crying. It brought a sour taste to Katherine's mouth. Given his line of job as a biotechnical agent in the CIA and how he acted all macho with his coworkers and friends, she had expected him to put up a fight. To be glaring at her with contempt. All her previous targets had eventually succumbed to tears once she began the torture, but they'd always hit her with slurs in between breaks. Their lips didn't quiver like his did when he raised his head.

She dangled a patch of his skin in front of him with slender, manicured fingers. Cut in a box shape, the edges clean from any blood. Hair from his forearm brightened under the descending sunlight. She ignored the sweeps of disgust swirling within her. Was it self-disgust of having to torture her own husband or perhaps loathing of touching the cut-off skin? In the end, she couldn't hold on to it any longer, letting the skin fall on the white kitchen tiles. It hit the floor with a wet slap, like a piece of sliced ham.

"There will be more of this if you don't start talking."

Harry shook his head. "Please, Katherine," he blubbered, snot mingling with the tears and sweat. "Why are you doing this?"

Katherine's mouth thinned into a smooth line, and she covered the bristle of hair on her arms. How she had hated that name her superiors had given her for the mission. She had always managed to disguise her loathing whenever anyone called her by that name. She had even transformed it into a bright smile when Harry uttered that name. Now, she couldn't turn on the charm. It was over, anyway.

"My name is Katerina and that was not the answer I'm looking for." She grabbed the back of Harry's neck and placed the device on his naked bicep. She ran it down smoothly, as if she were slicing cheese. With her other hand, she thrust the cloth back into his mouth as he screamed. Usually, she didn't care when her targets screamed. The jazz music dampened them. But for some reason, her stomach churned if she heard Harry's. Another piece of flesh flopped down on the floor. "I won't stop until you give me all the information about *Project Milosnitse*."

Harry's eyes diluted in fear. "*Project Milosnitse*?" he panted. "I don't know what you're talking about."

A ghost of a smirk tugged at Katerina's lips. "Don't patronize me, Harry. I may have played the part of unsuspecting housewife for seven years, but you *know* what I'm talking about."

Katerina relished in her target's confusion. She had indeed been superb. She had monitored his routine, waiting for the perfect moment to strike up an innocent conversation while wearing her best clothes and the scents that he liked. It hadn't been long till they were dating. A few months after that, he had popped the question. The last seven years had sped by, but Katerina had always maintained her sight on her mission. Always looking for an opportunity that presented itself. It never did. Harry turned out be incredibly secretive about his line of work within the CIA, not even bringing his work back home. Katerina couldn't expose her frustration, so she played her part handing him a brown paper bag with his favorite, bologna sandwich, while giving him an affectionate kiss on the cheek every day. However, the KGB had grown impatient and demanded more intel.

Hence, the unsuspected torture in the middle of the afternoon.

"Katherine, please. Please, stop. Think about Sofia," Harry said and jerked his head to the wall of framed photos to his left.

Katerina's eyes darted to the wall. They immediately fell upon on the center frame that had a photo of a smiling little girl, holding up trout from a thin fishing line. Sofia, her little girl. She had inherited her father's wispy blond hair and charming mismatched eyes but the rest of her came from Katerina. The dimples. The plump lips, cherubic facial structure and her slender, ballerina frame. A memory of Sofia and herself dancing in front of the TV invaded her mind. Sofia's childish laugh always tickled Katerina's funny bone. A breath Katerina didn't know she had been holding in escaped. How could she have forgotten about her own daughter?

"You can stop this, Katherine. You don't have to do this anymore."

The device trembled in Katerina's hand. She glanced down. If she squinted, the Dermatome could be a simple cheese slicer that she was preparing as a snack for Sofia once she got back home. Why wasn't she doing that instead of torturing a man?

Harry straightened up in the chair. "You've created a great life here with me and Sofia. Don't you want to cherish that still? You don't have to follow orders anymore. You can step away from it all."

Katerina's lips parted, and words, barely audible streamed out. A mix of her orders from the KGB and images of Sofia assaulted her mind. She dropped the skin grafter and clutched her head, nausea sweeping over. What should she do? Abandon the mission? Run away? No, the other agents would know where Harry would hide his own family. And even if she did turn away from everything, what guarantee was there that they would patch things up? Harry would forever suspect Katerina of treason. He would never trust her again. But would Sofia? Yes, her innocence and dependance on her guaranteed that trust. Katerina bit the inside of her cheek to prevent her from screaming. Or vomiting.

Sofia was the only thing that mattered. But could she truly focus on her only child? Was her entire life worth throwing away for the sake of that little girl?

"Yes, that's right. Focus on Sofia. She needs you." Harry said, as if reading her thoughts. He leaned forward with a hopeful smile. "*I* need you," he whispered.

Katerina blinked. The two words *mission* and *Sofia* that flashed before Katerina's mind became one. Became equal.

"Katherine?" Harry asked tentatively.

Right, the mission. For a moment, Katerina had allowed her weakness to slip out, slithering like a worm through a minuscule crack in her armor. She squashed the worm and taped over the crack. *Never show weakness. Ever.* If she did, it'd be over for her and Sofia.

She took a deep breath, ridding herself of all emotion, and looked down at the creature bound in the chair. Half-naked and squealing, snot dribbling down its chin. She ought to put it out of its misery. It was too loyal to its work. It wouldn't give her what she wanted, no matter what kind of torture she would put it through. It would never give her what she *needed* to ensure Sofia's safety.

The KGB had been clear: *Finish the mission or we will erase everything*. Her past. Her present. Her future. *Sofia's future*. What the pathetic creature offered was merely what the Americans called "a pipe dream". Since birth, Katerina's life had belonged to Mother Russia, whose bony clasp would never release a simple sleeper agent like her. She wasn't even sure if they would let her go if she finished the mission. They'd send her to another place to infiltrate another target for sure. She and Sofia would have to constantly uproot their homes and change their identities. She clenched her fists. That was no life for her little girl.

Katerina let out a scoff. "I'm sorry, Harry. I've never belonged here. You know that now."

She hated the glint of despair shining in her husband's eyes as she pulled a dagger from her pocket. Hated how his last words garbled out of him as she ran the blade across his throat. Hated how he stared, not in disbelief or hate, but in pity as blood cascaded down his wound, dying his dirty white tank top crimson.

None of her previous targets had ever looked at her like that. But then again, she had never spent so much time with a target before. She had never felt anything for a target before.

"You gave me seven years of work," she mumbled into his ear as his life drained away. "Hard work that didn't pay off and I will suffer for that. But I will get that information one way or another."

Katerina glanced at the photo of her daughter. She had promised herself she'd feel nothing when she brought her into the world. But no amount of training had prepared her for the overwhelming feelings of love that enveloped her as soon as she cradled her baby in her arms. If they had known that they wouldn't have made women into sleeper agents. But she knew Mother Russia didn't care. Mother Russia expected, no, demanded love and devotion from her people, but she never reciprocated that emotion.

Sofia filled that chasm. Katerina wiped her nose on her sleeve and brushed the tears away. "But you gave me something that I will treasure for the rest of my life. I will protect her, both from the KGB and the CIA. Thank you, Harry."

Katerina gently pulled his eyelids down and began the cleanup. Each bead of sweat and the sore muscles in her arms felt like a small form of punishment for killing her husband, and she accepted it. As she scraped the tiles clean with a coarse brush, she reminded herself not to leave any traces behind. Armed with gloves, she placed the body in a barrel inside the garage and filled it with hydrofluoric acid. She wrinkled her nose at the strong chemical fumes that mixed with the disintegration of tissue and flesh. She left it there for anyone to find. Disposing of the barrel meant nothing to her at this point.

Once everything sparkled and the house reeked of bleach, Katerina went to Sofia's room. She lingered there, touching the bed and the desk. So many treasured memories. She knew her daughter wouldn't approve of leaving so abruptly, but she'd understand sooner or later. She put a few of Sofia's clothes, her favorite teddy bear, and other essentials in a bag. She snatched the photo album in the living room. A reminder of her past life. A reminder of what needed to be done. She reached for the telephone hanging on the wall and dialed the number for Harry's coworker, Ted.

"Hello, Ted?" Katerina asked, pulling the American accent as flawlessly as if she were a native. "Is Barbara there? No? Oh, she went to the park with the kids? Oh, it was nothing. I just wanted to drop off the casserole dish from last week. Are you sure it's all right that I come? Great, I'll see you in a bit."

She hung up, picked up the bag and slid the skin grafter and other trusty tools of the trade into it before going to the car. Sofia was at a friend's place, not far from where Ted and Barbara lived. She'd pick her up once she was finished with her mission.

SKÖTUMÓÐIR

Cold winter gales bit the bare skin of Detective Máni Steindórsson as he stood at the edge of Lake Lagarfljót in Egilsstaðir, at the east of Iceland. He cursed his forgetfulness of not bringing a scarf or something to protect himself against the harsh Icelandic winter. Despite having lived on this god-forsaken island all his life, he always underestimated the unpredictability of the weather.

"Anything?" he shouted to the Search and Rescue volunteer who passed him with a sniffer dog.

"Nothing yet," the volunteer called back.

Detective Máni shook his head and crossed his arms to preserve what little heat his coat contained.

It was a bizarre case. Three young adults from Reykjavík had been missing for the last two days. None of them had contacted their families after leaving the city. The only thing the families knew was that they were going to film themselves trying to catch sight of the mythical *Lagarfljótsormurinn*, the Icelandic equivalent to the Loch Ness Monster. Detective Máni couldn't help but scoff at the ridiculousness. There were a lot of tourists who visited the lake with the amusing but mild hope to see the serpentine monster, but he'd thought Icelanders were smart enough to know the being didn't exist. Or at least they were courteous enough to respect the monster's privacy, like they did with the *Huldufólk.*

But apparently, the missing trio had a YouTube page where they posted footage of themselves at known locations that supposed ghost sightings were. Everything was done to get their fifteen minutes of fame nowadays.

"Detective, we found something!" the SAR volunteer shouted a hundred meters to the right of the lake.

Detective Máni steeled himself for the worst, pushing the bubbling dread further into the abyss of his gut. He trudged along the uneven path of rocks that littered the lake to the volunteer. Barks from the sniffer dog filled the air for a second, only to be drowned in the howls of the elements. The volunteer held something small in his gloved hands.

A smartphone with its screen cracked.

"Does it still work?" Detective Máni asked, fumbling for the on button. He pushed it. Nothing happened. He suspected as much, but luckily, he carried an extra portable charger in his car. He asked a fellow police officer to retrieve it for him. Once he plugged the phone to it, he tried again. The screen flickered to life, showing a photo of a young woman with short, curly hair embracing a young man with cropped blond hair.

"That them?" the volunteer asked.

"Two of them, at least. The woman is Guðlaug and pretty boy here is her boyfriend, Hlynur. But no photo of their friend, Páll, who runs the YouTube page. Is this the only thing you found?"

The volunteer nodded. "But we're still looking. We're not giving up."

A smile tugged at Detective Máni's lips. The Search and Rescue Squad rarely ever gave up. That's what he loved about them.

He turned to the phone. If they were out here filming, where was the camera equipment? They had found nothing so far and he doubted the wind had swept it to the next town. He stared at the device. He swiped his finger up on the screen, and to his surprise, the phone presented him with a blurry, still photo.

Detective Máni squinted. No, not a photo. A paused video. Was it only just one video? He pushed the return button and the folder displayed six videos, all marked on the same day two days ago. Maybe those videos could shed some light into the trio's disappearance.

He selected the first video and pressed play.

Video 1 (January 15th, 21:34):

Brown curls obscure the screen while laughter and music resound from nearby speakers.

Male voice: Hey, are you filming right now?

Female voice (hesitant): No. Well, yeah, just a little.

Male voice (stern): I told you, we don't start filming until we reach the lake.

The screen zooms out and reveals Guðlaug wearing a coy smile before she shifts the view to the two boys at the front of the car. Hlynur sits at the passenger seat, sipping soda from a bottle. Páll is driving.

Guðlaug: Sorry, I just thought it'd be fun to shoot one of those "before reels". We could add it to the actual footage later or put it in with the bloopers.

Páll narrows his eyes into the screen.

Páll: No bloopers. We're trying to be professionals here, Gugga.

Guðlaug (clicking her tongue): C'mon, it'll be fun. Right, Hlynur?

Screen zooms at Hlynur whose eyes avoid the camera.

Hlynur: Don't bring me into this. I'm just here for the ride and helping you carry the camping stuff.

Páll: Don't forget about the free exposure.

Hlynur frowns at his friend.

Guðlaug: Don't worry. I can delete this video and we'll start all over again.

Páll (sighing in relief): That sounds better, thanks.

Video 2 (January 15th, 21:52):

Guðlaug's face appears in the back seat of the car, surrounded by camping equipment and sleeping bags.

Guðlaug: Hello everyone, and welcome to another segment of "Hunting the Myths". Tonight, we're going a little bit away from the comforts of the capital city and are heading east to Egilsstaðir. Hmm, I wonder why we're going there. Care to enlighten us, Hlynur?

The screen zooms onto Hlynur, who this time, smiles expectantly into the camera.

Hlynur: Sure thing. We're going to see if we can capture the legendary *Lagarfljótsormurinn* on film.

Guðlaug giggles behind the camera.

Guðlaug: But wait, our viewers probably have no idea what *Lagarfljótsormurinn* is. Can you perhaps tell us, Páll?

The camera pans to the left. Páll's profile shines in the light. He keeps his eyes on the road, but a smug smile spreads across his lips.

Páll: Of course, I can. The worm, if we can call it that, is said to have been around Lake Lagarfljót since 1345. According to legend, the worm was nothing but a heath worm that wrapped itself around a golden ring. Apparently, the gold was supposed to grow into, you know, more gold, but instead the worm grew. The owner of the golden ring was so petrified of the size of the worm that she tossed the ring along with the worm into the lake, where it kept growing into the huge serpentine being we all know and love today.

Guðlaug coos behind the camera.

Guðlaug: So, we could find treasure there as well.

The camera pans to the right, just as it captures Hlynur laughing.

Hlynur: I doubt it. It's probably been long taken.

The camera veers to reveal a pouty Guðlaug.

Guðlaug: Fine, no treasure, but do you think we'll capture footage of the serpent itself?

The question seems directed at Páll as the screen zooms in on his smirking profile.

Páll: I'm sure of it. There have been countless captured footage of it, the most recent one taken during the winter in 2012—

The camera quickly reverts to Guðlaug who's scowling.

Guðlaug: And this is why we're hunting it in the middle of winter, correct?

Camera goes back to Páll who glares above the screen.

Páll: Yes, I have reason to believe the serpent thrives better in colder climates. Most of our mythological beings have been sighted during the winter—

Hlynur snorts besides Páll.

Hlynur: Oh yeah? Like what?

Páll: *Bjarndýrakóngurinn, Nykur, Selamóðir,* just tons of them, really.

Guðlaug snickers.

Guðlaug: Let's hope we find at least some of them.

Páll: I'm certain we'll find the serpent at this time of year because not many travel to the lake. It's way too cold for us humans.

Guðlaug appears in front of the camera with a mischievous glint in her eyes.

Guðlaug: Not for us. We're prepared. It won't stand a chance against us. Stick around for the lake part.

Video 3 (January 15th, 23:09):

The camera comes back to life with a bleak scenery of grey rocks upon sludgy ice. The camera shakes slightly.

Guðlaug (trembling): So, here we are at Lake Lagarfljót. It's freezing, but thankfully no wind or we'd be icicles.

The camera pans over to the bright yellow car that's parked in the camp parking lot a few kilometers away. A lone murky green tent stands beside the car. The lake is silent, save for the breaths from Guðlaug as she joins the boys at the edge of the lake.

Páll turns to the camera and seems more enthusiastic for the hunt than Hlynur who huddles besides him, stomping his feet for warmth.

Páll: So, as you can see—

The camera pans to the front of the lake.

Páll: —the lake hasn't frozen yet, which makes it perfect for *Lagarfljótsormurinn* to come to the surface, so what we're going to do is walk around the edge of the lake in complete silence.

Hlynur (quietly): How fun…

The camera quickly zooms on the rocks below the boys' feet, but it catches the look of irritation on Páll's face.

Guðlaug (forcibly cheerfully): Great, sounds like fun. Hope we can find it soon.

Video 4 (January 15th, 23:29):

Guðlaug's apple-cheeked face breathes fog into the screen.

Guðlaug (whispering): So, we've been walking in silence for 20 minutes. I spared you all the boredom from recording it. I think Páll doesn't know how big the lake is. If we continue any further, we'll end up coming back to camp in the morning.

Páll (hissing): I said no recording unless we see something!

Guðlaug (flinching): Eep! Sorry!

Video 5 (January 16th, 00:11):

The camera shakes from side to side, its screen pointed at the flurry of rocks and ice. Guðlaug's frantic breath is heard in the background.

Páll's voice in the distance: Over here, I found something!

The camera pans to a small pond linked to the lake. Guðlaug gasps behind the camera.

Guðlaug: Ew, what is that?

The camera zooms in on the small, flat creature as it swims lazily in the ice-cold water. Translucent in the shape of a soaked leaf. A long, slender tail steers its course in the pond. Hlynur crouches down near it.

Hlynur: I think it's a stingray, but it looks smaller than the usual ones.

Guðlaug: But don't they live in the ocean? They're not found in freshwater lake, right?

Páll shoves Hlynur aside.

Páll: Who cares? This is great. We can use it as bait.

Páll grabs a large rock, lifts it up above his head and lets it crash upon the stingray. A horrible crunch mingles with the splash of water and Guðlaug's startled yelp.

Hlynur (yelling): What the hell are you doing?

Páll laughs as he rams the rock again on the animal carcass.

Páll: It's fine, it's fine.

Blood and chunks of flesh spatter the ground. The camera falls back and focuses on brown hiking shoes covered in gore.

Guðlaug: Ew, you got some on my shoes, Páll!

Hlynur (disgusted): Did you have to pulverize it?

Páll throws the rock into the lake, panting.

Páll: Well, I'm not carrying a knife. Are you?

Hlynur frowns and shakes his head. Páll stoops down and tosses the mangled pieces of slimy flesh into the lake.

Páll: I'm sure the serpent is an omnivore, like us. It'll appreciate some good grub.

Hlynur: We could have chucked the dried fish we have in the car, you know? Don't you have any compassion for living creatures?

Páll (snorting): Stingrays are gross. They killed Steve Irwin.

Hlynur stares shocked at his friend, his mouth agape.

Hlynur: And you think that justifies murder?

Páll furrows his brow in confusion as he pats his hands clean on his jeans.

Páll: What's the big deal? It's not like no one is going to know about it.

Hlynur jerks his head at the camera.

Hlynur: Think again, idiot.

Páll glances at the camera before smirking.

Páll: Well, I'm *counting* on Gugga to delete that part. Won't you, Gugga?

Páll stares intently above the screen with his arms crossed. Guðlaug lets out a nervous giggle.

Guðlaug (stammering): O-of course, Páll.

Páll gives the two of them a broad smile.

Páll: See? Problem solved.

Páll strides away, stooping to chuck a few more stingray pieces into the lake. The screen zooms in on Hlynur's conflicted expression before he reluctantly follows. The camera records the place where Páll threw the carcass pieces for a couple of minutes before the screen goes black.

Video 6 (January 16th, 02:15):

Guðlaug's defeated face appears. Dark bags hang underneath her drooping eyes. Her blue lips quiver. She yawns, fogging the screen for a moment.

Guðlaug (groggy): We've been at the lake for over 2 hours now. We're cold, we're tired and the damn serpent hasn't shown up at all. Not even after we fed it *yummy* stingray meat. So, I'm saddened to say our hunt wasn't fruitful this time around. Shit happens.

Páll swears loudly in the background. The camera pans over to him as he paces around, back hunched and hands shoved in his pockets. Hlynur stands a few meters away from him, his arms wrapped around himself for warmth.

Páll (mumbling): I was so sure of the time.

Hlynur (huffing): Well, it was a huge waste of time.

Páll throws up his hands in frustration.

Páll: No, it wasn't. I know it's down there, it's just hiding from us. Tomorrow, we'll rent a boat and—

Hlynur (scoffing): Fuck that! Guðlaug and I are going home. If you want to stay, be my guest.

Páll lets out a mirthless laugh while smacking his forehead.

Páll: I got it! If food won't lure *Lagarfljótsormurinn*, then perhaps this will.

He dangles a key chain with shiny bronze keys before throwing it into the lake.

Páll (thinking): But maybe that isn't enough. Gugga, give me your gold necklace.

Páll lunges at Guðlaug, hand groping for something below the camera's angle. Guðlaug yelps behind the camera and backs away. Páll's manic expression shines in the light just before Hlynur charges at Páll, grabbing his coat and baring his teeth.

Hlynur (growling): Leave my girlfriend alone! What the fuck is wrong with you?

Hlynur raises his fist as Páll cowers, his arms protecting his face.

A large, wet plop comes from the lake.

Both boys freeze until Páll pushes Hlynur away. He stumbles on the uneven rocks and glares at his friend.

Guðlaug (whispering): What was that?

Hlynur (looking around): Probably a goose or something.

Páll screams.

The camera whips to the right where Páll is. No sign of him, yet he's still screaming.

Guðlaug: Where is he?

Hlynur: Up there! *He points up to the sky.*

The camera veers up. Páll dangles from the air, held up by something monstrous. The light from the camera doesn't reach that high.

Guðlaug: Oh my god, what is that?

Páll screams for help. An inhuman shriek fills the lake as the creature flies higher into the darkened sky.

Footsteps thump nearby and Hlynur's hurried breath comes near the camera.

Hlynur: Gugga, we need to get out of here.

Guðlaug: What about Páll?

Páll's screams intensify in volume at first but then come off vague and distant. Then nothing. A horrible crack breaks the hushed silence.

Hlynur: What was that?

The camera points down as Guðlaug and Hlynur approach the place of the sound. The sludge covering the rocks are spattered with crimson drops that increase in size the more they approach a boulder sitting next to the lake. Guðlaug gasps.

Guðlaug: Oh my god…

The camera zooms in on the broken heap of what used to be Páll. His chest is thrust forward at an odd angle where he landed on the boulder. Rib bones protrude out of his clothes like sharp teeth. His head has been ripped off.

Another shriek tears apart their collective shock.

Hlynur (shouting): We need to hide. Now!

The camera points down once more and captures only their shoes and Guðlaug's heaving sobs.

Guðlaug (sobbing): He's dead, he's dead, oh shit, oh shit, oh shit!

The camera shows a thicket of birch trees briefly before the screen focuses on the lake. Guðlaug's sobs are still audible, though muffled, as if she's covering her mouth with her other hand.

Guðlaug (whispering): What was that thing? Was it *Lagarfljótsormurinn*?

Hlynur shushes her.

Hlynur (whispering while panting): I don't think so. A serpent doesn't fly to my knowledge. But we need to stay quiet. It could still be out here.

The air whooshes and pushes the pair down, as if gravity is the one doing the pulling. Something flaps monstrous wings in quick successions. The screen captures scenes of the lake in rapid ascension. Guðlaug and Hlynur's screams carry out before they fade away as the screen flips between the sky and the ground.

A crash.

The screen zooms out from what appears to be a giant bird with the stringy body of a stingray carrying the pair into the darkness.

Detective Máni shut down the phone.

He rubbed his beard. He saw something in those videos, but he couldn't explain it. His mind denied the proof found in Guðlaug's videos.

"Detective, we found what appears to be the remains of an animal carcass," The SAR volunteer jogged over to him.

Detective Máni clenched his jaw. Further proof of the events. A headache gnawed at his temple. His footsteps felt heavy as he followed the volunteer to the small pond that had been captured in one of the videos. Sure enough, pieces of translucent stingray scattered the place.

"We don't know what kind of animal it is. Looks like a stingray to me, but we'll figure it out once we test it. Other than that, no signs of them."

Detective Máni sighed. "I don't think we're going to find them."

The volunteer nodded at the phone in Máni's hand. "Find anything useful in there?"

Detective Máni pocketed the phone. "Something like that. Call off the search for now. It's getting dark. We're not going to find anything in the dark unless it wants to be found."

As he got back to the car, he could have sworn he'd heard a distant shriek blend in with the ghoulish dirge that enveloped the lake.

THE
RESCUE

ebecca Harris peered through the one-way mirror, her mouth a thin line of concentration.

"She demanded to talk to someone from Child Protection Services, Miss Harris. She even mentioned your name. I'm relieved you managed to come so quickly," Detective Jones said as he handed Rebecca a few files.

"I was in the neighborhood on a different case," Rebecca muttered, not taking her eyes off the person sitting in holding. She glanced down at the files for a second, reading the most important bits, the ones that required her services. Her eyes narrowed. She was well aware of this case but had never been able to approach it. Not until today.

"Oh, I'm sorry, I didn't mean to take you away from a case," Detective Jones apologized, rubbing the back of his neck.

Rebecca's mouth twitched into a small smile before she erased it with a professional scowl. "It's fine, it was already finished. I was just doing a routine check. Now, tell me more about *her*."

Detective Jones heaved a sigh, as though reluctant to set his gaze forward at the woman. "There´s not much to tell. She only gave me one name; Remy, and that she just escaped a place called "Ha-kán's Haven". But she left her child there and apparently, that's where you come in."

Rebecca nodded. She knew about that place; a heathen, religious cult that had spread roots near the city a couple of years ago. She had seen those people out in the public parks, with their shaven heads and wearing nothing but linen robes, preaching their religious nonsense, hoping that someone vulnerable and gullible would take their bait. Usually Rebecca had nothing against people of religion. She just disliked their methods of spreading the words of their savior as well as how "their savior" took care of them. Case in point was the woman sitting there in the interrogation room. Shaved head, spotted with scabs, either from bugs or the continual scratching she's seen them do. Sunken eyes and gaunt, wax-like face. Indication of malnourishment and lack of sleep. The once pearl-white robe now crusted with dirt, from the dangerous risk of running away from the cult.

Rebecca wrinkled her nose in distaste. What kind of savior would do what to their people? An oppressor, that's who. Someone who delights in having people serving his every need, be it emotional or physical.

Rebecca knew all about it. Her mother had lost a sister to a cult back in the eighties. Rebecca never got the chance to know her aunt the way her mother had before a charismatic narcissist took her away to his place of worship. Her aunt had died, along with hundreds of others in a desperate attempt to reach a place that didn't exist.

Rebecca shook her head, pushing the memory of her mother wailing at the news to the back of her mind. "All right, I'll see if I can make her talk." She bunched up the papers and held them close.

She stood in front of the door leading to the interrogation room, closed her eyes for a second and wiped her mind clean of the judgmental thoughts. In this line of work, she had to be objective and professional. She had to be—it was all for the sake of the children.

She put what she hoped to be a sympathetic smile on her face and opened the door. "Miss Remy?"

The woman turned in her seat. Her gaze made Rebecca's stomach recoil. It was like staring into the bottom of an old well. A well that rapidly filled with water. Remy covered her face as she turned away, her thin shoulders quaking with sobs.

"Please, I need your help."

Rebecca's armor fell slightly as she sat down opposite Remy. She'd thought she would at least be met with some resistance. Brainwashed people are difficult to reason with and deprogramming those individuals would take months.

Rebecca cleared her throat. "That's what I'm here for, Miss Remy. But I need to know a few certain things first. Now, Detective Jones, the nice man with whom you spoke, told me that your child is still at the compound?"

145

Remy spread her fingers apart and gazed at Rebecca with those void eyes before nodding.

"How old is your child?" Rebecca pulled her notepad and pen from her bag and the pen hovered slightly above the paper.

Remy wiped her eyes and nose with her already dirty sleeve. A chink broke off in Rebecca's armor, allowing a drop of actual pity to trickle through. She handed Remy a couple of tissues from her bag.

"Thank you. Celia is only six years old."

Rebecca noted the girl's age in her notepad. "Was she born in the compound?"

Remy nodded. Rebecca glanced up. Remy dropped her trembling chin to her chest. "Yes, our gracious leader insisted that we women have children to strengthen the bond of our family."

Rebecca's eyes narrowed. She had to ease the grip she had on the pen. "Is that so? Were you happy with that?"

Remy bit her bottom lip. Rebecca noticed that she kept rubbing her hands on the dirty fabric on her thighs. "I thought so at first, but not anymore."

"And why is that? What made you change your mind after so many years in the presence of your leader?"

Remy's gaunt face turned ashen. Her hoarse voice lowered to a whisper. "Because they're going to kill my daughter."

Rebecca stopped writing and gave Remy her full attention. "What do you mean?"

"Please, you must help me save her. She's all I've got. I can't let them take her." Remy broke into hysterics and flung herself on the table, sobbing loudly.

Rebecca took a deep breath, reached a hesitant hand forward and patted Remy's shoulder. "I am going to help you, Miss Remy, but first you need to tell me why they're going to kill your little girl."

Remy took a few moments to regain her composure. Detective Jones helped when he brought the two of them cups of coffee. Remy didn't touch hers, though; only cradled the warm cup in her bony hands. "It's because of the harvest. Our crops are dying. They've been dying for a while now. We've tried everything but nothing worked. Then our gracious leader received word from Ha-kán, our god. In order to survive, we would need a blood sacrifice to water our crops. Only the blood of an innocent will help our harvest."

Remy paused as she wiped the tears from her eyes. "Two days ago, our gracious leader told us that Ha-kán had chosen Celia."

"Why do you think your leader picked your child, specifically?"

Remy twisted the fabric of the robe underneath the table. Her sidelong glances at the mirror and then back at Rebecca confirmed what Rebecca had been thinking.

"You were having doubts about your family? About your leader? About your god?"

Remy nearly crumbled under Rebecca's scrutiny. She refused to look up in her eyes and merely gave a tiny nod.

"I see." Rebecca scribbled into her notepad.

"Why couldn't our lord have picked another instead? Despite my doubts, I had been diligent. I had been working hard keeping our family safe and content. Why did he have to pick my child?" Remy caught herself and clapped a hand on her mouth, eyes widening.

Rebecca put her pen away and steepling her fingers together, she gave Remy a stern, determined look. "Why don't we find out?"

"Are you sure about this?" Detective Jones asked Rebecca for the sixth time that evening.

Rebecca pressed her lips together as she gathered her things in a small sports bag. They were only a change of clothes—no valuables, no gun, nothing. Remy had said that the compound would confiscate such things at the entrance.

"Yes, Ben, I am. It's the only way we can get Remy's girl and perhaps some of the other children as well."

Detective Jones rubbed his chin, glancing at Remy who stood quiet by the exit, eyes gazing far away. "Yeah, but going with *her*? Isn't that a bit risky?"

Rebecca nodded. "It is, but how else am I going to get inside? They don't allow strangers to just waltz in, not when they've got armed men guarding the premises."

"Then at least take this," Detective Jones discreetly slipped a switchblade in Rebecca's hands. "Keep it in your sock. They usually forget to search there."

Rebecca nodded, dropped a shirt on the floor and pretended to pick it up while concealing the small switchblade inside her sock. Cold metal adjusted to the warmth of her skin.

"Are you ready?" Remy called anxiously, one leg already through the threshold, her hand clutching the fabric, as though it were the only thing keeping her intact in this world.

Rebecca zipped up her bag and looked up at Detective Jones. It warmed her heart to see the knitted eyebrows, the clenched jaw. Perhaps when she was done with this case, she might finally accept his offer of dinner. But for now, it was time for business. "Remember, if I'm not back by tomorrow evening, you will alert the troops."

Detective Jones exhales and then gave her a firm nod.

Rebecca smiled and gently squeezed his arm before turning away and exiting the police station with Remy.

The drive to the compound was a silent one. Remy hadn't said a word since they left the city except for giving Rebecca directions to their destination.

Rebecca wasn't fond of this tense silence. Or of her silent companion for that matter. She glanced at Remy for a second. The way she looked ahead with those sunken eyes gave Rebecca the creeps. Those eyes, however, were alight, with quiet determination for once. To get her child back? Rebecca hoped that was the case.

She cleared her throat. She needed to lift the air between them. Make them (or her, if she was honest) feel more comfortable. "Are you nervous about going back?"

Remy's hand shot up and picked at one of the scabs on her shaved head. "Nervous? That's an understatement. I've seen what they've done to caught deserters. They're...not the same as before." Her fingers scratched furiously at her scalp. Blood trickled down her temple.

Rebecca's stomach quivered. She hadn't noticed that she was gripping the steering wheel so tight her knuckles were white. She quickly pulled out a handkerchief from her breast pocket and gave it to Remy. "What do they do?"

Remy shook her head, her bottom lip trembling. She wrung the handkerchief in her hands but she didn't use it to clean the blood. "I can't tell you. It's too awful, but according to our leader, it was necessary to cleanse them of their betraying toxins."

Rebecca scoffed. "You know, you don't have to refer to him as your leader anymore. Once we get Celia, you'll be leaving that life forever."

Remy slowly nodded, even gave a weak chuckle. "I'm sorry. My head is still all dizzy. It's hard to throw away years' worth of what you believed to be the truth."

Rebecca patted her hand in what she hoped was motherly and reassuring. "It all takes time, but don't worry. We'll all be here for you and your daughter."

Remy said nothing, just clasped her hands together on her thighs and allowed the trickle of blood to drip down her jaw.

After an hour of driving, they were met with a sea of tall cyprus trees over the horizon.

"We're not far from home now," Remy muttered.

She told Rebecca to keep driving until the forest swallowed them. Until normal roads deserted them, and a worn-off gravel path embraced them with open arms. Thick canopy of trees engulfed the car from all sides. Their leaves almost obscured the setting sun from behind. The creeping shadow that followed them prickled Rebecca's scalp and she felt a sense of claustrophobia settling within that had never happened before. They really were isolated here. No wonder not many managed to escape. Where would they go, if they succeeded, having nothing but the cult's doctrine engraved in their minds?

"You should park the car here. Walking the rest of the way is safer." Remy said.

Rebecca's hand hovered over the keys. She didn't want to leave her trusted car in the middle of nowhere, but it was best to follow Remy's advice.

They walked up the hill, Rebecca's feet aching in the ascent. The path got narrower and steeper, only fit for one person at a time to walk. Remy walked ahead, her stride confident and firm. Rebecca raised an eyebrow.

Perhaps she was keeping a front, so that the others wouldn't notice her true intentions. She noticed that Remy had a peculiar scar on the back of her neck. She squinted her eyes. It was some kind of ancient runes that Rebecca couldn't read. She hadn't noticed it before, but then again, she hadn't been focused on anyone's neck so long as far as she could tell. She opened her mouth to ask Remy about it, but her words choked in her throat when she saw the wooden fortress.

High walls of wooden boards towered over them, barring them from seeing what was inside as well as barring them from it. Two men guarded each corner and immediately aimed their rifles at them.

"This is private property of Ha-kán's Haven. Trespassers will be shot." One of them announced in a loud, clear, authoritative voice.

"Don't shoot. It's me, Remy. I've come back from my recruiting journey. I've brought a friend over."

Remy pulled Rebecca close to her and the heady smell of dirt and sweat wafted into Rebecca's nostrils. She hadn't felt it in the enclosed car, but amid the forestry, it was all consuming. She resisted the urge to wrinkle her nose, even though her throat itched for it.

"Glad to see you returned in one piece, Remy. All right, open the gate." The guard nodded to someone hidden from below.

The ground trembled as the gate was pushed to the side. Remy marched ahead, not letting go of Rebecca's arm.

What Rebecca imagined to be lush greenery similar to the open forest around them burned to a crisp the moment she set foot inside the compound. The grass, grown tall yet wilted and sickly yellow, barely swayed in the breeze. A row or two remained of the crops of corn near the walls, insects feasting on them. The soil was wet with something crimson. Roofs of the houses were crooked and missing a log here and there. Rebecca suppressed a shudder at the thought of trying to survive the winter in those sheds.

People gathered as Remy and Rebecca approached the small square. Some looked up from their futile attempts at saving their gardens, others paused their wood chopping, axes raised above their heads. All of them looked the same; shaved heads, simple linen robes and those eyes devoid of any energy, of any life.

Rebecca gulped to moisten her already dry throat. She planted her feet firm on the ground to keep herself from bolting out the gate. She gave a half-hearted wave and an awkward smile to a group of bald children who stopped playing in the square and ogled at the two newcomers. One sat at the base of a statue that was in the middle of the square. Rebecca's eyes traveled up. She wished she hadn't. Cold dread crawled up her skin like maggots.

A being shrouded in heavy robes glowered over the cultists. It was taller than the largest man in the group, probably reaching eight feet in height. Hundreds of tiny, bulging eyes covered almost every thread of the robes, their irises all peering down, as if casting judgment upon the worshippers. The head was a huge skeletal beast. Not cast in cement like the rest of its body, but an actual skull, cracked and weathered but still retaining that ivory color. Not human in shape, but deer, its antlers reaching far and wide into the sky, as if ready to take flight at a moment's notice.

Rebecca had to remind herself that it was only a statue, a mere fabrication of a non-existent deity. Yet there was something about it, like the eyes themselves followed their every move.

"This is your god?" She couldn't help herself.

Remy nodded as she walked up to it in a slow, revered motion. She placed two fingers on her lips, then gently touched the wound on her head. It was still in the process of healing and her fingers came back red. She coated one of the deity's eyes with her blood. "I have returned, oh great one. Sorry for being away for so long."

The people around them then proceeded to mimic Remy's actions. After placing two fingers on their lips, all withdrew a knife from their robes. Rebecca tensed and got ready to bend down and draw out her own switchblade. They ignored her, however, and gave themselves a small cut on their forearms. The adults assisted the children by pricking their fingers with sewing needles. The children didn't even wince, a practice drilled into them since birth. They all smeared their blood on the statue's eyes, murmuring their praises to their monstrous god.

Rebecca swallowed the excessive, bitter tang of saliva in her mouth. She rolled her shoulders, unsure whether she should follow their leads. Unsure whether she even *could* follow them. The act of cutting herself and offering her blood to that monster sent her stomach churning. She caught Remy watching her with a faint smile.

"Don't worry, you'll catch on soon."

Rebecca tried to reciprocate the gesture, but it only turned into a tight grimace.

A man approached them from a house that looked a lot better than the rest of the sheds; painted white with a huge golden insignia (a blooming yew tree) hanging above the double door. The man himself looked more nourished, of stocky built and with a commanding air around him. It wouldn't have shocked Rebecca to find out that he was either in the leader's inner circle or the leader himself.

"Remy, Gracious Adlai wants to see you."

The muscles in Remy's neck tightened. Even though her back was turned against her, Rebecca sense that she was terrified. Was the leader going to punish her? She wanted to stay by her side, to let her know she wasn't alone, but that could blow her cover. She must act like everything was new to her. Which wasn't hard to do at all.

So, she feigned surprise and let out a gasp of wonder. "Oh, how marvelous that you get to meet the leader, Remy. I wonder when I will be blessed by his presence."

Remy turned and there was something dark in her sunken eyes. A small twitch in her mouth, as if suppressing a grin. "You will soon enough. Please, make yourself at home while I'm gone. I won't be long."

A chunk of ice fell into Rebecca's insides. Its ripples reverberated through her veins. She had been hoping to stay at Remy's side the entire time. As Remy followed the stocky man back to the white house, Rebecca felt abandoned. Tossed aside to fend for herself in a new surrounding. She imagined herself as a transfer student, trying to get along with the rest of the class. She had experienced that when her mother moved them to get closer to her sister's cult home. She felt those same eyes of judgment and distrust fell upon her now.

She shuffled the weight in her feet, eyes darting between each member who regarded her as something new and foreign. As something possibly dangerous and contaminating.

She focused on the children instead. Her line of work helped connect with them better than the adults. The children hesitated at first, glancing up at the adults for approval. When one woman gave a reluctant nod, they eagerly took Rebecca around their meagre homes. Each of them showed her a wooden toy they had made themselves. Most of the time, it was just a stick with small, broken branches.

"Is that all you have?" Rebecca asked.

A girl no older than eight nodded and squeezed her stick as she would a teddy bear. "We don't need anything else. Our leader told us our imagination was enough."

Rebecca bit the inside of her cheek, resisting the urge to grab them all and run towards the gate. They all deserved a better place. Somewhere far away from here. But she had to be patient.

She had until nightfall.

The cult's prayers were performed during the mornings, the afternoons and in the evenings. The cult members all gathered to the largest house in the compound, which acted as their prayer domain. Loud, shrill chants in a mixture of Gaelic and Hebrew could be heard throughout the compound. It sent a shiver down Rebecca's spine as she tiptoed around the corner of one of the sheds, seeing only the faded white silhouette of Remy ahead of her.

She was glad to be outside, under the pretense that Remy had to teach her the complex prayers. The leader apparently had ordered her to do it. If only he knew...

The thought of betraying his sorry ass burned bright in Rebecca's mind and strengthened her resolve. She was relieved that Remy seemed to feel the same way as she marched headstrong to the houses nearest the white one.

"The children are kept down in the basement during prayers. The leader dislikes their fussing, says it disrupts the power of the prayers." Remy scowled at the words.

Rebecca nodded, glancing behind her shoulder to make sure no one was following them. "And Celia will be down there?"

During her time with the children, she had asked them about Remy's girl. The children had gone silent until one boy spoke with reverence: "She's waiting in the cellar for her bright time."

When Rebecca had inquired more about this 'bright time', the kids shushed at the boy and quickly changed the subject. It was horrifying to know that even the children were aware of the cult's human sacrifice.

Remy nodded. "I can finally free my girl from that prison." A shudder went through her. Rebecca gave her an encouraging squeeze on her arm.

When they reached the second house to the left of the leader's quarters, Remy placed a finger on her lips. They could heart the squall of children playing inside the cellar.

Nervous butterflies fluttered chaotically inside Rebecca. She wished she had a flashlight, a candle, anything to see in the dark. The last thing she wanted to stumble upon at night are the despondent eyes of a cult member. But it was too risky, so she had to rely on her eyes adjusting to the darkness.

Remy led her to a storm hatch in the back. She gave a small knock and waited until a faint knock could be heard from behind the hatch. She opened it slowly, resulting in a loud creak that carried on into the night.

Rebecca froze. Her heart hammered in her chest. She waited to hear thunderous footsteps approach their place. When she heard nothing but the thrashing in her own ears, she unclenched her jaw. No one was near. No one had heard. They were all too busy chanting their prayers to their make-believe god.

"All right, let's do this."

Remy held the hatch open. "I'll stay watch. You go inside first."

Rebecca found that odd. She thought she'd be rushing down, frantically searching for her daughter amid the group of playing children. Then she detected how Remy's hand trembled and Rebecca knew that she was holding it all in. She was waiting until they were out of this god-forsaken place.

The old stairs leading down to the cellar groaned under Rebecca's weight. She cringed. This was why she hated old, wooden houses and why she preferred carpets over hardwood floors. The darkness inside swallowed her whole. She tasted copper in the air. But not just that. Something rotten tickled her nose. Rebecca strained her ears. Dead silence. Not even a childish giggle or the faintest of breaths of hidden children. Dread tugged at her sides. Were they in the right place? It was hard to tell, all of the houses looked the same.

"I don't see Cel—"

A white, sodden cloth thrust onto Rebecca's mouth, cutting her off. She gasped and inhaled the sweet, disinfectant odor. Chloroform. She recognized the smell from her juvenile days working the summers in a paper mill.

A hand shot from behind and secured Rebecca's arm, just as she was about to drive her elbow into the assailant. She stumbled down a step and clawed at her leg, trying to reach for the switchblade hidden in her sock.

Her head swam. Her eyelids grew heavier with each sedated breath. Her limbs lost all movement. Right before she passed out, she could have sworn she saw Remy with a broad smile on her gaunt face.

"Wake up, Rebecca Harris."

The words echoed in Rebecca's befuddled mind. She struggled to open her eyes. It was like they were glued shut. A breeze drifted by, spreading goosebumps all over her body. Nothing clung to her body, not even something as soft as a towel. She felt bare.

Hazy silhouettes formed in her vision as her eyes flickered open.

Three shaven heads, spotted with scabs, peered down at Rebecca. Bald men flanked Remy on both sides.

"You're finally awake. We can soon begin, then." Remy clapped her hands enthusiastically.

Rebecca tried to move. Something rough ground against her wrists and ankles. She glanced down. Rope bound her on a stone altar. She screamed when she noticed that they had stripped her of all her clothes.

"Oh, shut up." Remy slapped Rebecca hard. "No one is going to get you."

Rebecca's cheek stung horribly. But it didn't sting as much as the betrayal bubbling within her. She fought the angry tears welling up in her eyes. "This was a trap all along."

Remy nodded, smiling. "That's right. And you fell for it, hook, line and sinker."

Rebecca writhed against the bindings, ropes burning her skin. She gritted her teeth. "Why? I thought you wanted to save Celia."

Remy's sinister smile spread further, revealing yellowed, decaying teeth. "Oh, I have saved her. She won't be the sacrificial lamb. You will."

Cold struck Rebecca at her core, weakening her limbs. Numbness clutched hard. "What do you mean? Why me?"

Remy strolled around Rebecca, her fingers stroking Rebecca's bare body. Rebecca shuddered under her touch. "We've been watching, Miss Harris. You've been *very* interested in our community, thinking that we need saving. Well, I guess you're right to a certain extent. I wasn't lying when I said that our crops were dying. You witnessed it yourself. We tried to sacrifice our own to appease Ha-kán, to receive his grace, but our emaciated bodies weren't enough."

She gestured to the corner of the room, to the source of the foul, rotted stench Rebecca had detected earlier. Rebecca raised her head. Her stomach dropped. A pile of naked, dismembered bodies filled the corner. Dead eyes stared up at the ceiling. Rebecca remembered seeing something crimson on the corn soil. Had they really watered the crops with the blood of their own members? She wanted to curse but she had lost her voice at the sight of the massacre.

"As you can see, Ha-kán wasn't satisfied," Remy continued. "So, when I suggested someone meatier, someone whose blood ran righteous in their veins, he accepted. And I chose you. With you gone, our crops will be saved and Ha-kán will be free to roam the earth."

Rebecca broke free from her shock and scoffed. "It doesn't matter if I'm gone. The police will raid your fucking cult whether I live or die."

Remy leaned mere inches over Rebecca's head. Rebecca nearly gagged at her bad breath. "Let them try. They're no match to the power of Ha-kán."

Rebecca let out a hoarse laugh, devoid of mirth. "You actually think that this stupid god of yours exists. You're so deluded."

Remy's smile faltered. She pulled out a knife engraved with runes on the blade. The same runes that scarred the back of her neck. It glinted in the light that hung above Rebecca.

"Only one way to find out."

Footsteps clamored the room. Forlorn faces of all shapes and sizes gathered around the altar table, looming over Rebecca.

"Begin." Remy commanded as she climbed a small ladder and positioned herself across from the altar, hands clasped around the ceremonial knife.

They all opened their mouths simultaneously. Their voices boomed in aggravated chants. Some of the cult members adorned the altar by placing diseased corn next to Rebecca. Others smeared runic symbols in the congealed blood of their dead members across Rebecca's body.

A little girl stood on her toes to give Rebecca's forehead a kiss. She was the spitting image of the horrific cult leader who towered over her. "Thank you for your bounty," she said with a lisp and trotted to the back where the rest of the children danced and swayed to the rhythmic chants.

The voices rose higher, their eyes glazed over. Some began to convulse but all remained rooted to the spot.

"Now, my lord. Accept our sacrifice and rise above. Show this rotten world the rule of Ha-kán!" Remy shrieked, raised the blade above her head and jumped from her pedestal.

Rebecca screamed as the knife plunged into her abdomen. Blood bubbled from her mouth. Her stomach was on fire, like Remy had stuck a red-hot poker inside and twisted it.

Remy let go of the blade and raised her arms to the sides. "It has begun. I can feel him. He's coming."

The cult members never stopped their chants. On the contrary, they became more frantic as the air seemed electrified. Rebecca tried not to move. The blood spilling from the wound grew bigger around her. Cold gripped her limbs and threatened to freeze her. Breathing became a struggle until it transformed into low gurgles.

Her vision must have been the first thing that got damaged in the initial attack, because she could have sworn that something within Remy's skin *moved*. Her arms bulged, as if bitten by some insect and the allergic reaction went haywire. This reaction accelerated and soon, Remy's whole body expanded, like a balloon.

And like a balloon, she burst.

Bits of flesh, bones, organs, and blood splattered all over the room, painting the white robes in grotesque abstracts. No one screamed. No one had even flinched at the bodily explosion.

Rebecca wanted to but couldn't. Her voice had been stolen by the figure standing instead of Remy. Living, writhing darkness shrouded its entire body. Thousands of bulging eyes blinked and squirmed in the void, rinsing themselves of Remy's gory remains. The god's massive skeletal head surveyed Rebecca with amethyst glowing eyes. Dozens of arms sprang out from the cloaked shadows, like branches of a tree, and gripped each cult member's head. Never did they stop their chants, not even as its nails buried into their skulls. Blood mingled with their tears, but their mouths were spread in exultant smiles.

An enormous gap formed in the middle of the inky blackness. Rows upon rows of jagged teeth chomped eagerly at the fresh meal laid on the table.

SHED
THE NIGHT'S
SKIN

he digital clock on the nightstand read ten minutes after two when Eric Northcutt heard the knock on the front door. He'd been dreaming of the cave he'd visited on a class trip as a boy and sitting up he at first thought he was still there, under the earth, waiting for the black, cavernous depths to swallow him whole. Next to him in bed his girlfriend Michelle stirred in her sleep, and after a second rap from downstairs one of her hands nudged Eric's arm.

"Someone's out there," she said, a half-wakened murmur. "Go see who it is."

Eric rubbed his eyes. "It's two in the morning."

"It's probably your brother. I get sick of him showing up drunk all the time. He needs to work shit out with Kelly. This crap is getting old."

Eric sat there, hoping the visitor wouldn't knock again, but when another pounding echoed up the stairs, he grumbled and crawled from the covers. The night had been warm, and he'd only slept in his boxers; tossing on a t-shirt and flip-flops, Eric went to the bedroom door. "I'll be back, all right?"

There wasn't an answer beyond Michelle's snoring and, yawning, Eric made his way downstairs. The foyer was dark save for a slice of moonlight slashing across the tile, but it was enough to see the blobby shape of someone through the sidelight window.

It probably is *Nick,* he thought. Michelle had been right about that, sleepwalker logic or not; his brother's after-last-call visits weren't a rare occurrence anymore, and Eric wondered how long Nick would be passed out on the sofa this time. When he reached the door, though, the voice that answered the inquiry for identification wasn't his sibling's inebriated tone.

"It's Trevor, man. Open up."

"Trevor?" Massaging his eyelids once more, Eric fumbled with both deadbolt and knob before opening the door. Out on the porch a man stood half-obscured in the shadows of the awning, but when Eric clicked on the front light the tall, skinny frame and sloppy, wannabe rock-star hair of his best friend came into sharp focus. Trevor shielded his eyes from the sudden brightness, and Eric saw the sleeve of his suede jacket was spattered with mud.

"Dude, what the hell? You know what time it is?" He asked. Trevor lowered his hand and nodded, and Eric noticed how jittery he seemed; Trevor's movements were skittish, and his voice, when he spoke again, was uneasy.

"Yeah. I'm sorry, bro. I, uh, I need your help with something."

"At two in the morning? What, you get into another dust-up with some chick's boyfriend? Man, when are you gonna learn groupies are trouble?"

Trevor smiled; usually it was a dashing grin, the same one Eric had been familiar with since high school. Trevor had always been the confident one, the charismatic one—the frontman in a band, the rebel, the mischief maker, the babe magnet. Even now, two years beyond college, when Eric had knuckled under and gotten a job as a bank teller, Trevor was still the outlaw, playing in bands, holding life's reins instead of watching it go by. Everywhere he went a rush of booze and mayhem followed, but the smile Trevor wore was shaky, streaked by an uncertainty Eric had never seen on him before.

"What's wrong with you?" He asked, and any feigned levity in Trevor's expression disappeared.

"I told you. I need your help. *Now.*"

Eric pointed to Trevor's jacket; it wasn't just the sleeve covered in grime, but the whole front lapel, and the t-shirt beneath, too. When Eric took a step closer he noticed a spot on Trevor's cheek, darker than the rest, and his scrutiny deepened.

"Is that blood?"

Trevor's nerves, already apparent, unraveled further, and Eric saw his hands shaking.

"I killed someone, man." Trevor admitted. "I...I *killed* someone."

Eric smirked. "Yeah, *right.*" His mind wandered backwards to all the times Trevor had pulled pranks in the past, how he'd reveled in getting one over on people with some joke or other. It was part of his mystique, what made him cool. That cocksure, devil-may-care slyness that assured he was always one step ahead of the pack. Eric pointed to Trevor, his smirk a full-on chuckle. "Man, you *almost* had me. Dude, how buzzed are you to try and pull a stunt like this?"

"I'm *serious,* Eric." Trevor insisted again, more a growl than anything, and his face drew down into an anguished leer. "I *killed* a guy. I was leaving the nightclub after tonight's show and I'd drank a little too much and...*Jesus,* man, I didn't even *see* him. I swear to *God,* I don't even know where the *fuck* he came from. He was just there and..."

Trevor ran one unsettled hand through his hair while the other tightened into a fist that he bit on, so hard that the knuckle dripped blood. Slowly Eric reached one of his own hands out, but Trevor pulled away from the comforting touch.

"What happened next?" Eric asked. Trevor glared at him.

"You *believe* me?"

Eric hesitated. "You're too freaked out *not* to believe. But you better not be dicking with me, either, because if you are, I'm gonna beat the *shit* out of you."

"I'm *not* joking." Trevor continued, slightly calmer. "I think it was a homeless guy. He was crossing the side exit when I was backing out with the van," he gestured then to the tarnished vehicle parked haphazardly in Eric's driveway, the same one he used to transport his band's equipment in. "All I heard was a *thump!* That was it. Guy didn't even scream. Shit, at first I thought I'd run into the dumpster until I got out and saw him lying on the pavement." Trevor's voice rose and his eyes widened. "It was *sick,* man. Some of his bones were broken. Blood was *everywhere...*"

"You check for a pulse?"

"Fuck do you think? Of *course* I did. He was stone-cold *dead.* No breathing, no pulse, no *nothing.*"

"Shit." Eric said, feeling breathless himself. "W-What'd you do? I-I mean, what'd you do with...*him?* You just leave him there? You call the police?"

"Look, I *told* you, I was wasted at the concert tonight, Eric. I've got some D.U.I's already. I'm not calling the cops for shit. I get busted for this, I'm fucked." He stopped and pointed to the rear door of the van. "I put him in *there.*"

"What?" Eric's eyes bulged. "You're messing with me."

"I *swear*. Come and see." Trevor was already off the porch by then, and despite being in his underwear, Eric followed. By the time he reached the van, Trevor had the back doors open, but when Eric peeked in, all he saw was a crumpled pile of blankets coiled on the vehicle's floor. It was only as Trevor anxiously unfurled the top-most covering that the battered face of a middle-aged man emerged. If he hadn't heard Trevor's tale, Eric would've thought the fellow asleep; he was pale-skinned, with gray hair peeking beneath a ragged stocking cap and a short, unkempt beard lining a sagging face. But there was a stream of crimson connecting nose to mouth, and a similar stain smudging the chin. When Trevor turned to him a second time, it was with pure desperation.

"We need to get *rid* of him," Trevor said flatly, adding then: "Will you help me bury the body?"

Eric staggered backwards into the hedge beside the driveway. Rubbing the scratches on his calf, he couldn't help a nervous chuckle of his own. "Oh, I see, *now* you're pulling my leg. Very funny, man. Gotta admit you went all out this time. The dummy looks real and everything."

"It's *not* a dummy, Eric! He's *dead. I mean* it. We have to bury him," Trevor climbed into the van and brought out two shovels.

Eric raised an eyebrow. Trevor usually put some theatrics into his practical jokes, but Eric couldn't remember if he'd ever brought along actual props. He glanced down at the body. Morbid curiosity propelled a probing index finger forward, and he gingerly poked the body's cheek.

Ice cold and plump.

"Oh, God, he really *is* dead," Eric muttered.

"No shit, Sherlock. What've I been saying? Now hop in, we need to hurry."

The van zig-zagged through what little traffic the outskirts of the Sacramento metro area offered at three in the morning.

Eric held on to his seat. The fajitas he'd had for dinner continually threatened to repay him a visit ever since giving that investigative corpse-poke and Trevor's reckless driving did nothing to calm his stomach or his nerves.

"Will you slow it down, man? Do you *want* the cops following us?"

Trevor snorted at that, but Eric noticed his leg ease up on the accelerator. He then caught sight of the bundle swaying from side to side in the rear of the van and wished they'd secured the body better. He didn't want to see the man's mangled face every time Trevor took a curve.

"Where are we going, anyway?"

"The woods. Best place to bury our mistake."

Eric cocked an eyebrow. "You mean *your* mistake. You're the one who ran the poor bastard over, not me."

"I know, I know, fuck, you don't have to salt the wound." Trevor raked fingers across his perspiration-drenched chin, then haphazardly patted the front of his jacket. *"Fuck,* I forgot my smokes at the club. Got any cigarettes?"

Eric chuckled dryly, pointing at his T-shirt and boxers. "See any pockets?"

Trevor cursed again and gripped the steering wheel tighter. *To hide the tremors,* Eric noticed.

"Hey, you want me to take over? I'm not sure you're in a condition to—"

"I'm *fine.*" Trevor growled. "I sobered the hell up *real* quick when I felt that thud against my bumper."

Eric rolled his eyes and looked through the passenger's window. The city's warm illumination

171

slowly faded to the shrinking horizon. A few houses here and there blurred past until the darkness swallowed the van whole. The further they slipped away from civilization the tighter Eric's chest felt.

"Look, man, what if we turn around and go to the hospital? We can explain that it was all an accident. I'll vouch for you. I've got your back. Always have."

Trevor's fearful eyes flashed against an opposite car's headlights. "No *way*. Doctors would be right on the phone to the cops, and then I'm screwed in more ways than one. You have *any* idea what convicts do to guys like me?"

Eric bit back the retort he had concerning prison showers. The more serious side of him wanted to tell Trevor he'd help with the bail, but a sharp image of Michelle's disapproving face intruded into his thoughts. She'd surely reprimand him for treating Trevor better than his own brother. Still, wasn't that superior to having a dead guy on his conscience?

Could he live with that?

Could Trevor?

Eric glanced at his friend. Trevor's pallid features looked straight ahead, jaw set and gaze fixated on the road. Apart from his girlfriend, Trevor was probably the most stubborn person Eric knew. Once he decided on something, impulsive or not, he set out to do it. When Eric said so openly, though, Trevor didn't answer; he only ground his teeth and kept his sights aimed forward as Eric heaved a defeated sigh.

Into the woods they go.

Eric would never admit it to Trevor—or anyone else for that matter— but he hated the forest. The way the trees held that ominous aura, like they collected everyone's darkest secrets, gave Eric prickling gooseflesh. And now here they were, adding one of their own.

Eric shivered when he stepped out of the van, cursing himself for not bringing at least a pair of pants. Trevor walked briskly to the end of the van and vanished inside. A few moments later he reappeared with the shovels, banged them together and handed one to Eric. "You ready?"

Eric looked around. They had driven deep into the wilderness. The silence that surrounded them played tricks with Eric's anxious head: he jumped at the innocent croaking of frogs and windswept leaves, and his apprehension wasn't helped by the dark, rain-thickened clouds overhead.

"Yeah, let's do this and get the hell out of here."

"Grab the flashlight from the glove compartment, will you?" Trevor asked. Eric nodded, went to the front of the van and opened the passenger's door; rummaging around, he bypassed a roll of duct tape, some hand sanitizer and a pack of condoms to retrieve the flashlight when Trevor let out an abrupt cry, so piercing Eric hit his head on the door frame from surprise.

"What the hell is it *now?*" He barked; one hand probed the base of his skull, and he grunted when the fingertips returned smeared with blood.

"The fucker moved!" Trevor shouted, rife with panic. When Eric reached the open rear doors, he saw his friend had backpedaled ten feet, dropped his shovel and was pointing with childish, slack-jawed fright into the vehicle, babbling so fast his words verged on gibberish: "I went to grab his feet and he *moved,* man!"

Eric glanced into the van. The body remained where he'd seen it last, tight beneath the blankets and he gave Trevor a jagged glare.

"You're *nuts.*" He said, remembering the clamminess on his fingertip. Yet Trevor's distraught insistence remained:

"Go! Go look!"

Eric paused before heading towards the van. His hands shuddered as he flipped on the flashlight, aimed the beam and yanked down the outermost blanket concealing the corpse.

"The dude's *not* moving," Eric retorted, and for the first time fear surrendered to annoyance. *The booze, the stress...Trevor's heading for a breakdown and then I'm gonna to be stuck in the middle of nowhere with a cadaver, a lunatic and no idea how to get home. I swear this is the* last *time I answer the door after nine p.m.*

"He *was*...I saw him," Trevor sputtered again. This time Eric marched over, grabbed the lapel of his blood-caked jacket, and jerked him forward.

"Keep it together a little while longer, all right? We go out, dig a hole, dump his ass and then *both* forget this *ever* happened. Until then keep your *fucking* head on."

Bewilderment still imprinted Trevor's face, but lucidity slowly crept into his tone. "Y-Yeah...You're right. Let's go." He took a few small steps backward, pointing with the tip of his shovel into the dark. "This way. There's a flat spot near a creek bed where I used to hang out with my cousin as a kid. He overdosed a few years ago and now nobody knows it's there but me. Come on."

He took the flashlight and stormed off, leaving Eric struggling to keep up. The trek thereafter was a nauseating nightmare of low-hanging branches and thorny brambles; Trevor stalked ten paces ahead, the flashlight's bobbing halo the only key to his position, and Eric cursed at every scratch and stab his bare arms and legs received. Finally, they arrived at a stony outcropping that sloped down to a low-lying grassy area, and Eric heard the soft rippling of water over nearby rocks. The light halted, spun, and Trevor's silhouette came back into view.

"Here," he commanded, and set the flashlight down. The next forty minutes was dripping, dirty drudgery as the pair dug, silent save for groans and heavy breath. Eric twice felt himself fade from exhaustion, yet each time he roused and extracted another spade of earth until, at last, the rectangular outline of a shallow grave was carved into the ground. When the pit reached their knees,

Trevor stopped, tossed his shovel down and clamored from the hole.

"Come on. This looks deep enough," he said.

Eric hauled himself up, slower than when he started, and tried vainly to wipe mud from his shins. "How am I gonna explain this to Michelle when I get home? I'm filthy."

"You can shower, and I'll give you some clean clothes at my place," Trevor assured him. "Let's go back to the van."

He turned to take a step when there was a sharp rustling in the leaves behind him—*crunch, crunch, crunch*—echoed by a deep, rhythmic pant that faded as it passed by. Trevor haphazardly whirled the flashlight beam around, and the alarm in his voice renewed.

"What was *that?*" He hissed. Then, louder: *"Who's there?"*

Eric heard the commotion, too, and the sound made his pulse quicken. Reaching out, he lightly touched Trevor's shoulder, but Trevor flinched, pivoted, and frantically lashed the flashlight's handle across the right side of Eric's head. Eric grunted, more from shock than actual pain, and lurched back before falling to one knee.

"What the hell, man?" He shouted. "What's gotten *into* you?"

"Jesus hell, I'm sorry!" Trevor snapped, immediately pulling Eric up by an arm. "I...I didn't mean to..."

At least now my head doesn't hurt where I hit it on the van, Eric told himself as he pushed away from Trevor. Snaring a glimpse of his friend's eyes, though, told him

Trevor's reaction didn't just stem from merely being startled—he was terrified.

"I'm sorry, I thought you were...I thought you..." Trevor paused, then slumped his shoulders. "It was probably a deer or something. Y-You okay?"

Eric managed a grim grin. "I'm thinking if I'm not careful I might end up taking the dirt nap myself tonight."

Trevor lit the path they'd taken; leaving their shovels at the makeshift burial plot, the return hike wasn't any easier than the original foray, and though a part of Eric wanted to cheer when the van appeared he dreaded the idea that the next journey would be burdened with dead weight. Ahead of him, Trevor was walking with long, determined strides, but just prior to reaching the vehicle he stopped, and Eric watched his posture stiffen.

"What is it?" He asked, but Trevor didn't respond. Instead, he raised his left hand, and in the dullness Eric saw each finger tremble as Trevor pointed to the van's still-open rear doors.

"He's...he's *gone.*"

"What?" Eric rushed to Trevor's side and peered into the van.

Unbelievably, Trevor was right. Nothing remained except the dirty blankets the body had been wrapped in.

"How. In. The fuck?" Eric mumbled as he grabbed one of the ragged covers; it felt wet to the touch.

"This can't be happening." Trevor's voice shook so badly Eric almost couldn't understand him. He backed away, hands gripping his head, chest heaving, the whites of his eyes manic as he swiveled to and fro.

"Calm down, Trev." Eric took a cautious step to his friend. "There's an obvious explanation behind this. M-Maybe the body fell off when we were out there digging. We didn't exactly have it secured very well."

Eric knew he was only grasping invisible straws with his attempts at rationale; worse was that Trevor did, too, and he violently shook his head. "NO. We *both* know it was here when we left. But it's gone, Eric. It's *gone.*"

He began to laugh; a fit of suppressed giggles escaped his lips and he playfully stooped to check beneath the van.

"Nope. Not *here."* Trevor cackled, repeating the phrase after he ducked behind one pair of crooked trees, then another, and his eruption of hysterical guffaws encased Eric's veins in ice. Earlier he'd worried about his best friend's mental state; watching him spiral further down the rabbit hole was something else altogether, and when Trevor abruptly snapped his fingers Eric actually jumped.

"It walked away. Got up on his two feet and waltzed right outta here," Trevor jabbered and imitated a zombie, arms raised forward and dragging his legs in a shuffle. He cackled again, then descended into incoherence: *I need to stop drinking and smoking so much weed, this is the fuckin' government's fault, toxic waste and a hole in the ozone and Global Warming, fuck this, what the fuck are we gonna do now? FUCK!*

Eric stood there, feet rooted to the spot, speechless and afraid, this time of Trevor; slowly he held up a hand and spoke with as smooth and soothing a tone as he could muster.

"C'mon, Trev, if it's gone, it's gone, and we don't need to worry about it anymore. If anything, it's problem solved. Let's just go back home and forget about the whole thing." Eric's feet uprooted and he inched towards his friend, clutching the blanket tight with the thought he might need to wrap it around Trevor as a straitjacket.

The idea, however, and the action, were stillborn; from the silent woods there came the crash of hurried, thunderous steps as branches snapped and gravel crunched right behind Eric.

He turned around and something struck hard into his shoulder. In the dark the intruder seemed mountainous, like a bear, but he felt no fur on the shadowy figure, though it was strong enough to knock the wind from his chest as he crashed to the dirt. Eric gasped and rolled, but the thing had bypassed him to launch in Trevor's direction; the flashlight fell once the two collided, and the pair became blackened outlines to Eric's eyes. The screams, though, were savage in the night, and though his intention was to rush to Trevor's aid, Eric's lungs choked for air and instead he felt himself getting dizzy before he didn't feel anything at all.

Trevor's disorientation lasted barely five seconds after the figure tackled him to the ground.

"The fuck?! Get *off* me, creep!" He shouted as he tried to shove the figure away.

The thing atop him raised its arms and clawed at Trevor's clothes. He yelped in pain as shreds of his shirt tore from sharp fingernails.

A harsh stench of dirt, sweat and old urine assaulted Trevor's nostrils as he dug his own nails into the attacker's sunken cheeks. Something wet plopped onto his bare chest. Pieces of torn flesh, spattered with blood and crumpled like bacon strips. Trevor's heart palpitated against his ribcage, and he closed his eyes at the grisly sight until the thing above him spoke.

"Look. At. Me."

Trevor blinked in shock when he recognized both the stink and the person who owned it. It was the homeless man, that he was sure of, but there was something wrong, something that set his senses on edge; the man's voice was almost exactly like his own, though the inflection sounded off, like a baby trying a phrase for the first time.

Fingers caked in soil and dried blood grabbed Trevor's chin, forced it upward, and Trevor thought for sure then he had gone insane. His own eyes were looking back at him. His cheekbone peeked through the wet slabs of flesh dangling from the man's face. The dimples—his own dimples— popped as the man's mouth stretched into a sinister smile.

"What..." Trevor's shocked mind only managed a single word.

The man chuckled (Trevor's laugh!) as he continued what Trevor started; he tore pieces from his body like flaky, sunburned skin that sizzled upon hitting the ground as if the gravel were a huge pan with which the man was making a grotesque breakfast.

Trevor watched in frozen, awed terror as the stranger contorted his limbs and torso a final time before letting out a contended sigh. He looked down at Trevor, only now the image of himself, butterfly from chrysalis, was complete.

"Now *there's* a handsome fella." The duplicate said, and the voice sounded perfectly like Trevor's. "Can't have two bucks strutting around, though, can we?"

Before Trevor could reply, the doppelgänger raised its fist and struck. Trevor's ribs cracked, splintered bone pierced his innards and ruptured arteries drowned it all in coppery, crimson stew. Blood spurted from his gasping mouth. His vision blurred, but Trevor still spotted the imposter holding something in its hands: his own pulsating heart, liberated from the bodily prison but trapped like a suddenly freed bird in the talons of a cat.

"Normally I'm not the vindictive type, but you ran over me, man. And you know what they say—" the thing gave that cocksure grin Trevor himself had worn so many times before squeezing the ripened-tomato heart. "Karma's a *bitch.*"

Eric felt like a stampede trampled him once his eyes fluttered open. His head ached, his forearm was twisted, and his shoulder was sore. He groaned, sat up, and was impressed by silence; the last thing he remembered was being blindsided, but where he expected the sounds of struggle there was grim silence.

"Trevor," he called out, groggy with concussion. "You okay, man?"

There wasn't an answer, and when he turned, Eric blinked. A person stood a few feet from him, blood smeared on their bare chest. Eric frowned. When had Trevor taken off his shirt?

Then he spotted the lifeless body, spotted Trevor's blank, open eyes staring back at him. His shirt and jacket were ribbon, but worse was the fractured breastbone, pulp from the inside pulled out and mauled. And yet Trevor was standing there, too, eating something cupped in his palms with slovenly, animal ferocity; the scene made no sense, and Eric labored to align the twin visuals.

"Trev, what's going—"

The question hung, unanswered, when Trevor—and it *was* Trevor, down to the last chin whisker—turned and dropped the partially-devoured heart he held.

"Hey, bro," he said, smirking scarlet. "Couldn't resist a snack."

Eric opened his mouth, to speak, to scream, but any verbal distress was stifled as Trevor rushed him; there

182

was simply no time to react before knuckles connected with his jaw, and Eric's consciousness crumbled. From there everything he witnessed was in hazy, piecemeal clips—Trevor retrieving the duct tape from the van to bind Eric's wrists; Trevor disappearing into the forest with the mutilated carcass and Trevor returning alone. When Eric roused the fourth time strong hands clasped each arm and his feet were dragging a trail through the woods; unexpectedly he dropped onto one side, and when Eric raised his head there was Trevor, squatting beside him, eyes beastly, reflective, and amber in the flashlight's glow.

"What...What the hell *are* you?" Eric rasped, and Trevor shrugged.

"All depends on who you ask, doesn't it? Some of the old Indian tribes 'round these parts used to have more than a few names for my kind, but they're long dead and names don't mean shit in the end. Skin's all that matters. That's what people see, so that's who you are, what you become. Yesterday I was an old drunk named Radecher. Right now, I'm your asshole buddy. Tomorrow I'll be somebody else. Sometimes it's hard never seeing your own true face, but sometimes life hands you little gifts that even the score." His eyes flared. "I heard everything you two lunkheads said on the drive out here. Girlfriend of yours sounds like a feisty little kitten. Think I might pay her a visit once I'm settled with you. 'Course, I couldn't show up on the doorstep looking like *this* and expect a warm welcome, could I?"

Eric flinched when the thing wearing Trevor's face stood and stretched its arms, grunted and writhed. It hunched over, tearing at its chest, and when the creature reeled upright again half the flesh from the abdomen was missing. To Eric's eyes the molting was like a man changing a shirt--the ripped husk slid smoothly off, and as the metamorphosis neared completion Trevor's splitting brow caused a scream to bubble in Eric's throat when he saw the all-too-familiar guise glistening beneath it.

"Anything you want me to tell Michelle for you?" The creature asked, and it was with Eric's own voice. His bubbling scream burst, but by then it was useless; the thing wearing his features pitched forward and gave Eric a forceful shove. Eric tried to raise his taped hands to defend himself, but he rolled backwards and thought for a moment he was tumbling down the rocky hillside. He was startled to land on something soft, and in the glow of the flashlight he saw Trevor, the *real* Trevor, half-buried beneath worm-ridden soil, and Eric knew then where he was.

Above him, the doppelgänger hefted one of the shovels, and as the first spadeful of earth spattered upon his face, Eric remembered again that cave he'd visited as a boy, felt himself slipping into its dreamy, subterranean grottos before all feeling suffocated into oblivion. It wasn't long until the pit was filled in completely and for some time after the forest became solemnly still; as daybreak approached a snake slithered across the grave's freshly packed surface, its thin outer sheath frayed and ready to shed. The serpent stopped, flexed its muscles, and wriggled fiercely before it was able to leave the old skin behind and move on, hungry for another meal.

RECEIVING IS BETTER THAN GIVING

I ripped the wrapping paper apart and tore the box.

A pale blue buttoned up cardigan with tiny silver stars twinkled out of it. My excited smile disappeared.

"Oh, Brynjar! Isn't it pretty?" Mom cooed, snatching the cardigan and lifting it up for all to see. It felt like the winking stars were mocking me. I tucked my arms at the sides, shrinking under the fanfare. Could she be more embarrassing?

Helga, my little sister, snickered before grabbing another present from underneath the Christmas tree.

Heat buried deep in my cheeks. My chest tightened in embarrassment. "Mom, this is a *girl's* sweater. I'm not wearing that."

"No, grandma told me that the salesperson told her that it was unisex. It suits both girls *and* boys. So, of course you can wear it and you will, don't you?" Mom folded the cardigan as a professional retailer would and handed it back to me. Her narrowed eyes dared me to object.

I hitched up a fake smile, flushing down the disappointment. "Fine, then."

186

"Then you better call your grandma later tonight and thank her for the lovely gift," Mom said while stuffing the wrapping paper into a large, black garbage bag. I got the biggest urge to sneak the cardigan into the garbage bag, but Mom guarded it like a dragon would a treasure.

I looked at the loot next to me and then drifted to the cardigan on my lap. The crime noir books, the video games, even the towel my dad's girlfriend gave me were better than that ugly cardigan.

I had been adamant. No clothes for Christmas. It was a pact everyone in my environmental class had agreed on. The teacher had shown us dozens of pollution documentaries and had asked us what we could do to halt climate change. Our protests at Alþingi had gained us nothing, except a few hundred likes on our social media. But that wasn't enough. We had to become more proactive but nothing to the extremes. Sigrún, the girl I liked, suggested that we deny ourselves new clothes for three months, leading to the new year. Clothing factories were one of the most polluting industries in the world and after watching a particularly invasive documentary about the *H&M* factories in Southeast Asia, we felt guilty contributing to said pollution. Besides, we would be able to show the baby boomers that we're capable of saving our money and use it for a better cause.

But apparently, Grandma didn't get that memo, or she chose to ignore it because she always gives us clothes for Christmas. I asked Mom why and she said that Grandma held on to traditions. Like inviting us to eat putrefied skate on December twenty-third, which is fucking disgusting. Our traditional food sucks. To make matter worse, Grandma also used to tell Helga and me the old Christmas stories. Every year she would recite the poems about the thirteen Yule lads, their heinous troll mother Grýla and the huge Yule Cat. She used to threaten us that she would write to Grýla and beg her to come down from the mountain and take us if we were ever being naughty. She always told us to appreciate the clothes we got for Christmas because then the Yule Cat wouldn't come and eat us. As little kids, we believed her. But then we grew up and knew that it was all make-believe and just part of our Icelandic tradition. Traditions aside, she got Helga nice pajamas this year. I poked at one of the stars on the cardigan, as it were a piece of boiled sheep's eyeball. My lips curled. Maybe Grandma's dementia had kicked in. No way this was going to look good on me!

"Are you going to wear it?" Helga whispered as we both assisted Mom tidying up our small living room.

I wheeled toward her, thrusting my chest out. "Hell no! I'm going to pawn it off to Ragnar as a back-up to the prank gift I gave him. It's his style, so he should be thrilled." I only used two fingers to stuff the sweater back into the box. I'm not touching it more than I have to.

Helga took a step back and goggled. "Are you meeting up tonight?"

I nodded. "Same place as usual. Paradísardalur park."

"Can I come with you this time? Please, pretty please?" Helga danced on her toes and tugged my sleeve. It wasn't the impromptu choreography that got me, though. It was her deadliest weapon. The one that killed

188

all hope of a sweet, uncomplicated party with my pals. The one that wouldn't help me get closer to Sigrún tonight.

Puppy-dog eyes.

Damn.

I hesitated, glancing toward the kitchen where Mom prepared the traditional, homemade Christmas ice cream. Helga was only fifteen, two years younger than me. The Paradísardalur party was an opportunity for my friends and I to blow off some steam after the whole stress from work and school. The kind of party that involved alcohol—bought by an older sibling among our friends. Helga wasn't ready for something like that.

I leaned away from my sister. I tried to ignore the slight tenseness of my muscles. "I don't know, Helga. I'm not in the mood for babysitter duty tonight."

Helga's eyes narrowed. "If I can't come, I'll tell Mom what you guys really do in those parties."

I folded my arms, pressing my lips together into a thin line. "You wouldn't."

The breath whistled through Helga's nostrils as she inhaled, tilted her head in Mom's direction, and dropped her jaw, ready to shout.

My stomach dropped. Shit, she was actually serious. I clamped my hand to her mouth. "All right, all right. You can come, you little squealer!" I hissed.

An abrupt bang against the living room window interrupted her muffled giggles. Both of us jumped.

"What was that?" Helga asked, pushing me away.

I shrugged. "Dunno."

Helga stayed put, staring at me.

"What?"

"Aren't you going to check it out?" she asked. "It could be a burglar."

I snorted with laughter. "Yeah, like burglars would break and enter a house on Christmas Eve, when everyone in Iceland is at home. It was probably a bird or something." I walked over to the living room window, pulled the blinds apart and scanned the area. The colorful lights decorating the bushes in the yard revealed nothing. However, I noticed a dirty smudge in the middle of the window. It looked like a paw print. The yard was covered in pristine snow. Where had that dirt come from?

A pair of glowing eyes met mine.

My heart rate quickened. I squinted against the glass.

It was a small, dirty cat, hiding within the bush. I tried to conceal the small breath of relief that escaped my lips. I chuckled. Man, cats are eerie at night. I've never liked them, and apparently no one liked that one, considering how tangled the fur was and how thin it looked. Probably a stray cat or something. I'm definitely not letting it in, no matter how many times it begs for food.

"What was it?" Helga inquired, still rooted to the spot.

"It was nothing. It was probably some kids throwing snowballs at windows. Remember, we used to do that." I lied. Helga would have brought the cat in. We'd spend hours cleaning it and giving it leftovers. It would have ruined my night off. No, thanks.

Helga's mouth twitched at the memory. "Stupid kids."

I nodded as the two of us went into the kitchen to devour Mom's homemade ice cream.

Snow had been piling on the streets of Reykjavík all December. Some days it reached up to people's knees, but the roads were cleared up daily, thanks to the city's snow plowing trucks. My small Honda Civic wouldn't have been able to reach Paradísardalur without their efforts.

Driving through Miklabraut main road was peaceful; No brown, icy sludge splattering against the windshield through the daily traffic. The warm light twinkled on the white fluffy hills that flanked the road. The colorful lights adorning each and every house on every street repelled the ever-lasting darkness. It was one of the few things that I liked about winter. Christmas really became a celebration of lights in Iceland. No one was outside at this time of night. Everyone usually retreated to their rooms after eating ice cream, snuggling in bed with the latest book they got for Christmas. Some would get together in the living room and play the board game they got as a prize for finding an almond in their cinnamon rice porridge that afternoon. I wished I were there right now as a grunt of complaint came from the passenger seat.

Helga blew air on her hands. "Can't you turn on the heater? It's freezing in here."

I scowled. "It's already on. It just takes a while for it to heat up. You should have dressed warmer."

She tapped on the box that was crammed between her legs. "Gee, maybe I could have borrowed your *awesome* sweater."

I took my foot off the accelerator and the car slowed down as we approached Ártúnsbrekka. "Do you want to walk the rest of the way?"

Helga pouted a plump lower lip and hugged herself tight against her thin, neon pink windbreaker. "No. Besides if I wore that stupid sweater, Haukur won't lend me his coat. He is coming, right?"

I rolled my eyes. Haukur was in my year. He played football. He was a total jock and always tried to be funny by playing crude jokes on everyone. The girls in my year really liked him, and my sister was no exception. "Yeah, he is."

Helga squirmed in her seat, giggling. "I'm so excited. My first Christmas Eve party."

My eyes narrowed till my eyebrows formed a straight line. "You remember our deal, right? No drinking and no wandering out of sight. I don't want Mom chewing my head off if you get lost and freeze to death."

Helga gazed up the ceiling while she tapped her finger on her chin. "I think she'll do more than that. Take your car, maybe? Feed you nothing but boiled sheep heads? Destroy your phone?"

My hand slid down to my jean pocket. My phone was thankfully still there. The thought of it made me shudder. "Enough! Are you going to stick to our deal or not?"

Helga nodded eagerly. "Don't worry. I'll stay close… to Haukur."

I drowned out her shrieking giggles by whacking the radio volume to the max. I suppressed a snort. Like Haukur is *ever* going to be interested in my geeky little sister. I mean, look at her. Who wears a neon pink windbreaker when everyone in Iceland wears a 66°North parka? And even if he did, it was going to be the most awkward *menage a trois* ever because I'd have to chain my little sister to my leg.

The Honda Civic's little engine whined as it trudged through the snow. I clenched my hands on the steering wheel, foot nailed to the accelerator as we climbed higher toward the small Rauðavatn Lake. The frozen water of the lake trapped the moon in its slick, mirrored surface, holding it fast. Like all the old folks and their dumb traditions. An irritated fingernail worried at the leather of the steering wheel.

It would be gone, though, when the spring thaw came. Melt away. Maybe then I'd stop getting stupid presents like girly sweaters.

I looked again at the immobile moon shining in the lake. Then I blinked. For a moment, a shadow floated above it, as if the last cloud of the race had reached the finish line. I tilted my head up, squinting through the frost-framed windshield. The shadow, cloud, whatever it was, was gone. Only the stars winked down at me. My hands tightened on the steering wheel, then loosened. It was probably just an abnormally big goose or something. I hummed with the song, pushing the uneasy feeling to the back of my mind.

We parked in the Morgunblaðið Newspaper's factory's near empty parking lot. The grey building, absent of festive decorations except for the lights within the windows, looked bleak compared to the houses that blinked red, green, and white across the hill. I scoffed at the sight of few cars scattered around it. Even though it's Christmas Eve, people still have to get their newspaper ready for tomorrow. How sad is that?

Helga stamped on the snow and slapped mitten hands on her thin arms. "How much further?"

I wrapped a scarf around my neck as I picked up the box containing that ugly cardigan. "It's about a twenty-minute walk from here."

Helga groaned. "Why didn't we park closer to the party?"

"Because it's way off in the woods. Now quit bitching and help me carry these bags." I handed her two of the lighter bags, filled with snacks and a metal canister of mulled wine. Sigrún, the girl I liked, enjoyed drinking that in the winter. I overheard her say that to her friends in the school's hallway. I'm sure to score points when I give her a glass.

Helga frowned at the canister. "When did you make this?"

I shrugged. "When Mom was working. You even think about telling her and I'll drive you back home."

Helga ran after me, the bags bouncing in her hands. "Cross my heart and hope to die."

I scowled at her over-enthusiastic grin.

Let's hope it doesn't come to that.

Even though it was only a twenty-minute walk, it felt a hell of a lot longer when carrying a box and a heavy bag full of beer. The snow hadn't been plowed away on the trail, so Helga and I were knee-deep in leg-numbing frigidness.

I squinted through the dim light, searching for familiar markers on the path. Helga yipped like a frightened dog as birch branches snagged her hair. The thin white sentinels guarded the trail, knotty fingers groping through the inky black of night. But that's not how I saw the forest. No, I saw a winter wonderland. Snow dusting the limbs of the trees, like sugary peppermint sticks. A cautious rabbit nosing through the snow for a morsel of food. Though, come to think of it, I actually hadn't seen any of the woodland creatures I usually saw out here. Not a mink, nor a rabbit. Not even a rat.

I shrugged and cast a glance through the skeletal fingers of the tree-tops. Stars strung across the velvety blackness of the sky like twinkle lights. I grinned. Perfect for a Christmas Eve party.

I looked back toward the path and scowled.

It was also perfect for getting lost.

My toe caught a rock hidden under the snow. I stumbled. Helga rammed right into me.

She rubbed her nose. "Hey, what's the big deal?"

I frowned as I looked down. There should have been footprints. Tracks from all my friends. I wasn't expecting a deep hole in the snow. It was a massive crater. Like a group of people had all cannon-balled into a drift of powdered white.

"Brynjar, I'm freezing. Let's go." Helga whined, pushing me ahead.

I glanced behind my shoulder at the hole. It was the second weirdest thing I'd seen tonight if you counted the sweater. At least the sweater could be explained by Grandma's bad taste. Nothing explained the bizarre void in the winter snow.

The longer we walked, the brighter the horizon became. The birch trees gave way to pine. Orange lights danced across them. An audible sigh escaped Helga's lips as we heard upbeat music drumming ahead. The pine trees swayed, beckoning us to the party like sirens.

"Yo, Brynjar!" Ragnar called. The crowd gathered at the small bonfire within the clearing cheered.

The gnawing unease I had felt over the hole in the woods dissolved in an instant. I was happy to see my friends, but I was ecstatic to see *her*.

Sigrún chatted with her friends by the fire. Her ginger hair looked like an extension of the flames. She looked like a fire spirit. I wasn't even close to the bonfire and yet heat enveloped my entire body when I stared at her smiling face.

Our eyes locked. Her cheeks pinked. She waved and jumped into a hurried conversation with her best friend.

I made a decision. If I got some alone time with Sigrún tonight, I'd man up and ask her out. It'd be a bold move. No one had successfully asked her out. She reminded me of our Hidden People, the elves, and fairies of Iceland. If you wanted to see one, you'd have to be patient and make a wish. Well, I made a wish when I made that mulled wine. I hope it comes true tonight.

Helga nudged me in my elbow. "Where am I supposed to put this?" She held up the bags with an annoying pout.

I shook my head, dispelling the early punch-drunk love. "Right by the fire. That way the drinks won't freeze."

Ragnar came over and gave us hearty hugs. His cheeks were dull red from both the cold and booze. "Merry Christmas. P.S, loved the pecker condoms you gave me for Christmas. They're not my size, but they gave my family a good laugh, though."

I chortled. "Sorry, I couldn't resist. Here, I got you a proper gift."

Ragnar took the box, lifted it up against his ear and shook it. "It's not a game or a puzzle."

Sudden regret tugged at me. My brilliant re-gifting plan had a flaw. We'd all agreed not to accept clothes for Christmas. I grit my teeth. He removed the lid. His blue eyes lit up. "Hey, that's pretty nice. Thanks, man."

I unclenched my jaw. In his intoxicated state, he seemed to have forgotten about our pact.

"Glad you like it." I patted him on the shoulder.

Ragnar put on the cardigan over his coat while Helga and I unloaded the bags. He looked ridiculous, but at least he was happy.

The snacks were immediately snatched up by hungry classmates. There was barely anything left for me. I chuckled. Never underestimate the bottomless wells of the teenage stomach.

"There's Haukur." Helga indiscreetly pointed at a guy with a shaved undercut who was surrounded by girls.

I sniffed as I opened a can of beer. Helga didn't stand a chance when most of the popular girls in our year were in the way. But I admired Helga's courage as she joined the girls and laughed at Haukur's jokes.

Since Helga was within sight, I grabbed the mulled wine and hurried over to Sigrún. I slipped on a patch of ice in my haste. She giggled. The sound of her sweet voice dissolved my lightheadedness, but it didn't ease my rapid heartbeat.

"Hey, Brynjar. I thought for a minute that you wouldn't come." Sigrún breathed.

"Sorry, I had to help Mom tidy up and Helga insisted to come as well. So that took time." I kept the canister hidden behind my back. No need to reveal it just yet.

Sigrún glanced at the group of girls, spotting Helga in her neon pink windbreaker. Her brow furrowed. "She's got competition. I hope she can handle it."

I waved a dismissive hand. "Don't worry about Helga. She'll be fine. She's tough."

Sigrún nodded, a smile tugging at her lips. "Like her older brother." She softly touched my arm.

An electrical jolt ran through me at the slight touch. My heart banged in my chest. Is this for real? Is she interested? I mean, she touched me first, so that must mean I've got a shot. *Now's your chance,* the daredevil within me cheered.

"I brought you something." I fumbled with the lid of the canister. The pungent aroma of cloves, nutmeg and cinnamon mingled with red wine wafted through the air.

Sigrún inhaled deeply. "I love that smell. Where did you buy it?"

She thought I had bought it? I bit my lip as I poured her a mug. My heart shrunk a tiny fraction. I tilted my chin down and had to bite the inside of my cheek to conceal the frown. "Oh, I, um, I made it myself."

"You did?" Sigrún's nose wrinkled from the first sip. She quickly disguised it into a smile. "Oh, it's great. Thank you."

"You think so? I can send you the recipe if you want. *Tasty* has some great ones." I rocked back and forth, a sudden giddiness taking hold. She liked my wine. Score one for me.

"Thanks, I'd like that. You can send it to me now if you want." Sigrún pulled out her phone. "Wait, I don't have your Snapchat, do I?"

My heart resumed doing jumping jacks. My palms became moist within my gloves. I never had the courage to ask her for it, even when the class went around claiming each other handles. There's also the fact that my Snapchat handle was stupid.

She looked up expectantly, phone and app at the ready. I shuffled my feet in the downtrodden snow. "Oh, it's, um, brynjar_the_stud," I mumbled into my scarf. Heat gathered in my ears.

Sigrún smirked but she didn't say anything else. She was kind that way. Unlike the other girls, she kept it to herself. "Found you and added to my group."

My phone pinged in my pocket. I pulled it out and gazed at her handle. It was normal, just her full name and her birth year. But it suited her. "Thanks."

Her sweet smile returned. "Don't mention it."

I rubbed the back of my neck. I found it hard not to stare at the cluster of freckles that resembled the stars of the sky on her nose and cheeks. "So, what did you get for Christmas?" I cringed. Oh, *that* was original.

"I got lots of nice books. I can't wait to read them in bed tomorrow. What about you?"

I almost didn't hear her question. I was preoccupied with something over her shoulder. Haukur and the gang of girls were going deeper into the forest, away from the bonfire. Helga tagged along.

"Helga! Where are you going?"

"We saw a cat, but it didn't seem to have a leash. We're going to search for it." Her voice trailed off as she disappeared into the darkness. A cat? Rabbit, sure. Mink? Nasty little creatures, but yeah, okay. But a cat? I bristled. The only animal I was really worried about was a fox. Not the furry Arctic kind but the sly kind. The ones called Haukur.

I took a step forward, my brotherly instinct hovering on the attack switch. Sigrún's hand touched my arm.

"They'll be fine It's not like you can get lost here." She chuckled.

I joined in, although half-heartedly. My eyes scanned the tall pine trees. A shadow flitted between them. I blinked and rubbed my eyes, trying to clear my vision. When I opened them, it was still there, swaying. I breathed. It was just the shadow from the bonfire. The bright light seemed to dim. My gaze searched upwards. Clouds gathered in the sky. That's odd. The weather forecast said that the sky would be clear.

One by one the stars disappeared, snuffed out by the thick clouds. Even the moon said goodbye. The sky turned pitch black. Our only source of light was the bonfire that was losing embers by the second. Ragnar poked at the dying flames with a long stick.

"Hey, any of you geniuses remember to bring dry wood?" he bellowed to an emptying clearing. He stumbled a bit and plonked on a log. He looked down at his feet where Helga had dropped our bags.

"No? That's all right, then. At least we've got the beer."

He fished out a new can. The crack of the pop top echoed, and he chugged it back.

I tugged at my scarf, wrapping it closer around my neck. A chill seeped through my skin. A chill deeper than could be explained by a dying fire. My scalp prickled.

My glance darted among the remaining party-goers. No one else seemed affected by the pervading cold. Everybody continued to chat, drinking their beer, as if nothing was wrong. But something was off. Or maybe I was just too sober.

A blood-curdling scream pierced the night.

Ragnar fumbled with the radio, turning off the music. Confused silence fell upon the group. My heart clenched. The scream came from the direction of Haukur and the girls. Of Helga.

A second scream echoed through the woods.

My classmates muttered among themselves, shuffling closer to the perceived safety of the fire.

"Helga!" I bolted to the woods. Dread burned through my veins like acid.

Someone collided into me. One of the girls. Eyes bulging and out of breath.

"What happened?" I gripped her arms before she could bolt.

"I-I don't know. Something grabbed Haukur and pulled him into the trees. He screamed. We screamed." The girl sobbed, yanked herself free and ran away. Ran for the clutching birch. Anything to get away from...whatever she had seen.

The rest of my classmates weren't too far behind. Sigrún and Ragnar ran up to me. Soon, it was just us alone with cans of beer littered around the clearing and the sparks of the dying embers.

Sigrún stayed close to my side. Her shivers reverberated through her whole being. The red patches on Ragnar's cheeks had dissolved and his eyes were more focused than earlier.

"What the fuck was that?" Ragnar asked.

"No idea, but I have to find my sister." My mouth went dry, like I'd eaten a mouthful of the Sprengisandur black beach sand. Clenching clammy hands, I fought my flight instinct and ventured into the darkness. Helga needed me.

The quiet smothered. My breath choked in my throat. Why wasn't anyone screaming anymore? My mind went through haphazard scenes from the crime noir books I got for Christmas. Like how the villain buried a young woman alive near Esja mountain. I shook my head. Iceland doesn't have any serial killers. I tried rationalizing. Haukur must have just played a cruel joke on the girls.

"If this is Haukur's idea of a joke, he's being an asshole right now," Sigrún whispered, mirroring my thoughts. Her hand clutched my arm so hard it felt numb.

"I'm sure they're fi—"

Something stubbed my toe. I involuntarily gasped. It must have been a branch, hidden beneath the snow. I turned on the flashlight app on my phone. The artificial light beamed down on speckles of crimson on the snow.

My pulse jumped up. I guided the light further ahead. I saw an arm. Only an arm. I dropped the phone. The cold snow swallowed the light.

Sigrún clamped her hand on her mouth, muffling her horrified gasp. Ragnar swore under his breath. "It's probably just a prop from the school theater."

Cold sweat gathered in my armpits. My rapid breath crystalized in the air and my heart thrashed in my ears. It didn't look fake to me. I scrambled in the snow for my lost phone. Ignoring the cold soaking through my gloves, I dug until I gripped stiff fingers around its case and pulled it from the drift.

"I see something. Over there, to your left." Sigrún tugged on my coat and pointed into the darkness.

I turned it to the left. A torn off leg hung in one of the branches. The dripping blood tapped a disconcerting rhythm on the exposed tree roots below.

"Let's get out of here, Brynjar." Sigrún's tugging became more aggressive and her whispers hoarser.

A whimper sounded to my right. I shone the light there. One of the girls, Heiðdís, lay on her stomach, her hand stretching out toward us. There were ugly, long scratches across her back.

"Help me," she wheezed.

"What's going on? Who did this to you?" I asked.

Sigrún hurried over to her, scrutinizing over the wounds with a grimace. "She's hurt really bad. We need to call an ambulance."

"Wait, I want to know the fucker who did this. Was it Haukur? Is this some kind of sick joke?" Ragnar's voice rose higher as he circled the two of them.

Heiðdís's eyes squeezed shut, shaking her head. "It was huge… furry…yellow eyes…it's real."

I moved closer to her. My mind recalled the hole I stumbled into earlier. Thing was, it hadn't just been a single hole. As I had looked back over my shoulder, I now remembered seeing four smaller indentations curved over one edge of the larger one. A paw shape.

"Brynjar, please, before it comes back," Heiðdís crawled toward me. Sigrún bent over, sliding an arm under her shoulder.

I knelt, ready to hoist her up.

A gigantic paw slammed down on Heiðdís. Bones crunched. Heiðdís spewed blood. It splattered my coat. Sigrún screamed.

Teeth chattering, I looked up.

Glistening eyes met mine. Full of malice. Brimming with hunger. The fur was matted with earth and blood, blending in with the trees as it crouched down on all fours. Stringy drool, tinged pink from blood traveled down from its opened maw. Its hot breath reeked of dank and rotted flesh.

A cat. Not the cute cuddly kind they make YouTube videos about. It took a step forward. The ground trembled under its massive paw.

"Brynjar," Heiðdís's gurgles were near inaudible.

"Brynjar, help me," Sigrún sobbed as she stretched out her left arm. Her right one was trapped under Heiðdís's crushed body.

The cat kept its gaze locked on mine. At the same time, it bowed its head and ripped the girl in half. It didn't even bother to chew. It swallowed Heiðdís's upper half whole and took Sigrún's arm along for the ride.

Her agonizing wails punctured my soul.

Ragnar bolted, screaming. The cat's pupils dilated as it followed him. The ground shook with each of its steps. The blank snow canvas splattered with pink as drool fell from its mouth. It raised its claws and swiped at Ragnar's back. Ragnar hit a pine tree and crumbled like a rag doll. It towered over my friend and the hideous purr resounded through the forest. It bent down its head once again, ready to swallow him whole. Ragnar whimpered. Then it stopped and sniffed him. The cardigan over his coat tugged with each inhale. It gave a nasty hiss, but it turned away, strolling to where Sigrún and the rest of Heiðdís' body was.

Warm urine cascaded down the inside of my pant leg. I wanted to help. I wanted to run. I wanted to snap out of it and realize this was all just a fucked-up nightmare. The weight of hundreds of years of tradition rooted me to the spot. This can't be real. This thing was only a myth. A cautionary tale to appreciate what you got during harsh times. I've never heard of people actually getting eaten by a humongous cat here. Something with an appetite that huge would have undoubtedly left a scar on the planet's face. You'd think we'd have noticed.

The cat yowled as it pushed the ripped lower half of Heiðdís's body around. Sigrún clutched at the stump where her forearm had been, tears streaking her freckled face. The blood streamed down, painting the ground crimson. The cat's whiskers bristled as it touched the gore. Sigrún shook her head and pushed backwards.

"No, please don't," she begged.

The cat cocked its head to the side, as if considering mercy upon the girl. Then it bent low on all fours, ears tugged away, and pounced.

I clamped my hands on my ears, shutting out the bone breaking as it feasted on the girl I loved. With it, it ate my heart. I kept muttering, "This can't be happening, this can't be happening," as I took cautious steps backwards. Careful not to alert the damn cat.

Then, my mind connected the dots. Heiðdís, Sigrún, Haukur and the others were all in the environmental class with me. We all had agreed on no clothes. The old poem Grandma used to recite to us when Christmas neared flooded into my mind:

You all know the Yule Cat
And that Cat was huge indeed.
People didn't know where he came from
Or where he went.

He opened his glaring eyes wide,
The two of them glowing bright.
It took a really brave man
To look straight into them.

His whiskers, sharp as bristles,
His back arched up high.
And the claws of his hairy paws
Were a terrible sight.

He gave a wave of his strong tail,
He jumped and he clawed and he hissed.
Sometimes up in the valley,
Sometimes down by the shore.

He roamed at large, hungry and evil
In the freezing Yule snow.
In every home
People shuddered at his name.

If one heard a pitiful "meow"
Something evil would happen soon.
Everybody knew he hunted men
But didn't care for mice.

It all clicked. The small cat in the yard. It could have been working for the Yule Cat or maybe it had been the cat itself. The flitting shadow above the sky as we cruised to the park. The damn cat must have known. It must have been waiting for all of us to gather. This party had been an easy target.

The Yule Cat didn't eat Ragnar because I had given him the cardigan that Grandma gave me. For some reason, it doesn't eat people who receive clothes for

Christmas. My fingers tingled. He was safe from its clutches. But what about Helga?

Not moving an inch, I scanned the area. A pair of frightened eyes within a neon pink windbreaker stared back at me, concealed within a clutter of birch to my right. I couldn't help exhaling in relief. Tears welled up behind my eyelids. If I had any urine left in me, I would have expelled all of it right now.

Thank God! Helga was safe. Grandma had given her pajamas for Christmas. The Yule Cat couldn't touch her. That was all that mattered.

"Run, Helga. Take Ragnar and get to safety."

Helga shook her head violently. Her bulging eyes seemed to say, *what about you?*

I let out a weak chuckle that ended in a long exhale. "It's too late for me. For any of us who didn't get clothes tonight. We got what we deserved. Honor the old ways. Never forget that and spread the word. Go to Hagkaup and buy mittens, socks, any clothing for the rest of the class. Save the rest of them for me, if you can." My teeth chattered. I clenched my fists. "I'll stay here and hold it off."

A choked sob caught my ears as Helga crawled out of her hiding spot. I watched her pull a possibly concussed Ragnar from beneath the pine tree and the two of them ran away. Both looked back, their eyes wide in fear and disbelief.

My muscles softened to jelly. Numbness enveloped my whole being. My chin trembled. I could no longer tell if it came from the cold or from fear. I glanced at the puddle of blood where Sigrún had been. Nothing was left of her. I couldn't save her. I didn't get my wish. Nausea filled my senses. My stomach threatened to empty the contents of it onto the already splattered snow. I could smell the Yule Cat's fetid breath, see the torn flesh hanging from its yellowed teeth.

In a weird, nasty way, my mind reminded me that I had forgotten to call my wisest relative and thank her for the gift before I left for the party. A huge lump lodged in my throat. Next time, we'll be wiser. Next time, we'll really listen and heed the words and traditions of the old.

"I'm sorry, Grandma," I whispered before the cat's stinking jaw unhinged and obscured the world.

KOKKURI-SAN

Michiko means "beautiful, wise child", derived from the kanji symbols beauty (美) knowledge (□) and child (□).

But Michiko wasn't two of those things. Not according to her classmates, Satori, Akiko and Maya. To them, she was poor, gloomy and always trying to set herself apart from the others, even when she wasn't.

She didn't fit in, and the trio made sure to remind her of that fact every single day.

One day, she would find her gym clothes missing. The next, her desk had been pushed way into the furthest corner with crude messages scribbled in permanent ink all over it:

"Die, ugly."

"Just do us a favor and kill yourself."

"Fat whore."

"No one loves you."

"Leave, trash."

For not obeying the messages her desk would be filled with trash the next day.

Blinking away tears and quelling the surge of injustice in her belly, Michiko quietly sat down. Her mouse-colored hair, a bright reminder of how she didn't fit in a sea of dark hair, obscured her face as she bowed her head.

She tried to ignore the giggles and the occasional wad of paper thrown at her desk.

"Please be seated," Mr. Eishi, the homeroom teacher, said as he entered the classroom.

"Excuse me, sensei," Akiko piped up, her voice almost shrill with glee. "Michiko's desk stinks."

Mr. Eishi turned towards Michiko. A flash of pity sparked in his tired eyes. He shuffled a stack of papers on his desk. "Could you clean out your desk, Michiko, before the smells get worse?"

Michiko gave a somber nod as she rose from her chair and scooped filth out of the cubby built in her desk. Plastic sandwich wrappers, rotting fruit and leftover yakisoba noodles spilled across the sleeve of her school uniform, staining it brown.

Few students murmured their disgust at the stench. Others giggled, but none of them came to help her. Not even Mr. Eishi. He figured it wasn't his place to meddle into the lives and affairs of his students. He was only paid to teach, after all. Besides, he feared the wrath of Akiko's father, who was a big shot in the city. So, he allowed the bullying, or at least, ignored it because he didn't want to stand out among the crowd, following the old Japanese motto: "The nail that sticks out gets hammered down."

It pained Michiko, but she was following that motto as well. She didn't fight back, she didn't tattle the bullies and she made sure she ran every errand Akiko, Satori, and Maya asked her to do, hoping they would grow bored with her.

But it was no use. Once they had chosen a target, they stuck to her like a cicada on a tree, their shrieking laughter droning in her ears.

How she wished she could make them stop.

Michiko contemplated skipping school but banished the thought away. Her parents would worry and ask questions. She wouldn't involve them in her suffering.

As if on autopilot, muscle memory steering her along, Michiko dragged her feet through the school hallway and all the way into her classroom.

She froze by the door frame.

Akiko, Satori and Maya circled her desk like coyotes. Akiko held up an A3 sized piece of paper, a smirk stretching on her thin lips. Eyes traveling up, she caught Michiko by the door. Those raccoon eyes narrowed.

"Good morning, Michiko. I didn't know you played Kokkuri-san."

Heat gathered in Michiko's cheeks. She marched into the classroom with her arm outstretched for the paper.

Akiko yanked it out of sight behind her back and Satori caught it.

"Please, give it back," Michiko pleaded in her small voice and moved closer to Satori.

Satori pushed her back with a harsh laugh and passed the paper to Maya.

"No, really, what were you asking the spirit? How to make you pretty?" Maya giggled and sidestepped Michiko's feeble attempt at groping for the paper.

"Only if she was wishing to look like an ugly fox or a raccoon," Satori sneered.

Michiko let out a whimper. "No, I didn't," she whispered, her fingers balling into fists. She fought the urge to push back, to punch. Nothing good would come out of it.

"Hey, I have an idea." Akiko's honeyed voice sidled up closer to Michiko's ear. "How about the four of us play a game of Kokkuri-san after school?"

Michiko's lower lip trembled. Their ideas of games were never fun, and always resulted in Michiko being the butt of the joke. She couldn't refuse, though. Only worse suffering would await her if she did.

"How about it?" Akiko repeated, her tone harsh and firm, the honey all dried up.

Michiko hastened to nod and focused on looking at her shoes. Her heart pounded in her chest.

"Good," Akiko was chipper again as she waved the paper in front of Michiko. "I'll be holding on to this until we play."

The three of them passed her. Satori walked deliberately into Michiko's shoulder, hissing, "don't get in my way," before getting to her seat.

Michiko's stomach soured. She rubbed her throbbing shoulder as the knot grew ever tighter in her gut.

The sun cast an orange hue across the classroom. Three dark shadows stood waiting for their prey.

"Are you ready?" Akiko asked as she unfolded the paper and placed it down on her desk.

Michiko carefully entered the room. Her eyes flitted to the setting sun on the vast horizon and wished it could have overstayed its welcome. Playing that game during the day would be safer.

"What are you waiting for? Get over here and let's play." Maya beckoned with a twisted grin.

No use stalling. Michiko suppressed a whimper and went over to her tormentors. She glanced down at their latest toy, their latest torture device.

All the characters of the hiragana alphabet centered on the paper while numbers from zero to nine were written below the last of them. The characters that spelled "yes" and "no" stood at each upper corner and between them rose a *tori* gate colored in deep red. The traditional Japanese *shinto* gate allowed Kokkuri-san, a spirit who is said to resemble either a fox or raccoon, passage from the spirit world and into the mundane one. The gate usually symbolized tranquility and sacred space. But now, it would be violated by the cruelty of three girls.

"Who's got a ten yen?" Akiko asked.

Maya and Satori rummaged through their pockets and bags, not bothering to ask if Michiko carried one. They'd think she'd be too poor to carry small change.

"Found one!" Maya exclaimed and pulled her arm from the black hole inside her bag. A shiny ten yen sparkled between her fingers in the last rays of the sun.

A cruel smile spread across Akiko's face. Smiles usually made a person more beautiful. Not Akiko. It contorted her features, revealing the horrid monster underneath.

"You go first, Michiko," she said, snatched the coin and placed it in Michiko's palm.

The coin dug hard into Michiko's skin as she looked from Akiko, Maya and Satori. "We-we all have to play together."

Maya wrinkled her nose. "I don't wanna touch trash."

"It's fine. Michiko washed her hands before coming, didn't you, Michiko?"

Akiko leaned closer as if trying to catch a whiff of any bad odor.

Cold sweat gathered under Michiko's arms. She couldn't remember if she had cleaned up after hiding in the library all day.

"Let's just get this over with," Satori grunted.

Michiko gulped and placed the coin down on the shrine gate with quivering fingers.

The girls then put their index fingers on the coin and chanted in unison: "Kokkuri-san, Kokkuri-san, please come. If you're here, please say yes."

Then they waited.

216

The silence would have been thrilling and full of suppressed giggles if Michiko were playing with a group of friends. But they were no friends of hers.

"This is boring," Maya blew air out of her cheeks.

"Let's try the chant again," Akiko offered. "If it doesn't work after that, we've marked a toilet stall for Michiko."

Ice ran through Michiko's veins. She shut her eyes closed and prayed in her mind, willed the coin to move across the paper.

The coin shifted for a second.

Satori rolled her eyes, "Who moved it?"

The coin slid sharply to the left before anyone got a chance to reply.

The girls gasped, then squealed with delight as the coin obscured "yes".

"Finally," Akiko said. "Now we can start."

The object of the game was to ask Kokkuri-san questions, similar to the western ouija board. The trio asked a few mundane questions, like if there was going to be a pop quiz in English, or if the cafeteria would run out of yakisoba bread during lunch. Michiko remained silent the whole time, watching the coin move from yes and no at intervals.

Akiko noticed, for she changed the topics of the question toward her. "Tell me, Kokkuri-san, will Michiko wet the bed after tonight's event?"

Michiko knew better than to look up and see the malice in Akiko's eyes. Dread wrapped its tendrils around her muscles and threatened to squeeze what liquid remained in her body.

Maya and Satori snickered.

The coin slowly slid towards affirmative, and the girls burst out laughing, their shrill shrieks bouncing from each wall of the room.

Michiko's cheeks burned from humiliation, but she held onto her own vow of silence, biting the inside of her mouth until she tasted copper.

"Wait, I've got one," Maya leaned closer to the board. "I know that Michiko likes Takashi. Will he reject her if she confesses?"

Michiko's gut sunk deeper into the never ending well. She pinched her thigh to prevent herself from breaking the link and endured another torment as the coin once again confirmed the question.

"Of course, he will. Even Takashi has standards," Akiko scoffed.

"Do you think Michiko will ever get rich?" Satori asked, earning a snicker from the other two.

The coin went right and halted under "no".

Michiko knew that wasn't a possibility, what with her parents working minimum wage jobs and living paycheck by paycheck, but the spirit's assertion hurt nonetheless.

"Enough about her, I wanna know my prospects. Will I remain as beautiful as I am now?" Maya asked and flipped back her shiny, wavy hair.

They watched as the coin drifted away from the usual "yes" and "no" answer and slid towards the characters below.

Even hotter, Kokkuri-san spelled out.

The trio looked at one another, a greedy spark reflected in their eyes.

"Me next." Satori almost shoved Michiko out of their circle. "Will Shinji-senpai notice me?"

The coin traveled across the board in quick, fluid motions. *He will only see you.*

Satori squealed in happiness.

"Will I become famous?" Akiko asked, her hungry eyes fixated on the small coin and its spirit inhabitant.

Their hands jerked as the coin flew across the board so fast they barely caught the characters it landed on.

They will never forget you, Kokkuri-san replied.

Akiko released a sigh of contentment and gave the coin her nod of approval.

"I'm hungry. Let's go to Mosburger," Satori said.

The three of them told the spirit to return home to its world. Michiko stayed silent.

"Remember to burn the board, Michiko," Akiko called over her shoulder as they exited the classroom.

Michiko stood alone in the darkness, gazing down at the board and hating it. Hating everything that happened tonight.

"It's not fair. I wish I could make them pay," she whispered.

Something breezed past her. A cold wind that carried the stench of incense and rotten fish through the door, manifesting into a hulking shadow.

The girls waited for Michiko the next day.

They stood next to her desk, Satori and Maya leaning closer to Akiko, who was in the middle, and whispering something in her ear. A devilish smile tugged at Akiko's lips and she gave a nod.

"Good morning, Michiko." Maya waved to her, the enthusiasm way too cheery to be authentic.

The familiar serpent stirred in Michiko's stomach, twisting her entrails.

"Get over here," Akiko said. Not a gesture, but a command.

Palms sweating, Michiko took careful steps. She scanned the classroom; only a handful of students had arrived. Not enough to have a spectacle. The trip always wanted everyone to watch them torment her.

"The girls and I were talking last night," Akiko began, her voice syrupy sweet.

Michiko's throat constricted, barely allowing air to slip through her mouth.

"We actually think you've got a shot with Takashi. Why don't you go and confess to him later?"

Michiko's head whipped up, her eyes wide with fear. She looked behind her shoulder, a horrible feeling that Takashi was there, leaning against his desk and chatting with his friends. But he usually came late during first period.

"Yeah, you could do it during lunch. We'll come with you. You know, for support," Maya said.

Michiko shook her head violently from side to side. "Thanks, but I'm good."

She turned to leave, going for the library, her sanctuary, but Satori grabbed her wrist. She grabbed it hard, her callous hand reddening Michiko's skin. Michiko let out a whimper.

"Either you confess during lunch or you won't be able to take down notes for the rest of the semester," Satori said, her tone low and dangerous.

Michiko glanced at Akiko, thinking for some stupid reason she was going to tell Satori to go easy on her, but that accursed smile told otherwise.

Choking back a sob that had lodged in the back of her throat, Michiko gave a feeble nod.

"Excellent. You better prepare what you're going to say to him."

The girls brushed past her and went for their as desks as the bell chimed in the first lesson of the day.

Michiko had the sudden urge to bolt out of the classroom. One of her feet had taken a step, but halted when Mr. Eishi walked in, crushing her last opportunity. She couldn't storm off. Mr. Eishi would have to mark her absence and then report it to her parents. She had sworn to herself not to get them involved. They already had so much on their plate that she couldn't bear to add her own problems too. No, this was her issue, not theirs.

So, she sat down and endured the long hours until the bell chimed for lunch.

Defeated, Michiko allowed Maya and Satori to tug at her arms as they led her up to the roof. Students were normally forbidden from going up there, but no one stopped them. As long as they weren't causing trouble, the teachers didn't care. Therefore, the roof had become the most popular spot for love confessions.

Coughs of suppressed giggles came from the pair, but Michiko ignored it. Best to get it over with. She could expel the hurt once she could find a bathroom stall far away from those demons.

The bright sunlight stung Michiko's eyes when Satori opened the roof door. She blinked and shielded them with her hand.

Takashi stood in front of the fence surrounding the roof. Locks of his dark brown hair danced in the mild breeze. Michiko dreamed of touching just a strand of his hair. For a moment, she only saw him in his perfect stance and loosened school tie. Then a figure appeared behind him.

Akiko.

They engaged in light chatter. Akiko played with a piece of her hair between her fingers, occasionally touching Takashi's arm as she giggled. The way he smiled at her made Michiko ache in her heart. Then Akiko got on her tiptoes and planted a light kiss on Takashi's cheek.

Michiko wanted to scream. She dug her heels on the last step, not wishing to go any further, not wanting to see the rouge color Takashi's cheeks. That he might have feelings for the girl who's making her life a living hell caused bile to gather in her esophagus.

"He's right over there. Now's your chance, Michiko," Maya cooed, pulling her wrist.

"Get over there or I'll send you to the infirmary," Satori hissed.

They pushed Michiko out into the roof. She stumbled a bit but grabbed the fence for balance. She was close to fainting. Her head swam and sweat drenched her in all the worst places.

"Michiko."

Akiko's tone was sweet, but Michiko had long recognized the authority and arrogance hidden underneath the syrup.

Michiko forced herself to look up.

They stood side by side, the perfect couple, a peculiar look scrunching up Takashi's features while Akiko wore a mask of the supporting friend.

"Don't you have anything to say to Takashi?"

Michiko chewed on her bottom lip, nails digging at her sides. She squeezed her eyes shut and bowed. "I've liked you for a long time, Takashi, Wi-will you go out with me?"

The words ran through like a gushing river with a slight hiccup at the end. Michiko didn't dare open her eyes, but she imagined either a look of pity or incredulity on Takashi.

"I-I'm sorry," he began.

Michiko shook her head, body still bowed at an awkward angle. She knew she hadn't stood a chance against someone like Akiko. Knew that Takashi wouldn't even spare a second glance at the bullied girl. But it still hurt.

And that's what mattered to Akiko. A cough escaped those cursed lips of hers. A disguise for her laugh.

Michiko clenched her teeth to stop herself from bursting into tears. She turned on her heels and sprinted downstairs, the shrill laughter following her to her sanctuary. A sandalwood scent mixed with the sea lingered on the roof.

Maya was in good spirits on her way home. She had aced her pop quiz, run 500-meter dash in P.E. without breaking a sweat and played around with Michiko. All while looking fabulous.

Maya wasn't vain, but she knew she was pretty. Even on her way home, she managed to turn some heads.

Maya smirked. She enjoyed dangling that bait. She usually got what she wanted, simply by flipping her hair and fluttering her fake eyelashes.

She noticed a certain mouse-colored hair bobbing along a few yards in front of her. She considered hollering after Michiko but decided against it. Akiko was really the one who came up with the best ideas to torment the gloomy girl. Maya let her be, thinking that tomorrow would be a better time to bully her.

She knew her mom was home after seeing the lights through the window as she neared her house. She was probably busy making dinner for her and her father who was always late to come home.

Maya didn't want to spend the evening with her mom and her boring questions. She'd just come home, drop her school bag in her room and then go for karaoke with Akiko and Satori.

"Mom, I'm home," Maya called dully, the greeting a habitual drone.

Something sizzled in the kitchen. A quiet snark.

Maya frowned. Her mother always returned the greeting with a happy "welcome back," even when she was out in the backyard, hanging up wet laundry to dry.

A rotting stink tickled Maya's nose. She coughed, cupping a hand to her mouth. It smelled like fish and sweet decay. Had something gone bad in the fridge and her mom had forgotten to throw it out?

"Mom, something stinks," Maya called out, marching toward the kitchen.

The stench intensified. Eyes stinging, Maya kept her hand clamped against her mouth. It mingled with the aromatic scent of sesame oil. A horrible mixture.

Maya pictured her mom in some kind of experimental mode, trying out a new recipe she had seen on one of her favorite cooking shows. She couldn't help rolling her eyes.

A pair of feet lay on the floor from the corner of the kitchen.

Maya froze.

The feet had fluffy, pink slippers on, its soles almost worn out.

Maya's heart hammered in her chest. She didn't know what to do. Sizzling snarks and horrifying scenarios of meeting a bloody body occupied her mind.

"Mom?" she croaked, inching closer inside the kitchen.

Her mother lied still on her stomach, her face obscured by frazzled hair. Her hand clutched an empty bottle of oil. Maya hurried over to her side. Her foot slipped on a small puddle of oil, hidden by the shadow of the cabinets.

Sliding forward, she slammed her forehead on the counter. Her hands flailed around, searching for something for balance. She grabbed a handle as she slid on her knees, next to her mother.

The sizzle stopped for a second as hot, amber liquid tumbled down from the frying pan in her hand and splashed her face.

The sear drilled deep into Maya's skull. Each crackling snark blistered an ugly balloon on her beautiful face. She smelled what she could only describe as bacon before the oil took away most of her sense of smell.

Her skin tightened in angry, red blotches. As she tried to blink, Maya thought she caught sight of Michiko standing behind the window, watching her, an expression of triumph dazzling her face. One more blink and she was gone. Her eyelashes burned, the fake plastic sealing her eyes shut. Even her tears of agony couldn't escape their prison.

As the oil painted her lips purple, her tongue swelled, and blisters popped into her mouth with each choked scream.

Something furred with claws brushed burnt hair from her face. Amid her screams, she heard a faint growl, followed by the scent of incense:

"You're even hotter than before."

Satori chewed a hangnail from her thumb, the calcified flesh grinding against her molars as she fought against the tears.

She had heard about what had happened to Maya last night. Maya's father had called her mom and explained the awful, tragic event. She had spent last night numbly scrolling through their LINE conversation, her heart hollow from the news.

She and Akiko couldn't go and visit Maya in the hospital. Apparently, the pain of the burns was too severe, and the doctors were keeping her heavily medicated. Satori couldn't help but scoff. Maya had always been a klutz. A pretty klutz that could get away with anything. Well, not anymore.

A snicker slipped past and Satori slapped a hand to her mouth. She felt awful for thinking that. She glanced at Akiko who sat two desks to her right, by the wall. Eyes down, staring at the screen of her phone on her lap, not paying attention to the lesson. By the looks of things, it seemed like she didn't quite care what had happened to their friend. She hadn't looked distressed or worried when they talked about it before class started.

Didn't Akiko value them as much as they valued her?

Satori shook her head and focused on the blackboard. The mathematical problems swirled before her, forming the words of her worried mind. She gripped the pencil in her hand tighter. She was just overreacting. Of course, Akiko needed her and Maya. They were the most popular girls in their year. No one could shoulder the burden of popularity alone. They needed similar pillars. Someone they could lean onto. Without her or Maya, Akiko wouldn't be able to handle the stress. She was just dealing with the grief in her own way.

Satori exhaled in relief.

She had no cause to worry. Their foundation hadn't been broken.

Satori shielded her eyes from the glaring sunlight, frowning at the baseball field. The girls in her baseball club all carried the same grumpy look. Their advisor had told them late last night that she had to postpone their practice till the afternoon instead of the regular morning practice.

Like most of the girls, Satori had made plans to go shopping with Akiko after school but had to cancel it. As much as she loved her friend, baseball always came first for Satori, what with her being the star player in their club.

Her frown dissipated when she came across a boy talking to their advisor. It was Shinji Honda, an upperclassman who had agreed to become their manager and part coach due to his superior baseball skills in the boys' club. He was the second reason why Satori loved playing baseball.

"All right, let's do a practice match," Shinji called, beckoning the girls to gather in the front of him.

Satori ran ahead and made sure to stay in the center, meeting Shinji's gaze directly. She had applied pink gloss on her lips just before practice started. She puckered them ever so slightly when Shinji glanced in her direction.

He cleared his throat and went over today's goals.

Satori smiled to herself. The spirit had been right. Shinji-senpai only saw her.

She grabbed a baseball bat, threw on a helmet—even though she hated how it flattened her short hair— and jogged to the pitch, positioning herself next to the catcher squatting in front of the home plate.

The sun glowed directly above them, so it wouldn't interfere with her batting. She swung the bat and let it hover slightly over her right shoulder, ready to hit the ball.

"C'mon, Fukuhara. Show us what you've got," Shinji-senpai shouted behind her on the benches.

Butterflies floated in her stomach as she smirked. She loved it when Shinji-senpai called her by her last name. Imagine the explosion in her belly when he finally used her first name.

Satori nodded to the pitcher as she tightened the grip on the bat's handle.

Then she noticed something in the distance, through the fence behind the pitcher.

A furred, humanoid form clutched at the mesh wire. Eyes glowing amber against the sunlight.

Satori blinked and straightened her posture, staring ahead.

Whatever had hunched behind that fence was gone.

She furrowed her brow. It must have been someone in costume for the anime club or the theatre club. She vaguely remembered Akiko telling her they were putting on a Beauty and The Beast performance for the culture festival. A shit show waiting to happen.

"You ready?" the pitcher called, her stance low and arm holding the ball behind her back.

Satori shook it off and resumed her position, eyes focused on the pitcher's body language, anticipating her next move.

The pitcher swung her arm forward, launching the ball fast in Satori's direction.

A sudden breeze flew by, carrying a sickening odor of meat and produce decay. It punched Satori hard in the nostrils.

Along with the white cowhide, red-stitched ball.

The crunch reverberated through Satori's ears. The impact knocked her skull against the back of her helmet. Blood gushed in rivers down her chin, ruining her white jersey. The shock held her pain at bay, but once Satori tried to breathe through her nose, it pounded in sync to her heart.

"Fukuhara!" she heard Shinji-senpai yell in shock.

"I'm so sorry," the pitcher squealed in fright.

Satori had to go to the infirmary. She didn't know how bad it looked, only knew how horrible it felt.

"I'll take you there," Shinji-senpai gently snaked his arm under hers and guided her toward the school building. "Try not to speak."

Satori grunted, trying to ignore the blinding pain that had traveled from her nose and settled around her mouth. Her lips felt like marshmallows, its gooey content ready to burst and ooze out at lava speed. Blood continued to stream down her nose. She tilted her head back to stop the flow.

"It's better to tilt down. That way any excess blood won't go down your throat," Shinji-senpai said as he pressed her head at a low angle.

Even the gentle motion made everything hurt.

Something clattered within Satori's mouth. Her eyes widened. She unclenched her jaw just a fraction. A blood-stained tooth fell out. It skittered along the linoleum ahead of Satori and Shinji.

"What was that?" he asked.

A gurgle spat out from Satori's mouth, sending a few more of her teeth tumbling down in rows.

"Oh, god," Shinji-senpai muttered, stepping away.

Unable to breathe through her nose, Satori tried to inhale. Her front incisors came loose and got sucked back into her gullet. They lodged themselves in her trachea. Satori gasped, clawing at her throat.

Mouth overflowed with thick crimson. It slithered down, congealing the path of oxygen. Obstructing her only means of breathing.

Her already purple-bruised face turned a shade of blue.

Satori fell to her knees, one hand outreached to the boy she liked who could only stare in horror, feet rooted to the spot. She noticed Michiko standing by the corner, hand resting against the wall. She made no effort to rush to Satori's aid. A small smile twitched her lips. A furred creature loomed behind her.

As Satori's vision blurred and her limbs became weak, she heard a faint growl in her ear:

"He only sees you."

The classroom was silent.

The students' heads bowed low as they offered a prayer to the girls absent from their year.

Akiko turned her puffy, bloodshot eyes to the two desks with flower vases on top. The red spider lilies hung from them as if dead, symbolizing the dreadful passing of her friends.

She was alone now. For the first time in her school life, she felt truly alone. She hated that feeling. It made her skin crawl with goose flesh.

The rest of the class moved on with today's lesson, as if the mere prayer had been enough to consolidate the horror they had endured. What Akiko had endured.

She was only a single star now, her bright companions snuffed from the sky too early. She had always thought she would graduate high school together with Satori and Maya. Would even enter the same university together.

Grief clutched at her heart. She had to do something to push it away. Her eyes caught mouse-colored hair at the front. They narrowed.

There was one thing the three of them had enjoyed together. A day of torturing her would cheer her up.

Akiko tossed a hundred-yen coin at Michiko's desk. "I'm thirsty. Go buy me green tea."

Michiko's dull, droopy eyes lingered on the coin before she picked it up and went for the hallway.

Moments later, she handed Akiko a chilled bottle of green tea. The condensation melted in Akiko's hand. Without looking at it, Akiko gave a scoff and tossed it at Michiko. "I wanted the premium type, you idiot. God, can't you do anything right?"

The bottle hit Michiko in the arm with a thump. She barely reacted to it.

Akiko frowned. Usually the mousy-haired girl would flinch or whimper or apologize profusely. Now she stood opposite her, shoulders squared, a blazing fire in her eyes.

"Go get it yourself, then," Michiko said while fishing her phone out of her skirt pocket.

Akiko blinked. Talking back now? What's gotten into her? Was it because she was facing her all by herself? Didn't she feel threatened? No, fear was usually achieved by numbers. She bit the inside of her cheek while she fumed. She wasn't going to let her get away with it.

"Have you seen the news lately?" Michiko asked, breaking the stunned silence before Akiko could open her mouth to hurl an insult at her.

"No, why?" Akiko couldn't help asking.

What seemed like a small grin tugged at Michiko's lips. Dread unraveled from the depths of Akiko's gut. Michiko flipped the phone, revealing a news article flashing on the screen.

Akiko squinted at the small font. It spelled out her father's name. Her stomach plummeted. Her hand reached out to snatch the device, but Michiko pulled back.

"You can read it on your own phone, but I'm warning you; it looks bad."

Akiko glared daggers at her as she pulled up the news article on her phone. It didn't take long. It was the first one on the website. Her eyes scanned the news, her brain registering the unfolding events, but her heart refused to believe it. Her father had been caught embezzling from the bank where he worked. Her diligent father? How could that be?

The classroom buzzed with whispers and murmurs. Akiko looked up. Every student had their nose down their screens, eyes reflecting the news article.

Like flies on a turd, their eyes darted from the screen and then to her.

Judging her family.

Judging *her*.

"I hope you don't believe what's written there," Akiko called, her voice shaking with undiluted fury. "They're all lies."

Her classmates stared for a moment, then the buzzing got louder, groups forming, leaving only her and Michiko left.

"I hope your mom and dad are all right," Michiko said.

Akiko's head snapped back to Michiko.

A smile crept across her face. It made her pretty. It destroyed the hard work Akiko and her fallen friends had put into breaking her.

Had they even ever achieved that? Was she stronger than them?

"What do you mean by that?" Akiko hated the fear dripping from her voice.

Michiko shrugged. "I'm just saying, this kind of scandal would be difficult to recover from."

Akiko stared at her. Worry seeped into her skin and mottled her bones. She was right. Her mother was of the weak constitution. Akiko had inherited her father's ambition and tenacity. Had her father's own ambition been his downfall?

235

"I mean, if I were you, I'd go and check on them," Michiko said and sat down at her desk, pulling out a book and reading it.

How could she be so calm? When the buzzing was so loud, so clattering that Akiko felt like she was going mad. She punched in her father's phone number on her phone and pressed the screen hard against her ear. The line was busy. She tried reaching her mother. No one answered.

Her fingers felt numb. A sudden coldness struck her core. Nothing could have happened. Her family was strong. A scandal—if it was one, that is— wouldn't hurt them.

The hallway filled with the sound of ushering footsteps. Curious students from other classes clamored into the small door frame.

"Hey, Kanda, is it true? Your dad's a crook?" One boy asked loudly.

Akiko flinched. Those stupid rumors were already spreading.

"No, of course not," she spat.

"My aunt is a reporter. She told me that her newspaper has all the evidence," a girl said while reading from her phone.

"Wow, no wonder you got rich so fast," another student sniffed.

Akiko couldn't take it any longer. Those lies would crush her if she stayed in the classroom.

She pushed the students aside and stormed out. She needed answers and she knew her father would tell her the truth.

The train ride home was hell.

Everyone was gawking at Akiko like she was some kind of freak. One of the news websites had uploaded a photo of her and her parents together to go along with the embezzlement scandal. It had taken every nerve of self-control and poise to not lash out at them. Even when she noticed some of the passengers took subtle photos of her when they thought she wasn't looking.

Akiko ran like zombies were after her all the way home, her pounding heart lodged in her throat. Why hadn't her parents called her already? Were they not home? Why weren't they answering her messages?

These thoughts crowded her mind, adding fuel to the emptying tank. She had to know what was going on.

When she reached her house, her insides flooded with relief. No reporters lurked around the gate. Her father's car was parked in the driveway. The place was silent save for the occasional cry of the cicadas nestled in the trees nearby.

As she approached, she realized that cicadas usually roam around during the mornings and evenings. Not in the middle of the afternoon.

The cry carried through from her house. A hoarse wailing.

Fear squeezed the remaining puff of air from Akiko's lungs as she ran inside.

Her mother knelt in the middle of the narrow hallway, her shoulders quaking in violent sobs.

"Mom?" Akiko panted while cold sweat slithered down her back.

She had eyes only for her mother. But she thought she'd seen something from the corner of her eye.

It moved. Or more like swayed from side to side.

Akiko's heart fought against her rib cage. If she didn't move, she wouldn't have to look at it.

"Where's Dad?"

Her mother rocked back and forth, hands covering her face, muffling the horrid screeches. Then she pointed a shaking finger to her left.

Morbid curiosity possessed Akiko as her head swiveled left.

She wished she could blink what she had seen away. She could only stare, her own scream lost to the void that had taken her heart. Her hope.

Feet dangled from the floor. Dressed in bamboo socks and drenched in dank urine.

Her eyes betrayed her and traveled further up, following the stain. Her father's trousers were ruined. It was the only thing she could think of; the only thing that held the fragile pieces of her shattered mind together.

Her father's lifeless eyes stared down at her. Tongue out and swollen. His tie wrapped around his raw throat and was tied to the ceiling fan. The living room stank of his expelled excrement, but Akiko smelled a rank fish stench as well.

Her father held a note in his hand.

Akiko reached for it, amazed that she could move at all. She smoothed the paper, wondering if she should let her mother read it first. But she decided against it. She had every right to know why he had betrayed his family.

She read it.

She paled.

-They will never forget you-

A flash momentarily blinded Akiko. She blinked rapidly. It had come from the window.

A camera.

More flashes pierced her vision as the window filled with eager photographers and reporters, forever capturing them in their worst moments.

It was then that Akiko broke down and screamed.

Michiko scrolled through the latest news report. A photo of Akiko screaming next to her dead father was pinned as the front news.

-Daughter of Exec. Banker Witnesses Father's Death- the headline said.

Michiko looked up. The last student had just left the classroom. She was finally alone.

She rummaged in her cubby until she held a large, folded piece of paper. She spread it on her desk. The red *Tori* gate of the Kokkuri-board winked at her. She was supposed to burn it, but it had never been her intention.

She pulled out a black candle, placed it on the gate and lit it. She dug out a ten-yen coin, the same one she and the girls had used a few days ago and placed it on the board.

Resting her index finger on the coin, Michiko whispered, "Kokkuri-san, are you there?"

A gust of wind brushed past her, flickering the candlelight. It brought forth a stench of sweet decay. A stench she had already gotten used to.

She raised her head.

A slender, hulking creature stood before her. It wore a black, frayed *haori* and a dirty, ripped *hakama*. Congealed blood matted its frazzled fur. A part of its ribcage was exposed, displaying leaking guts and viscera that trickled on the floor. Its long snout wrinkled in a permanent snarl; sharp, yellowed teeth bared. Its eyes were black as coal, yet Michiko knew it looked directly at her.

"Were you pleased with my work?" it growled, white foam of spittle trailing down its mouth.

Michiko smiled. "You delivered perfectly."

Kokkuri-san extended a clawed hand to her. "You remember our agreement? A soul for me to keep in exchange for the destruction of three souls."

Michiko nodded and took its hand, not even flinching at the sharp claws digging into her flesh. She had endured much worse.

Now she was free.

WHAT
THE CHEF
RECOMMENDS

Candlelight flickered in the dim dining room, casting warm illuminations upon the long, elaborate table. Yet, the guest who sat in the high back chair remained in the shadows. The only sound they made was the soft clattering of cutlery against porcelain, an elegant knife slicing into broiled meat.

Mona stood in the background, hands clutching the metal serving tray. It was the only thing that kept her from breaking down completely. Her blood-shot eyes fixated on the black cloak that swirled in tantalizing tendrils below the high back chair. One movement and the guest's meal would be interrupted. It would mean a certain death to her and her remaining two children. It was too late for Phil, her husband.

He had become the guest's meal.

Mona clenched her teeth so hard she feared her molars would crack. Why did Phil have to be so damn hospitable? They had drilled into their children to never accept candy from a stranger, and yet Phil would always invite one to their rural home. Mona had always warned him people would take advantage of his kindness and look at him now: One of his legs was being eaten by a monster that had appeared at their doorstep.

Each scrape of the knife sent nauseous chills down Mona's spine. She tried to think of something else, but images of the monster's angler fish teeth chomping on Phil's flesh assaulted her mind.

Be strong, she chanted inwardly. *Don't show fear, or else Max and Diane will end up as desserts.*

The monster let out a satisfied moan. "That was delicious. I've never had a blackberry reduction with a human leg before. You really are a master of the craft, Mrs. Viridian—ah, pardon me, *Miss* Viridian." It turned its head sideways, glowing blue eyes staring intently, gauging Mona's reaction.

Mona forced herself to remain professionally stoic, even though hate and disgust bubbled beneath the surface. She wanted nothing more than to smash the tray on that bony face, pummeling it until dust remained. She knew she couldn't, though, and thanked the years of being a chef that resulted in her restraint. "Thank you. I aim to please my guests."

A hideous smile stretched upon the monster's paper-thin lips. "I'm delighted to hear that. I hope tomorrow's dish will surpass tonight's."

It rose out of the chair and four, fleshy horns tickled the ceiling. A dark cloak billowed like fog on the floor as it glided toward the front door, leaving a scorched trail in its wake.

Mona stood in the hallway, silently begging it to leave. Her legs threatened to buckle under the sheer fear of what tomorrow might bring, but she never let it show on her face. The monster turned to her before opening the door. A slight, greenish tinge marred the monster's bone-white skin underneath sunken eyes. Hope fluttered in Mona's chest. Was it getting ill?

The creature bowed its horned head. "Thank you for preparing a part of your husband for dinner. It was wonderful. I can't wait to see what you'll make of his remains. Have a pleasant night."

Another bow and it allowed the darkness to swallow it whole as the front door swung shut.

Mona collapsed, barely registering the dull pain in her knees. The hallway filled with her heaving sobs as she finally processed the atrocity the demon had forced her to do.

"I'm so sorry, Phil," she sobbed again and again, pleading for his forgiveness.

"Mom?" A small, terrified voice crept up behind her.

Small hands caressed her back. She almost laughed at the role reversal. "Come here, baby," she said, hiccupping and embracing her nine-year-old son, Max, holding him tight. Thirteen-year-old Diane knelt beside her, fist clutching the strings of Mona's apron.

"Take it off. I-It's got Dad's blood on it," Diane whispered, every word halting between her chattering teeth.

Mona said nothing as delicate fingers pulled and tugged at the strings, releasing the reminder of her horrifying act onto the floor.

"Will it be back?" asked Diane, while sweeping the apron away with her foot.

Mona nodded.

"We have to get out, Mom. We can't be here when it comes back."

Hours of slaughter teetered on the edge of Mona's mind. She was so tired. All she wanted was to take a rest on the floor, hoping it'd engulf her until nothing was left. But eventually she nodded for the second time. This was no time for grief. She'd have to lock it inside until all three of them were safe from that monster. She wiped her nose clean with her chef sleeve, gave an encouraging smile to Max, and stood up.

They all went for the door with nothing but the clothes on their bodies. Mona wasn't sure if they'd ever come back to this house. It had been filled with wonderful memories, but tonight's ordeal had destroyed all that.

Max had the honor of pulling on the door handle. He looked up at Mona with uncertain eyes, and she gave his shoulder a reassuring squeeze. He pulled and walked into a brick wall. He yelped and clasped his bruised nose.

Mona's heart plummeted. "No," she mumbled, hands feeling the rough texture. There was no way out the front door. "No, no, no."

"What about the back door?" Diane asked.

Mona took Max's hand and led them through the hallway. She abruptly stopped when they reached the kitchen entrance. The back door was located inside the kitchen, but she couldn't bear to have her children walk through it. Bile rose from her throat. Phil's remains were still there inside the walk-in fridge with splatters of gore on the floor and on the stainless-steel counter.

"Mom?"

Mona exhaled sharply and covered Max's eyes. She made Diane do the same while she held on to her chef shirt. "No matter what, don't open your eyes. Do you hear me?"

They both gave a shaky nod; Diane's lips trembled. She moved them quickly through the kitchen, sidestepping the puddles of blood scattered on the linoleum floor. The back door beckoned; a pot of holy basil hung in the middle as a green lantern to safety. She reached for the handle and pulled.

Another brick wall.

Mona cursed loudly, slamming her fists against the demonic lock.

"So, we can't get out? We're stuck here?" asked Diane, peeking from her spread fingers.

"Mommy, I'm scared," Max whimpered. "Is the monster going to eat us?"

Mona was certain of it. That bastard was planning on forcing her to cook her children in the same vile way it had forced her to do with Phil. She didn't need to confirm her youngest's suspicions. It wouldn't do them any good to wallow in grief and despair before the final hour.

Think, Mona. Think!

Mona paced the floor, her eyes fixated on the holy basil. She had an arsenal of knives in the kitchen. She could try to stab the demon when it came back. Abrupt images of the monster swiftly slicing Phil's body in

245

pieces as soon as it was allowed entrance flashed in her mind like a strobe light. Phil had been in peak physical shape. How could Mona stand a chance against it, armed with a butcher's knife?

She scrapped that idea and dug further. What could she do to kill it? Or at least render it immobile and vulnerable enough to strike the killing blow?

She caught Max reaching for some dark berries in the adjacent greenhouse, where she grew most of her ingredients for food and other medicinal purposes. Her eyes widened in fear.

"Max, no!" She rushed to his side and slapped the berries from his hand. "No, those are nightshade berries. They're poisonous. Have you forgotten how to distinguish edible ones from the poisonous types?"

Max burrowed his chin into his chest. "I'm hungry, but I don't want anything from the kitchen. It looks scary."

Mona glanced over her shoulder. She still hadn't cleaned up the blood. "I understand. There are tomatoes and apples in the crates on the other side of the greenhouse. Get some for your sister as well."

She picked up the berries from the dirt and studied them. She only used those berries as crow and insect repellent. She rolled them around in her hand. Would feeding them to the creature work?

She looked around the greenhouse. Most were common vegetables and plants but having grown up in a hippie commune taught her to utilize all parts of what nature had to offer. Including poisons.

She set out to work. She grabbed a wicker basket and plucked all the nightshade berries from the bush. She ran over to the darkest corner of the greenhouse where the lights couldn't reach. Armed with a trowel, she dug through the dirt and unearthed a few mandrake roots.

Max gasped when he appeared beside Mona. "Is that a human?"

Mona grinned. "It looks like one, doesn't it? Don't worry, sweetie. It's perfectly harmless, that is if you don't consume large quantities of it. Are you done with the apple?"

Max nodded, holding the half-eaten fruit.

"Good. I need you and Diane to collect all the apple seeds from the apples. Can you do that?"

A shadow of a smile flickered past Max's pale face as he nodded. Relief rushed through Mona. She knew keeping them busy with a worthy project would deter their despair and fear.

As her children sat down with small, carving knives and spoons around the crate of apples, Mona picked a bunch of fiddlehead ferns. The plant itself with its furled fronds reminded Mona of some Lovecraftian display, but she knew eating it raw or undercooked would cause vomiting and abdominal cramps. She had learned that the hard way growing up.

She then walked up to the rows of plant bushes lined up against the plastic of the greenhouse and picked castor beans. She grew those plants for the benefits of the castor oil, but not many knew the bean itself was highly poisonous.

Lastly, she pulled on gloves to tear hemlock leaves and cut off its roots. She gazed down into the unique ingredients resting in her basket. She had enough poison to kill an army.

Now she had to make a mouth-watering dish out of them.

Mona wiped sweat from her brow. She had been grinding down a majority of the plants into a wet paste for most of the night. She glanced over at the greenhouse entrance. The kids were tucked away on the wicker lounge chairs, sleeping peacefully. The knot in her stomach unraveled slightly, seeing them together and safe. They hadn't wanted to leave her all night, but she suspected they didn't dare enter what now had become a forest abattoir.

She had used grass to soak up the blood on the floor, which cushioned the awful squelch every time her soles stepped on it. She'd clean the kitchen properly later or burn it. Either way, after tonight, she was done with it.

Mona turned to the walk-in fridge… and Phil. The nausea she had been keeping down during the first feast came crashing back. Her head swam. She staggered backwards, holding onto the counter for balance. Tears burned her eyes. The lump in her throat threatened to suffocate her. To think she'd have to desecrate her husband's remains almost threw her off the edge. Mona took deep breaths, in through the nose and out the mouth. If Phil's body parts assisted in bringing that monster down, Mona felt certain he'd encourage it.

Her resolve returned and she stepped into the fridge.

Phil's blank eyes stared at her. Mona swallowed hard, willing herself not to throw up. His severed head rested on a metal tray on the upper shelf while the rest of his dismembered remains lied underneath. Mona closed her eyes, imagining his torso as a particularly thick hog ready for the *luau*. The coldness of his skin seeped into her fingers, almost rendering her immobile. She slapped some warmth into her arms and brought the trays into the kitchen. Once out of the frigidness, a distinct odor of decay slowly misted the air. Mona wrinkled her nose, holding back her gagging. She reminded herself that spoiled meat smelled just the same. She put on gloves and rubbed Phil's skin with a mixture of olive oil, rosemary, and thyme. Then she placed holy basil and parsley nearby, knowing the strong-scented herbs would mask the stench a bit.

She filled a turkey baster with the poison paste and injected it into small cuts within the fatty tissues and the muscles, making sure that no nook and cranny was spared.

She managed to disassociate her mind from the gruesome task, convincing herself this was just another day at the restaurant dealing with a particularly eccentric and demanding customer.

She cut off strips of meat and sawed-off bones to make it look aesthetically pleasing to the eye. She did that to all the body parts, even taking delicate care in shaving off

Phil's hair and eyebrows. Nobody wanted hair in their food. She scooped his eyes out with a melon baller and buried them in the greenhouse. Her mother had told her from a young age that the eyes could see everything, even in death. Mona didn't wish Phil to see any more carnage.

She boiled the head with an infusion of hibiscus, cinnamon, and hemlock. The sweet scent of spices engulfed the kitchen and Mona allowed herself to breathe it in, savoring the bitter sweetness.

Exhaustion fell upon her at last. She had done what she could in regard to preparation. The poison had to marinate within Phil's flesh for the remainder of the day before she could begin cooking. She stumbled into the greenhouse, into the warm embrace of her children, and buried her face in their sweet-smelling hair. Sleep soon swept over her.

The doorbell chimed.

Mona jumped; heart lodged in her throat. It was time.

Hands gripped her wrists. She glanced down. Her children's frightful eyes stared at her.

"Don't go," Max whispered.

Mona forced a smile and squeezed his tiny hand. "I have to. If I don't, it might come for you instead."

The little boy gulped. Diane looked at Mona. "What should we do?"

"Hide behind the bushes here. When I scream 'go,' you run for the door and go outside. Don't stop running, you hear me? Go to the Finnigans' and stay there until I get there."

Mona rose from the lounge chair, but hands still tugged at her wrist.

"I don't want you to be alone with that thing," said Diane quietly, tears glistening in her wide eyes.

"Neither do I," admitted Mona, heat spreading from her heart and into her fingertips. "But you are all I have left. That thing will *not* get you."

She gently pried their fingers off and waited until they were out of sight, hidden within the rose bushes. She gave them an approving nod and walked to greet their gruesome guest.

She stood in front of the entrance, wondering if not opening the door would help keep the monster outside. They'd be stuck inside for unlimited time, but it was better than what waited in the dark.

Tendrils of inky blackness slithered from under the door. One ghastly appendage reached for the handle, pulling it down. The door creaked open, revealing a body of writhing darkness, as if thousands of rats crawled underneath the black cloak. The monster bowed its head as it glided over the threshold. Its four horns seemed to pulsate with anticipation. "Good evening, Miss Viridian." Its hollow voice reverberated through every nerve in Mona's body.

Mona bit her bottom lip as she dared herself to face the creature that had brutally killed her husband. It was

251

proper etiquette to greet customers with a smile and eye-contact. She almost shriveled under its glowing, inhuman, blue eyes that seemed to float in the middle of wormhole eye sockets. "Good evening."

"I look forward to tonight's feast," it rumbled.

The greenish tinge still corrupted the creature's skin. There was still hope her plan could work. She gave it a curt nod before showing it to the dining room.

"If it's all right with you, I'd like to see you at work."

Mona froze. She looked at the monster over her shoulder. "Why?"

The mouth of angler fish teeth stretched wide. "I've always wanted to watch a chef work their magic, especially one as renowned as you."

Sweat gathered in Mona's armpits. Her heart pounded against her ribs like a caged bird. Did it suspect anything? She shook off the nagging doubt, put on her best professional smile, and gestured toward the kitchen. "As you wish."

Her legs performed an awful dance of turning into stone and jelly in tandem as she guided the monster into what used to be her sanctuary. The body parts were laid out on the stainless-steel counter along with the condiments and vegetables needed for each dish.

"I'm in no mood for appetizers—they tend to ruin the joy for the entrées," said the demon, leering down at the cut off fingers and toes coated in panko breadcrumbs.

Mona nodded. "Then I hope you'll enjoy what I've considered for the main dishes. First, we'll have human leg roast with peeled onions and carrots, topped with a honey bourbon glaze. Then we'll move on to my version of cock au vin, except I'll be substituting the chicken with the arms. The head I'll boil along with fall vegetables—celery, carrots, potatoes, and parsnip and with a dash of beef and human bone broth for a nice fall stew. And lastly, the torso I'm going to braise with soy and star anise."

Drool dripped from the monster's mouth. "It all sounds delicious. You may begin."

Mona said nothing while she dressed in a clean chef jacket, pulled her hair up in a bun, rolled her sleeves, and began chopping the vegetables. The monster floated behind her, its rattling breath ever closer as it monitored her movements.

Mona pretended it was nothing but a safety health inspector, although a real one would have something to say about her main ingredients—hidden and otherwise.

"Do you wish to join me for dinner? It is awfully lonely to be dining by myself," the monster said, a black tendril softly touching Mona's shoulder.

Goosebumps prickled her arms. The audacity of the bastard. Forcing her to cook the love of her life after it brutally killed him was already traumatizing but asking her to eat him too was unspeakable. She pressed her lips together to prevent from spouting any profanities that might cause the monster to attack. "I'm afraid that speaks against chef etiquette. We're not allowed to dine with the guests."

The monster tutted. "What a shame. Your husband tasted delicious. I wish you could give it a try."

The knife in Mona's hand quivered. Oh, how she wanted to plunge it deep into its hideous skull. She was sure it was expecting a reaction like that. She breathed in and out, imagining the potato as the demon and chopped it in half. Some of her anger submerged into the act which helped focusing on the task easier.

A sudden yelp startled her. Mona turned around. Her veins constricted. Max writhed in the monster's claws.

"What are you doing?" Mona shrieked.

The glowing eyes narrowed. "I believe that's my question." It held up a glass bottle with a clear liquid and a few garlic cloves in the bottom. "What is your intention with this? Answer truthfully or your child's head goes flying, much like the head of his father."

Mona's eyes darted between the bottle and her whimpering child. A dark stain gradually blossomed in the middle of his pants, pooling around his feet. Mona detected small movement from the corner of her eye, telling her Diane stood frozen by the entrance, not knowing what to do to get her brother back.

"Answer me, Miss Viridian," it rasped.

Mona's shoulders sagged. "It's holy water infused with garlic. I've heard it works against demons and I had some left after we blessed the children. I was going to mix it into the stew."

The monster let out a sound akin to a laugh, but it was more like a mix between a bat shriek and a bear growl. "That biblical nonsense doesn't work on me. I'm beyond that." It threw the bottle on the floor, smashing it to pieces.

Mona flinched, watching the glass shards scatter across the linoleum along with her supposed hope.

It continued to wheeze that nasty laugh, its breath of decay and destruction wafting in Mona's direction. She turned away, clenching her teeth.

"I love humans' feeble attempts at revenge. It makes for a nice appetizer." The monster released Max who scurried over to Diane's open arms. Diane and Mona's eyes met, and her daughter gave her a firm nod before retreating to their hiding place.

The monster swept over the kitchen, sniffing in various jars and looking into drawers. It taunted Mona whenever it found a stereotypical artifact, such as a crucifix or an iron horseshoe. Mona countered with lips trembling and slamming her fists on the counter, aiming curses at the creature. "I shall await in the dining room for the feast," it drawled, the raspy laughs echoing throughout the house as the shadow receded out of sight.

Mona's back was slick with cold sweat. She breathed a long-held sigh of relief. She thought it was never going to leave. Her motherly instincts compelled her to rush into the greenhouse and hug her children, but she stayed put. She needed to focus on her revenge, on their survival. It all relied on her skills as a chef and how well she could mask the poison.

"You may be beyond biblical artifacts, but you should never fuck with Mother Nature," she muttered under her breath.

The cart creaked under the weight of the four-course meal Mona pushed into the dining room.

Black candles with blue flames floated in the air, casting a grim blue hue on the once white walls. The demonic entity sat in the high back chair facing the entrance, bony claws clasped together in anticipation. The wretched skull looked up; glowing eyes ablaze.

"Ah, at last. Tonight's feast."

Mona placed each course gingerly on the table. Despite the horrid circumstances, pride bloomed within her. She had managed to turn a corpse into an alluring meal that could fool even the best food critics in the world.

Drool cascaded through the slits of angler fish teeth as the demon pulled closer the human leg roast. Hunger seemed to overpower the proper etiquette it had displayed previously as it ignored the cutlery laid down beside the dish. It grasped the whole leg with its claws and tore off a huge piece. The meat barely clung to the bone. Juices ran down its thin mouth while it gobbled flesh after flesh, discarding the bones on the floor.

Mona's stomach turned when it bit off Phil's tongue from his head, slurping the stew into its gullet. She wanted to leave. She didn't want to watch that horror show, but the cold blade nestled beneath the chef jacket convinced her to wait it out.

The monster moaned with delight as it pushed the final empty tray. It had only taken thirty minutes for Phil to completely disappear into the monster's belly. "That was divine, Miss Viridian. You spoil me."

Mona bowed her head. "I'm glad you enjoyed it."

"I've never tasted anything like it before. It was—" It let out a rattling cough.

A fire ignited in Mona. She carefully slid her hand behind her back, fingers touching the wooden handle.

The entity continued to cough painfully, as if a ton of mud plucked up each hole in its lungs. Coarse green sludge splattered the dining table as it hacked and wheezed.

Mona tightened the grip on the handle. It was almost time. Her heart screamed bloody murder.

White smoke puffed out of every orifice, obscuring those piercing eyes. The haunting elegance it possessed disappeared when it leaned over the table, regurgitating a fuzzy, moss-like substance. The monster's long limbs jerked and writhed like entwining snakes. Angry pustules burrowed out of the skin of its fleshy horns, pulsating with wriggling maggots.

Mona stared in utter bewilderment. She had no idea the poisons would create such horrifying agony. She silently withdrew the butcher's knife from behind her back. It was no ax. If she had to chop multiple times, then so fucking be it. She tiptoed behind the flinching creature, arms raised above her head.

The blue eyes flickered wide as it saw the sharp edge fling down upon its thin neck. Tar squirted from the wound, tainting Mona's stark, white jacket. She pulled the blade from the neck and swung again, hacking until the body slumped on the floor and its head remained wheezing on the table.

"Yo-You bitch."

"That's what happens when you mess with me and my family. GO!"

Footsteps thundered across the hardwood. Diane, squeezing Max's hand, ran with her brother toward the front door. She tore it open. The brick wall stood in their way, but shimmered in and out of focus, as if its illusion was running low on batteries.

Mona lifted a sack of rock salt they kept for winter into her arms. She cut it open with a swing of the butcher's knife and doused the monster with it. She made extra sure to drown the head in it.

Black fire erupted amid shrieks of pain. The brick wall shimmer shattered into glass pieces with the rush of the evening breeze kissing the children's cheeks. Without hesitation, Mona pulled Max into her arms, took Diane's hand, and together they jumped outside, the hot blaze licking at their shoes.

Into the darkness, they ran. Mona knew, despite what the cautionary tales her mother had drilled into her, that it was safer out there than within their sanctum. She spared one glance over her shoulder. A beacon of light within the gloom, the flames soon engulfed their last house of horror. Mona squeezed her eyes shut and led her children forward as the night devoured what remained of the Viridian family.

THE
BANQUET

Maria held the delicate card between her fingers.
The gold embossed letters danced along the shimmering white surface. To the unsuspecting eye, it was just a normal card, but Maria knew the power it had.

> *You are cordially invited to*
>
> ### The Banquet
>
> *Please wait for further information in regards to time and location.*
> *Formal dress.*
>
> *We look forward to seeing you.*
> *The Committee*

Maria's mouth felt dry.

The Banquet had long been considered a myth among women such as Maria, something they told each other on nights when their minds were on the verge of drowning in the darkness.

She never imagined she would receive an invitation.

Maria studied the card, fearing it might be a prank. She wouldn't be able to bear it. She had suffered too much to face more humiliation and shame.

It felt real, authentic, like actual money had been spent on making such a lavish card. Pranksters wouldn't go that far. Would they?

She rose from her booth and looked around the vast office floor. Tops of head bobbed above the surface of grey cubicles. There was no one there she could speak to or show the card to. She wasn't sure if anyone had experienced the same kind of traumatic event that she had.

Unfortunately, she knew of one person who shared a similar trauma. Her stomach simultaneously hardened and soured as she picked up her cell phone and searched through her contact information. Her parched mouth itched when she dialed the number. She steadied her shaking hand.

Maria hadn't heard from her since college. Since the incident. But she had been keeping tabs on her through social media. The guilt propelled her to do so. To make sure she was doing all right.

"Hello?" a voice on the other line said.

"Nicole? It's Maria. Listen, I got an invitation."

aria fidgeted with everything as she waited in the café: her sleeves, the hem of her shirt, her hair, the cracked lining of her cup. A coffee wouldn't help her anxiety but she would have felt weird ordering just water.

She hadn't expected Nicole to accept meeting her that day. She wouldn't have blamed her if she had declined or never showed up at all. After what had happened in college, Nicole had every right to not want to see anyone.

Chewing her bottom lip, Maria contemplated whether she should order another cup of coffee as the bell above the café door chimed.

Maria looked up. Seeing Nicole, she let out a sudden breath she hadn't known she'd been holding.

Nicole had a tight grip on her purse's handle. She scanned the café in the suspicious way Maria had caught herself doing before she arrived.

She's looking for predators, Maria thought, and her heart ached.

"Nicole? Over here." Maria waved her over, hoping her smile appeared genuine rather than fake.

Nicole's hard expression didn't lift as Maria had hoped when she strode over.

"Thank you for coming. I was kind of worried that you wouldn't show." Maria scooted to the other side of the sofa.

Nicole sat down in the chair opposite her without a word.

They sat in silence for a while. Nicole observed Maria, as if looking for something. To criticize her? To belittle? She had every right to, considering Maria had done the same thing when Nicole was assaulted in college. She was supposed to be a friend in a time of need. Instead, she hadn't believed her, and peer pressure from a clique she wanted to join caused her to spread gossip about her. In short, she had let her friend down in the worst possible way.

Stomach acid threatened to bubble over into her esophagus. "Look, I just want to say that I'm sor—"

"You said you got an invitation," Nicole interjected. The glare in her eyes matched the sharpness of her words.

Maria nodded.

Nicole extended a hand. "Let me see it."

Maria fumbled with the clasp of her purse, aware her hands were shaking. With fright or anticipation, she wasn't sure.

She slid the card across the table and Nicole picked it up, studying it.

"You've heard of The Banquet, haven't you? Do you think it's real?" Maria asked.

Nicole paid her no mind. Her fingers caressed the card fondly, as she would a pet or lover. The ice in her eyes seemed to melt away.

"It's real. I've been there."

Maria's heart nearly stopped. Every nerve in her body compelled her to lunge forward, but she contained herself. "How? When?" she blurted out.

Nicole smiled. It was a distant one, like she was recalling a fond memory. "Last year in July. I'd planned a trip to the Bahamas that month. I cancelled it. I wouldn't have missed The Banquet for the life of me."

Maria leaned closer, the tips of her hair almost swimming in her coffee. "How was it?"

Nicole shook her head. "I can't tell you. I signed an NDA."

Maria fell back on the sofa, not bothering to disguise her disappointment. She had hoped to glean a little bit of information. At least what to expect if she were to go.

"I can tell you one thing," Nicole said as she handed Maria back her invitation.

Maria raised an expectant eyebrow.

"It's worth everything."

Maria received the secret location and time later that week. On that fated evening, she paced back and forth in the tiny hallway of her apartment. She grabbed a tissue from the living room to wipe off her sweaty hands. She wasn't going to dry them on the fancy, emerald-green velvet gown she had rented. She felt like she was going to a Victorian ball and it made her more anxious. She had no idea how she was supposed to act at balls. Poised? Dignified? Silent?

Before her trauma, Maria had been outgoing, a chatterbox who just enjoyed life. That had all been taken away from her that awful night, that night when she stayed longer at the office at the request of her boss. She had ignored the jokes, the way he stood close enough for her to smell his cologne. She had typed it up as normal office behavior between a superior and a subordinate.

She had feared being fired if she spoke up against his lewdness.

Cold seeped into her skin. Maria froze as it spread through her nerves.

"No," she moaned and squeezed her eyes shut.

Her cruel mind was reliving the assault, creating that same feeling of helplessness and terror. The way her boss had held her down in the copy room. How he had robbed her of her joy, her freedom, her life.

"Stop it," she whispered, pushing her fists against her eyes.

She began counting down the street names of her childhood neighborhood—a coping technique given to her by her therapist. She forced her mind to focus on the signs at each corner, spelled them out loud until the numbness faded away. Until her breathing quieted down.

Cold sweat glided down her back. Maria felt as if she'd just finished a sprint. She walked to the mirror and flinched at the reflection. She hated that person. How weak she felt, a mere fragment of who she used to be.

Her phone vibrated on the counter. A message on the screen told her a car was waiting in front of the apartment complex.

Maria took a shuddering breath, quickly fixed her make-up and grabbed the card.

She was done feeling weak.

*M*aria noticed the number of houses diminishing each time she glanced through the car window. Fields soon replaced quaint suburban neighborhoods. Streetlights blinked away one by one behind the horizon until the only illumination came from the car's headlights.

Maria wanted to ask the driver where they were going. Going this far away with a complete stranger gave her goosebumps. Alarm bells rang in her head. Instinctively, she placed her keys between her fingers.

The driver caught her movement in the rearview mirror. He gave her a somber smile before pushing a button.

The small, blank screen below the fiberglass shield came alive and the face of an elderly woman with gray streaked hair wrapped tightly in a bun appeared. Maria recognized her as Rowan Ethers, the former mayor.

"Good evening, Miss Lopez," Rowan said, sending Maria a kind smile. "I want to thank you for accepting my invitation, and I want to assure you that you're in good hands. You may not have a lot of trust in men, which I completely understand, but I have faith in my personal driver. However, as a safety precaution, I've asked him to wear a shock collar on the off chance that he'll misbehave."

Maria glanced up at the driver.

He nodded as he pulled down his coat collar, revealing a black belt wrapped around his neck. He pushed another button. A compartment beside the screen popped open. A small device resembling a walkie-talkie was nestled inside.

"You have the power if you suspect any misdeeds," Rowan said. "I look forward to seeing you in person, Miss Lopez."

The screen went black, forcing the car into awkward silence once again. Maria reached a hesitant hand for the device, her eyes never straying from the driver.

It was cool in her hand and heavier than she had expected, but the mayor was right. It gave her comfort and safety. And more importantly, power.

"We've arrived, Miss," the driver said.

Maria looked through the window. She had suspected that the home of the Banquet would be big, but her jaw dropped, nonetheless.

A gigantic gothic mansion rose above them. Spires guarded each side of the mansion with ivy crawling on the walls. Steel bars kept anyone from breaking in its many windows. Though ominous and old, it looked well-kept with the grass freshly cut and the topiaries of griffins and lions trimmed to perfection.

Maria suddenly worried that her gown wasn't fancy enough for such a mysterious home.

She reached the top step where intricately carved mahogany doors greeted her. The carvings depicted various goddesses from multiple religions; Artemis from Greek mythology with her bow and arrows; Kali from Hindu stomped on piles of men and Frigg from Norse mythology sat proud in her throne in the center.

She hesitated before the door. She wasn't sure whether to knock or simply let herself in. Thankfully she was spared either when the doors opened. The former mayor herself gave off a warmth Maria hadn't felt in someone since she had last visited her mother.

"Miss Lopez, so good of you to come. Please, come in and make yourself at home." She placed her hand gently on Maria's shoulder and guided her inside.

Maria gazed at the double staircase that was lit with candles at every step. Portraits lined the wall at each corner. Maria tilted her head while walking toward one of them. An oil painting of the woman standing next to her captured every detail. She even wore the same high-collared dress.

"Every chairman gets a painting. It's silly but it's tradition," Rowan said.

"How long have you been doing this?" Maria asked.

Rowan grinned as she pushed her glasses further up her nose. "Longer than I expected."

She walked to a desk beside the staircase. "Before you go inside, I'm going to have to ask you to sign the non-disclosure agreement. Whatever happens in the Banquet stays between you and the committee. Contacting the women invited is prohibited. If you violate the contract, we'll be forced out of the shadows and the world is not ready to witness what we have been doing for decades."

Maria gulped and stared at the piece of official parchment. She had gone this far. There was no backing out now. She grabbed the pen and left her signature on the paper.

Rowan smiled. "Excellent. Follow me."

They walked down a narrow hall absent of home décor. The stark white walls and multiple doors reminded Maria of hospitals. She had hated the harsh antiseptic stench that permeated every floor when she had stayed in the hospital after the attack. It made her feel unclean. She caught herself rubbing her arms together to get rid of invisible filth. She glanced sideways to one of the doors.

A face pressed itself against the tiny center window, eyes bulging out of their sockets.

Maria shrieked and backpedaled until she hit the wall.

It was a man's face, but something looked horribly wrong. An iron framework enclosed his head. A muzzle with a curved plate seemed to press down on his tongue, hindering his speech. A stream of drool slithered down his chin.

Why on earth was a man like that behind that door?

"How do you like the scold's bridle?" Rowan asked, following Maria's line of sight.

Maria didn't know what to say. It was the first time she had ever seen anything like that. She couldn't stop staring, her heart doing jumping jacks.

"They were used against women in order to control and subjugate them in the past. I figured it'd be good if they got a little taste of humiliation before the main event," Rowan continued, a ghost of a smile tugging at her lips.

Maria raised an eyebrow.

They?

She looked into the window of another door. Another man, wearing a white shirt and black trousers, wrestled against the bridle, claw marks etched on the sides of his face. Every single room contained a silenced man.

"Come, the gathering is further down the hall. Ignore the banging. They'll tire themselves out sooner or later." Rowan looped her arm around Maria's and led her away from the doors.

Maria couldn't help but glance over her shoulders. Moans and feeble bangs followed their steps.

The main hall was like walking onto the set of *Pride and Prejudice*.

Cushy armchairs and sofas claimed every corner of the spacious dance hall. Dark-purple velvet curtains blocked the view from the tall windows. A red theater curtain obscured a shape that reminded Maria of a large, wide box at the end of the hall. Small groups of women in beautiful dresses and with elegant hairdos stood together, wine in hand, and chatted. Some of them seemed confident, excited even, at the promise of the evening. Others, like Maria, wore looks of nervousness, the question of why they should be here burning in their darting eyes. They huddled together, arms either crossed or fists clenched at their side, biting their lips.

Had they seen the men behind the doors as well?

"I'll let you mingle." Before Maria could politely object, Rowan released her gentle hold and wandered off, disappearing amongst the crowd.

Serpents coiled around Maria's gut, lunging at each other. She wasn't a fan of crowds, whether she was surrounded by fellow women or not. But this was the time to reclaim her bravery. To be outgoing again. She could do that with her peers. She wiped her clammy hands on her dress and walked to the nearest groups of women to her left. Some sat on the sofa while the others warmed themselves to the lit fireplace.

"Did you see the men out there?" Maria blurted out in a chuckle.

The women all turned in her direction. She blushed, cursing her sudden bluntness.

An Asian woman with an ornamental hairpin sticking out of her bun smirked. "I did. It was creepy at first, reminded me of mental patients, but then, I don't know, it looked *right* on them."

Most of them nodded.

"It means we don't have to listen to their bullshit tonight," a plump, middle-aged woman in a leather jacket piped up from the sofa.

Maria laughed. The others joined in and their laughter filled the hall. It warmed Maria's heart.

"Why are they there, though?" A young woman with curly red hair tied loosely in a braided updo asked as she fiddled with her gloves. Her pale eyes shot toward the door that led to the narrow hall.

The middle-aged woman snorted. "They're here for us."

"What do you mean?" the redhead asked.

The middle-aged woman leaned forward in her seat, a mixture of pity and trepidation painted on her face. "It's your first time getting an invitation, isn't it?"

The redhead nodded. So did Maria.

The middle-aged woman stretched her arms before getting comfortable against the velvet cushions. "This is my second time. You're in for a treat."

Maria's stomach sank. That meant she had experienced the trauma *twice*. She wanted to take that woman's hand, squeeze it and tell her it would be all right. That she wasn't alone. But the defiant glint in her eyes told Maria she didn't need to.

"What are we supposed to do?" Maria found herself asking out loud.

The woman turned to her with a wide smile, but then she shook her head. "Can't tell you because of the NDA. But you'll see sooner or later."

"I recognized one of the men inside the rooms," a blonde who sat next to the middle-aged woman muttered. Her posture stiffened, and her hands were balled into fists on her lap. Beads of tears sparkled in the corners of her smoky eyes.

"Really?" Maria asked. She didn't know anyone there, but then again, she hadn't looked into all the rooms. Glancing into two had been creepy enough. "Was it anyone you knew?"

The blonde clenched her jaw as she nodded. "That bastard attacked me."

Maria blinked. She turned toward the door. Cold realization seeped into her skin, creating gooseflesh across her arms. Did that mean *he* was here?

Rowan gave a low chuckle as she joined the group. "I thought you knew, Miss Lopez."

"How did you find him and the rest?" Maria searched Rowan's face for answers, but her smile kept all the secrets tightly locked.

"That is for me and the committee to know and worry about, my dear. However, he's here for the same reason as the rest."

A bell chimed before Rowan could explain further. The sound came from behind the dais. A woman around Rowan's age with cropped grey hair, emerged through the curtain, holding a bell in her hands. She nodded toward Rowan.

"Ah, I believe showing you would be a better explanation. For all of you, that is." Rowan gave Maria's hand a small squeeze before she left to join the woman in front of the curtain.

Both of them carried two large fishbowls to stone pedestals standing a few feet from the curtain. Small, folded pieces of paper filled both bowls.

Murmurs and whispers grew louder and more excited as women gathered around, forming a crescent opposite the pedestals. Maria's group stood tight knit in the center.

The instrumental background music faded away until the silence became nearly overpowering.

"Welcome, my dear ladies, to The Banquet, a secret annual event held by yours truly and my fellow committee members." Rowan flashed the women a gentle smile. "I'm sure you've all heard a rumor or two about our get-together?"

The Asian woman and the blonde stood between Maria and nodded. Others, including the redhead, shuffled their feet with their chins dipped, embarrassed that they believed in rumors. Maria felt that way, at least.

"Well, the rumors are true. This bowl here—" Rowan pointed to the bowl on her right, "—has all your names written on pieces of paper. I will draw one of those papers and read that name. The person whose name it belongs to will come up here and draw a slip from the second bowl." Rowan indicated the left pedestal.

A tense silence fell upon the group as they watched Rowan step to the first bowl. No one dared to ask what this all entailed, not even Maria. She could only watch, enthralled, breath trapped in her throat.

Rowan placed her hand inside and rummaged through the folded papers for a moment until her fingers enclosed around one. She unfolded the piece of paper, ran her eyes over the name, and looked up.

"Emma Thomas. Would you step up front, please?"

A slight whimper came from the redhead to Maria's left. The curly strands tickled her bare shoulders. Her gloved hands clutched the side of her dress as she took frightened steps toward the former mayor.

"Miss Thomas, you were assaulted by Richard Bower on February tenth, two years ago, is that correct?" Rowan asked.

Emma blanched, her eyes darting back and forth from Rowan to Maria and the rest of the women. Dull patches of shame bloomed on her pale cheeks. Her bottom lip trembled as she nodded.

"Bower went through trial, but due to the horrid state of our justice system, he was never convicted of his crime," Rowan stated.

Emma's eyes welled with tears. She gripped the dress so tightly Maria saw it crease badly in the light. "The judge said there wasn't sufficient evidence. It was only my word against his. He even said that I shouldn't tarnish the reputation of a good man with my lies." Emma's voice shook with barely contained rage.

Maria wanted to hug her. She knew that injustice far too well. It had happened at her trial. A lot, if not all, the women shared their sentiments. They glared at Rowan, as if angry that she had brought that unforgivable act back to the surface. Some of them wanted it buried deep, not to touch it ever again.

Rowan took hold of Emma's shoulders and embraced her. "I believe you, Emma. We all do." Rowan stroked Emma's hair, taking utmost care to not ruin her hairdo.

Emma's entire body quivered. Maria knew she was close to snapping, to releasing all her emotions and crying until she lost her voice. Maria had been standing on the verge of that cliff as well, but every time she had backed away, bottled everything, and kept it locked away in her heart. She heard sniffles among the group.

"I also believe in the term 'an eye for an eye, tooth for a tooth.' No bad deeds should go unpunished, especially one as heinous as this." Rowan led Emma to the second bowl, where a slightly smaller pile of folded paper awaited them.

Without words, Emma stuck her hand inside the bowl and fished out a paper slip. Afraid to see what was written, she handed it to Rowan, who opened it and read the contents. A glint of triumph gleamed in her eyes.

"Boots," she simply said.

The woman standing next to her nodded and strode out of the hall.

Whispers began anew, pondering what that word meant. The middle-aged woman's smirk grew wider as she smashed her fist into her palm. "This is going to be good."

Bees buzzed in Maria's head. She glanced at Rowan and the closed door between the women in the back. Suddenly she heard stomping and muffled voices approach the hall, but the noise never burst inside. Instead, it faded into the darkness.

"May I please direct your attention to the dais?" Rowan asked, standing beside it. She pulled on a rope dangling beside the heavy curtain. The curtain rose up with a whoosh, revealing dozens of huge flat screens propped up against the dark wall.

A screen in the middle flashed alive, showing video footage from a surveillance camera. Two darkly dressed men in hoods pulled a lean bald man through a deserted hallway. Maria squinted. It wasn't the same one she and Rowan had been in. Was it on the other side of the mansion? The man had been freed of the bridle and he used every opportunity to scream profanities, spittle raining down from his raging mouth.

"Let me go, you fuckers!" he shouted and planted his heels on the floor in an attempt to stop the men as they ascended a spiraling staircase.

Emma's eyes widened in shock and she gasped. "It's him!"

Maria watched as the men approached a lone door at the top of the staircase. The video blinked and changed footage, revealing a room. It looked empty save for the metal chair and harnesses in the center. Something long and heavy poked in the corner but the lightbulb hanging from the ceiling showered only the chair with its light. The door opened and the men strapped the man to the chair. His feet were held down by a belt on the floor instead of the chair itself. Then they tied curved iron plates studded with spikes to his legs. Bower yelped when the spikes touched the bare skin.

Rowan grabbed a microphone that was plugged to the screens and turned it on.

"Mr. Bower," Rowan said firmly, her motherly smile vanishing, replaced by an indifferent line. "You were arrested for the assault against Emma Thomas."

Bower started from the chair. His head swiveled in all directions, trying to see where the voice came from. "That was two years ago. I was acquitted," he snarled, his voice echoing.

"From a failed justice system, yes, but you're in my land now," Rowan leaned in close to the screen, hatred sparking in her narrowed eyes, "—and here, I am judge and jury. The part of the executioner falls upon Miss Emma Thomas, if she agrees to it."

Emma flinched as though she'd been slapped. Her head whipped from Rowan to the screen, confusion etched on her freckled face.

"Mr. Bower, for your atrocious crimes, I hereby sentence you to torture by booting. May you never hunt down a woman again."

Rowan patted Emma on the shoulder and gestured to the lady with the cropped hair who stood ready by the door. Emma gave a weak nod before they both disappeared behind the door. Maria and the rest of the women in the Banquet Hall watched Emma advance towards the room on one screen while the big one in the center displayed the hooded men placing iron wedges between the casing and Bower's flesh.

"Are you fucking serious?" he spluttered and struggled against the harnesses.

The door opened and the two women entered the room. Maria swallowed the sour taste in her mouth as she watched the lady handing Emma a mallet that had been kept in the corner. She grunted against the weight but held on tight.

Finally, she stood alone with Bower. His chest heaved as he glared daggers at her.

Emma kept her eyes on the floor. Even through a live video stream, Maria saw that she was trembling from head to foot. She took a step forward, but a hand grabbed hers.

Rowan pulled her back and shook her head. "This is her decision. We should respect that." She turned to the group. "If anyone finds this unsettling, you are free to leave the Banquet. Just remember our agreement and never speak of it again."

Maria wanted to say something, but Rowan was right. It all depended on what Emma wanted to do. She heard receding footsteps and the door closing. She looked behind her shoulders, startled to see that more than half had stayed put. Hungry eyes seeking retribution shone from the faces of most of the women. Nostrils flared and heavy breathing droned in Maria's ears, but she was relieved to find uncertainty within a handful of them, fearful hesitation rooting their feet to the floor.

"You really think you can do this?" Bower's voice snapped the tense air.

Maria's head whipped to the front.

Bower let out a harsh bark of a laugh. "You're nothing but cunts. Walking vaginas for us to stick our dicks in. You don't have the guts to pull something like this. You're just weak, pathetic worms for us to ste—"

Emma raised the mallet and swung it down. It hit one of the iron wedges, causing pressure between the casing and Bower's flesh. The spikes punctured his legs.

He let out a howl of pain.

"Don't *ever* call us weak again," Emma panted as she raised the mallet once more, striking the wedge for the second time.

Screams burst from the throng of women. The middle-aged woman cheered Emma on and spat insults at Bower. The blonde went pale and stared horror-struck at the screen. The Asian woman grabbed Maria's arm with a gasp, but seconds later, a hysterical laugh escaped her lips.

Maria waged a tug-o-war with her emotions. On one hand, she found the ordeal horrifying and couldn't imagine being in Emma's shoes. On the other, she *had* been in Emma's shoes and that part of her wanted to whoop and whistle. That part didn't want the torture to stop. That part of her *wanted* to participate.

Emma struck the wedges again and again, a smile creeping on her lips with each blow. Her smile grew bigger with each agonized scream. She didn't pause when his shattered tibia made Bower let out a scream that pierced the room and resonated around the hall. She didn't even halt when blood from his legs peppered her face. She only stopped when Bower's eyes bulged in torment one last time, his throat raw and dry. His head hung limp on his chest.

Applause clamored throughout the hall.

Panting, Emma threw the mallet down and searched for the camera. She looked up, her makeup grimed by the spatters of blood, grabbed the sides of her dress and curtsied.

"Well done, Emma. Fantastic job," Rowan said as Emma reemerged into the Banquet Hall. "How do you feel?"

Emma pushed sweaty strands of hair away from her face and took a shuddering breath. "I feel free."

Maria thought so she looked free as well. It looked as if Emma had years taken off her. The light in her eyes gleamed brilliantly, far brighter than the dull glow reflected from her own. She had craved for that light to return to her ever since the attack.

Pride radiated from Rowan as she gave Emma one final pat on the shoulders before releasing her to the group.

Maria watched the blonde pick from the lottery next.

Learning her name, Allison Connor, made her come alive. She wasn't some unknown girl that no one cared about. Here, everyone commiserated with her as they learned her story, her plight. While still pale, Allison clutched the paper slip in her hand and strode with her head high out of the Banquet Hall. She met with her rapist in what seemed to be a dark dungeon. He was held by the hooded men and pleaded for mercy as they listened to Rowan's judgment. Behind him stood a life-sized bronze bull.

Maria recognized the bull. She had read about it when she and Nicole had taken a class in Greek history in college. She clasped her hands over her chest as her heart throbbed in anticipation.

Piles of cut wood stacked one corner of the room. A can of kerosene lay next to them. The man begged in a hoarse voice as the hooded men thrust him inside the bull. He banged against the bronze plating. With her back turned to the camera, Allison threw wood under the bull. Next, she sprayed kerosene on it and lit the pile on fire with a match. She waited patiently in front of the bull and listened to the frantic bangs that intensified as the heat increased.

Maria and the others waited with bated breath.

A bellow of a bull pierced the room.

Maria flinched. Even Allison had taken a step back in shock. The middle-aged woman blew raspberries until it turned into a raucous shriek of a laugh. The bellows continued and tickled everyone's funny bone. Maria wondered if they knew that a special apparatus within the bull converted the man's screams into bellows as he roasted to death.

She detected no horror in their hungry eyes. Only Maria seemed to know, and it frightened her how quickly she had become desensitized to the display of torture.

"We have time for one more," Rowan said, plucking the slip of paper with elegant fingers. Her smile stretched wide. "Maria Lopez."

Maria's heart skipped a beat.

She squared her shoulders and strode to the bowl. She tried to steady her hand as she fumbled for a paper slip burrowed deep in the bowl.

Heart hammering against the ribcage and fighting the giddy nausea raging in her belly, Maria unfolded the paper and read aloud: "Pear of Anguish."

"Ah, marvelous. We haven't used that in a while."

She returned with a small, pear-shaped metal instrument. It had spoon-like segments that could be operated by the turn of a heart-shaped screw on top.

Maria's brow wrinkled in bewilderment. Rowan chuckled, leaned into her ear and whispered its purpose and methods.

Maria clasped a hand to her mouth. She was given authority to use *that*?

She sensed movement from the corner of her eye.

The hooded men dragged *him* to another chamber.

A low pitch seemed to burrow itself in Maria's ears, drowning Rowan's explanation of his crime. She could only see his bored expression, the same one he wore during the failed trial.

A horrible memory crawled from the depths of her mind.

After he had finished, he had stooped low, his breath on her frozen cheek. "You were a boring lay. I had at least anticipated a struggle from a hot-blooded Mexican."

Maria felt a room full of eyes staring her down. For a moment, she thought she was standing in the courtroom, accusing glares piercing her thick skin, turning it brittle.

She swallowed the sour bile rising up her throat and clutched the pear. Her heartbeat thumped in her palms.

"Whenever you're ready, Miss Lopez," Rowan said.

Maria opened her eyes. The women standing before her did not judge her. They wore expressions of solidarity and trust. They all had experienced the same kind of trauma and they had survived. Emma and Allison stood together and nodded to her. She was among warriors. Wolves in sheep's clothing. Maria took a deep shuddering breath. *Remember, you're here because you want to reclaim your life,* she reminded herself. She walked with determined steps out of the Banquet Hall to cheers and pats on her shoulder.

*O*nly a single door stood between Maria and Don Graham.

Her rapist.

Her hand rested on the doorknob. She wanted to open it, but every nerve in her body banded together and pulled her away from the door. What was wrong with her? In the Banquet Hall, she had been ready to storm into the room and make him suffer. Was it because she was alone now? No one to cheer her on? No one to gently push on the small of her back? She glanced over her shoulders, expecting to see Rowan on her way, but the hallway was deserted.

Maria gritted her teeth. *Remember why you came here.*

With every ounce of willpower in her being, she gripped the doorknob tight and turned.

283

Bright, fluorescent light blinked alive as soon as she entered the room. A strong chemical scent reminiscent of bleach punched Maria's nostrils. A wooden dresser with a metal tray on top took the left side of the room while coat stands with black latex aprons and a small metal furnace occupied the right side. Two grates on the stark white tile floor stuck out between the large metal table in the center of the room.

The men had strapped Don Graham on the metal table, spread-eagled, his hands and feet in chains dangling at the sides. He didn't look like the confident CEO executive of a bank firm from that position. He had been a person Maria once admired and respected. She remembered how ecstatic she had been when she had beat hundreds of women for an office clerk job in his firm. How he had given himself time from his busy schedule to help her get adjusted. How he had crushed her body and soul that night when no one was around.

"Who's there?" His voice sounded like he had ingested gravel.

Centipedes of unease crawled down Maria's back. It had been three years, and yet his voice had enough power to freeze her.

"You one of the women I saw walking past my cell this evening? Come over here so I can see you."

Maria felt like she was wading through thirty inches of mud. The rest of the mud clogged her insides. She placed the sweat-drenched pear on the dresser, afraid it'd slip from her hand and clatter to the floor. She noticed the metal tray had various sets of knives neatly arranged in order of size.

He raised his eyebrows in surprise when Maria stood in front of him, her back hovering against the wall.

"Lopez? What the hell are you doing here?"

The authority in his voice made Maria flinch. Despite being chained down on a table he still had this overpowering aura. She felt as if he had clamped her mouth shut.

"Hello? Hablas inglés?" he sneered.

A crack split in the dam within her, threatening to let everything spill. She inhaled through her nose and balled her hands into fists. "You should know why you're here."

Don Graham shrugged with difficulty as he donned a mask of bewilderment. "Haven't the slightest. Why don't you tell me?"

Maria was transported to the courtroom. The way he demanded an explanation reminded her of his asshole lawyer who had loomed over her at the stand with a smug grin on his face. A bead of sweat trickled down her back. She gave her head a quick shake. "You're here after what you did to me three years ago."

He let out a short laugh. "Seriously? I'm held against my will over something that *never* happened?"

Flames ignited in Maria's belly and pumped her blood into action. She grabbed the nearest knife on the dresser and held it in front of her. She had dreamed of this happening, fantasized horrific things being done to him if he ever got caught again, but now, given the opportunity, she had no idea what to do.

His condescending leer drilled holes into her confidence. "What are you going to do with that knife? Cut me?"

Maria's hand shook. She flicked the blade on his bare arm before she lost her nerve.

He yelped and yanked on the chain. "That hurt, you bitch!"

Maria stared at the blood leaking from the minuscule wound. Her heart pounded. From fear? From excitement? She wasn't sure, but she was eager to find out. She moved to the back where his legs were. She rolled one of the pants legs up, exposing his tense calf. She ran the blunt side of the blade against his skin. His leg flinched. It made Maria smile. The bastard was afraid.

"You scared, Don?" she was surprised to hear herself asking. To hear the tease in her voice, the control.

"Shut up and let me go."

Maria chuckled quietly. "Not until I'm done."

She held the knife above his Achilles tendon, wondering if she should slice horizontally or vertically. Which would hurt more? She decided on both. She held the blade firm as she pushed the sharp edge into his flesh. The knife vibrated as the taut nerves snapped in two. Her ears rang amid his screams. Warm blood oozed from the wound, coating the knife and her fingers. Pressure lifted from her chest. It had been obstructing her breathing since that fateful night.

"Please, stop. You can't do this to me!" He wailed.

Maria's heart leapt with elation. She hadn't felt that in years.

She tugged on his pants until the pant legs hit the bleeding wounds above his heels, earning her another scream. He could scream all he wanted. She wasn't done with him. "Move your hips."

Don Graham refused to comply.

"Oh, *now* you don't want to whip your dick out?" Maria scoffed. She took a clean knife with a serrated edge from the dresser and brandished it in front of his face. "If you don't obey, I will slit your throat right now."

Something between a grunt and a whimper crawled out of his mouth. He moved his hips with a wince. His flaccid penis rolled into sight.

Maria tilted her head as she examined it. "I can't believe your tiny-ass dick is uncircumcised. But I can help with that."

She pinched the foreskin between her fingers. His penis shrunk even more against the cold blade. "Hmmm, I need a better tool."

None of the knives on the tray looked appealing. She found a boxcutter in one of the dresser drawers, its blade rusty and blunt. Her fingers tingled at the sight of it.

Slicing off the foreskin was difficult work, but Maria relished the job. She hadn't expected so much blood to pour out, but it made her giddy nonetheless. Don Graham's howls of pain were like a symphony to her ears. She hummed along to the tune. She flicked the cut foreskin into the furnace and watched it sizzle into nothing.

Tears ran down Don Graham's face, his mask crumbling to pieces. "Please, *please* stop. I'll do anything. Just let me go, please." He sobbed the last words.

It wasn't enough. He hadn't experienced the same level of pain, humiliation and despair she had endured all those years.

A stoker stood rigid next to the furnace. She placed its end inside it and cleaned the knives as she waited. "You really think that's it? The end? A couple of slices here and there and you can just walk out of here with a few months of physical therapy? Do you have any idea how much time in therapy I had to go through? How many times I would just lie in bed and wish I had never woken up? How many times the darkness almost choked me? Do you have any idea how many friends and family I lost because of you?"

He shook his head, mucus oozing from his nose and mixing with the drool in his mouth.

"Exactly. You don't care. Men like you never do. Not until you experience the same kind of pain all of us carry after you rape us." Maria pulled the stoker out of the furnace, its end glowing bright red. The handle burned her palm, but she ignored it as she positioned herself in front of his bare ass.

"No, no, no, please, *please!*" His voice was raw from screaming.

Maria grew tired of his pathetic pleading and rammed the stoker into his anus, impaling him. The stench of burning flesh and blood quickly filled the room. Without skipping a beat, she grabbed the Pear of Anguish and shoved it into his already open mouth.

"Clench your teeth," she ordered.

She heard a crack and delighted that he would need new teeth after this. She leaned close, her fingers gripping the heart-shaped screw. "You know what I realized? You're boring. I was anticipating a struggle from a piece of shit like you."

She turned the screw slowly, knowing the petals would bloom with each crank.

Each turn of the screw represented the anguish she had felt after the assault.

Each agonizing muffled yowl and the sight of his bulging eyes broke a chain that had held her prisoner since then.

Soon, she would be free like Emma and Nicole and countless other women who had received an invitation to The Banquet.

Tears mingled with her laughter.

Soon, she'd have her life back.

NIGHTLY ENCOUNTERS:
Acknowledgments and Inspirations

I don't know about you, but I really enjoy reading the final section of a short story collection where the author gives the reader a little bit more insight into their stories and the reasons behind their creations. So, of course I'm including a sneak peek into my depraved mind and hoping you won't be too appalled.

A MOTHER'S JOB

This story is actually the first short story that I wrote and actually completed. I had started on a short story while I was working on the second book of vampire horror series, but I never completed it (I will eventually, of course).

Being a huge zombie fan, I've always wanted to write a zombie story, but I never knew where to start. One of the favorite things I love about zombie stories is the moral and emotional aspect of them, like you see in *The Walking Dead*, for example. I love the gory stuff too, but seeing people struggle with their moral compass is more fascinating to me because I always start to wonder what *I* would do in that situation. Movies like *Cargo* and *Mandy* both deal with parental figures and their difficult decisions concerning their children in a zombie apocalypse and they're what inspired me to write this story.

I was ecstatic that it found a home in Jazz House Publications' autumn anthology *Of Cottages and Cauldrons* in 2020 and it boosted my confidence in continuing to write more short stories.

THE THRILL OF THE HUNT

This was the second story I ever wrote, and it came to me after listening nonstop to a podcast called Serial Killers on Spotify.

Like any horror fan, watching, reading, and listening to true crime stories is one of my favorite past times. Really, nothing gets me happier than going on a brisk walk around the neighborhood, listening to a podcaster describing horrid murder scenes. Serial killers in particular have always fascinated and horrified me at the same time, especially how most media tend to cover only the killer and not the victims. It's like stepping into a terrifying new world and I really wanted to explore that.

I'm not going to lie, I felt unclean writing in the serial killer's POV. I had a frown on my face the entire time. Thoughts of how most victims and their families don't get the proper justice raced through my mind, so you can imagine the immense pleasure I got while writing the serial killer's comeuppance. Revenge stories really are my guilty pleasures.

I was afraid no one would enjoy this little story of mine, but luckily Kandisha Press loved it and published it in their *The One Who Got Away: Women of Horror Volume 3* in March 2021.

TAUMUR

When people think of Iceland, the first things that come to mind are the northern lights, hot springs, the midnight sun, and our delightful Icelandic horses, just to name a few. They don't, however, think of monsters or mythical creatures (except for maybe the Huldufólk). I don't blame them. Iceland is just a tiny island way up in the north Atlantic. Tourists would rather focus on the beautiful landscape and the rough, almost non-touched environment.

I've also noticed a lack of the Icelandic folklore being used in horror, aside from the occasional supernatural crime noirs published in Iceland. It's a shame because monsters are abundant in Iceland, most of them are even allegedly recorded in our ancient history texts. One such creature is *Taumur*, the titular sea monster in this story. I wanted to explore some of the lesser-known Icelandic monsters and since I have a crippling fear of the sea, a story about Vikings, betrayal during the brutal winter night in the middle of the Atlantic Ocean slid silently into my head and attacked.

It was quite fun to attempt to write the dialogue a little bit differently as well as using Icelandic names. I can already picture the readers trying to pronounce them.

THE MOSS-COVERED VOLCANO

I wrote this story shortly after the eruption in Fagradalsfjall early this year (2021).

The eruption might still be ongoing even after this collection has been published, which would be insane! As with most volcanic eruptions, it attracted a lot of attention from both locals and tourists. As time went by, there were a lot of news and footages of people risking their lives by approaching the lava stream or even walk on the barely hardened lava. I was really annoyed that people wouldn't listen or respect the rules and boundaries set by us Icelanders and since I couldn't reprimand them myself, I decided to vent my frustrations into this story.

I sprinkled a little bit of Icelandic folklore with the Huldufólk and the result was immensely satisfying in my opinion. Moral of the story: Don't piss off writers. We might just kill you off in the most gruesome fashion.

NAILS

One of my worst fears is to break my teeth or have my fingernails extracted. The former almost happened to me when I was fourteen years old, and I was playing around in a sleeping bag and my little brother thought it'd be a good idea to *step* on the sleeping bag. I faceplanted on the floor, resulting in one of my front tooth's roots dying. Fun times.

So, naturally I can't read or watch anything that involves teeth or fingernails in horror without my stomach turning. But I'm a masochist because this little imp creature popped into my head, pulling out fingernails and eating them. It demanded to be put on paper and if I wanted to sleep peacefully again, I had to write it.

I was surprised how much I enjoyed writing it. I guess the advice "write what you fear" really helps. I was inspired by *The Twilight Zone*'s episode "Nightmare at 20,000 feet" where the protagonist is an unreliable narrator, and you don't really know if it's all in his head or not.

HOPE

This story was originally written and submitted to Scott J. Moses' *What One Wouldn't Do* anthology, but sadly it wasn't accepted.

Once I heard of the theme, an idea of a desperate father trying to do whatever it took to save his daughter crawled from the depths of my mind. I don't have children of my own, but I definitely understood Barry's despair. However, what scared me the most was I could picture it happen somewhere in the world. So, in a way this story could be interpreted as a cautionary tale for Tinder/online dating.

The werewolf mauling at the end of the story was actually inspired by Zack Snyder's *Army of the Dead*. I did not enjoy that movie as much as I would have wanted but Valentine the zombie tiger and the way it killed the traitor completely made up for it.

THE DOLL MUSEUM

I don't know about you, but dolls freak me out. I only had one doll as a kid, and it was child-sized Palm Pals doll that stuck out its tongue. It reminded me of Emil, the protagonist of the popular Swedish children's story *Emil i Lönneberge,* so naturally I named it that. I took him everywhere and didn't find him creepy at all. But it changed when my aunt once got me a porcelain doll for Christmas. There was something about those dead eyes that seemed to stare into your soul, grabbing your deepest secrets to keep until the time was right. Needless to say, that doll unnerved me, so I kept it staring out the window most of the time before I threw it away after coloring its hair with blue nail polish.

I got the idea for this story by mixing together my fear of dolls, the 1953 classic horror movie *House of Wax* and the real horrid story of Anatoly Moskvin who snatched up 29 corpses of girls and dressed them up as dolls.

Those who have read the books in my Nocturnal series might have noticed a connection between the world of vampires and the killer in this story.

SPLIT

I got the idea for this story when Dark Dispatch announced an identity horror theme for its *Dead Inside* anthology. I had never properly researched what identity horror was but after reading Sandra Ruttan's short story, I had a vague idea that transformed into a full-blown story. It ended up being shortlisted for the anthology but in the end, they had to pass on it.

I do enjoy reading and watching spy stories but most of them heavily rely on the action of being a spy with all the cool gadgets and speedy cars. I hadn't really delved deep into the psychological aspect on having these double identities until I watched *Red Sparrow*. I loved the dark atmosphere with second-guessing on who was the good guy and Jennifer Lawrence's performance in it was superb. There was one scene that really got to me and that was the torture scene, and I will admit that I borrowed elements from that scene to use in my story.

I really loved exploring the tug-o-war that raged inside Katerina's mind, whether she could continue on with the double identity but ultimately, she had to choose. Whether she chose the right thing, I'll leave it up to the readers.

SKÖTUMÓÐIR

I'm going to be honest here. Found footage horror is not one of my favorite horror genres. The shaky camera makes me queasy and most of them don't really scare me. But I had never written a found footage short story before, so I went out of my comfort zone and created this story, featuring another Icelandic monster.

I've always had this idea of writing a full-length Icelandic horror novel with this creature. This story is kind of a sampler for it since I haven't shelved that idea completely. So be on the lookout for this terrifying monster in the future.

THE RESCUE

Along with my morbid fascination with serial killers, cults are a phenomenon that really boggles my mind. I've always been a person who questions and overthinks everything. I consider myself lucky that I haven't stumbled upon a charismatic leader that'll whisk me off my feet and turn my life upside down in the name of some religion. Other people who are down on their luck haven't been so fortunate and reading about their lives in a cult is both engrossing and horrifying.

After listening to *Cults*, a podcast about, you guessed it, cults for an indecent amount of time, an idea struck me. I wanted to see if I could create a creepy little cult that worshipped a Lovecraftian deity. I've always wondered what would happen if the deities those cults worshipped actually existed and if their faith would withstand the horror it brought forth.

That I managed to creep out my alpha reader with my cult followers was a huge success in my books. I wonder if I managed the same success with you, dear reader?

SHED THE NIGHT'S SKIN

My friend Damascus approached me one night and asked if I'd be willing to write a collaborative story with him. I, of course, jumped at the chance since I quite enjoy Damascus' prose and his reanimated dialogue.

We both delight reading about Native American folklore and we settled on writing about a skin-walker. We took turns writing a part of the story and then combined them together, so you might have noticed the style change a little bit. It was a lot of fun and definitely cemented our path in co-writing more stories together.

RECEIVING IS BETTER THAN GIVING

Christmas traditions are important to us Icelanders and we still celebrate them even though the underlying meaning has escaped the modern times. Folklore lies deep within our Christmas traditions, particularly concerning the thirteen Yule lads, their heinous troll mother Grýla and her gigantic Yule cat.

Being a mother of two cats and having been raised in a home that always had cats, you can imagine the Yule Cat being my favorite of our Christmas folklore.

The legend of the Yule Cat was used by farmers to make sure that their workers would finish getting the wool ready before Christmas. Those who finished received new clothes, but those who were lazy got nothing and were threatened with the monstrous cat.

This legend still lives on in the hearts of Icelanders and it's very common to give at least one type of clothing, be it socks or even mittens, for Christmas so that the Yule Cat won't come and eat you.

It was very easy for me to come up with a haunting Christmas story when Jazz House Publications announced its submission call for Krampus Tales: A Killer anthology and I was overjoyed when my story found its home there.

KOKKURI-SAN

I'm a language nerd and can safely proclaim that I have some proficiency in at least three or four languages. Japanese and the culture within has always had special place in my heart, ever since *Akira* traumatized my young, tender mind as a child. I studied Japanese in university, eventually earning a BA degree in it. I spent two years living in Japan, so I'd like to think I'm well acquainted with the culture.

Everyone knows about Ouija boards, but few know that the Japanese have a similar "game". It became popular among elementary and junior high school students in Japan when the manga *Ushiro no Hyakutaro* depicted characters playing Kokkuri-san in 1970. Kids played it for fun most of the time but eventually teachers and parents had to step in and warn them not to play it anymore when it began taking its toll on them mentally. There were even rumors of children going crazy and even being hospitalized.

Bullying is a huge thing in Japan, especially if you're different from the rest. I've seen and read many depictions of bullying in Japanese movies and mangas and I wanted to write my own version of it.

While I delight in revenge stories, I wanted to show there are consequences when you summon a spirit. Especially if said spirit is known for trickery.

WHAT THE CHEF RECOMMENDS

There were two things that inspired me to write this story: the manga *The Promised Neverland* by Kaiu Shirai and Hailey Piper's short story "Recitation of the First Feeding". The demons and their insatiable appetite for human flesh from *The Promised Neverland* unnerved me and I loved the prose Hailey conjured up in her Cenobite-esque tale. I wanted to see if I could create something similar while still holding on to my favorite theme, the bonds of family.

I absolutely felt Mona's grief for her husband's death but loved how her determination to protect the rest of her family shone in her actions. I wanted the demon entity to be weak against the unsuspecting gems of nature, so I sought help from the horror community on Twitter, asking for uncommon ingredients that a chef could use. They certainly didn't disappoint, and I was flooded with suggestions. In the end, I couldn't just pick one ingredient because like Mona, I wasn't sure if one ingredient would be enough to take down an unknown demonic entity. So, I almost picked all of them, but in the end, poisonous herbs and berries were the real winner and it fitted Mona in two aspects: She was a woman, and it is believed that women typically killed using poison and her background in living in a hippie commune, learning about the good and bad side of nature.

THE BANQUET

The week from March 8th to March 15th was an emotional rollercoaster for women. We celebrated International Women's Day where the theme centered on achieving an equal future in leadership in a Covid-19 world.

While it was supposed to be a week where we celebrated our success, people lashed out when a woman mentioned in a controversial interview that she wasn't allowed proper mental health care in a time of need.

Then on March 9th, the world discovered the tragic murder of Sarah Everard. She had been on her way home from a friend's house, but a police officer had kidnapped and killed her. Her murder is but a drop in the bottomless ocean on how common it is that women are attacked. People got online and criticized her decision on walking by herself, why she hadn't taken a taxi or let her friend drive her home, basically victim-blaming her.

It made me mad.

The whole ordeal that women are expected to take great care in protecting themselves while going on a walk and yet still have to face accusations if they get attacked makes me furious.

The problem is not us.

It's with the bastards that attack us. Those who can't be civilized among us. Those who only look at us as objects. They are solely to blame.

I needed an outlet for my fury and thankfully, my outlet is writing. While I read the news and scrolled through various Tweets from women, sharing their experiences, I had an idea for a story. Survivors may not have a chance to get back at their attackers, but I could give them an example through my story. I shared this idea to the horror community on Twitter and received a positive response.

That is, until one man stepped up, quoted my tweet and said I shouldn't write it because there was enough man-bashing in the world already.

His tweet fueled my desire to write this story even more.

Because this story isn't meant for him or any other man who shares his misogynistic views.

It's meant for us.

ACKNOWLEDGEMENTS:

After working on my vampire horror series and producing 4 books with the 5th one in progress, it's always such a nice reprieve to let my mind wander into shorter stories.

Ever since reading Shirley Jackson's *The Lottery*, I've always had great respect and fascination for short stories. I knew writing a novel was hard but for some reason, I always figured writing short stories was even *harder.* I mean, I'm not wrong. Creating a full-blown story in such a short format is difficult but it's always invigorating and a great mental challenge.

For the last two years, I've been writing short stories and submitting them to various anthologies. Some managed to receive a nice home while others were comfortable in staying with little ol' me. Those ended up in this debut collection of mine and I want to express my thanks to the people who helped me reach this point in my publishing career.

Thank you, Becky Wright from Platform House for doing a spectacular interior design and formatting.

Thank you, Matt Wildasin, for designing a killer book cover. I approached him with some ideas of what I liked and it took him no more than a few days to create a haunting cover fitting for my stories.

Thank you to my alpha reader, Damascus Mincemeyer, my writing partner in crime, who was always willing to read my stories once I finished writing them and giving me great feedback.

Thank you to my beta readers, Richard, Jacob, Jim, Mitch and Cat, who read through my collection and gave me helpful tips and suggestions on making the stories better. Their advice gave me enough courage to submit my collection to indie presses.

Thank you to the horror community on Twitter that has always been so supportive of me and my writing, whether it's cheering me on when I get a fresh idea for a story or when I'm promoting my stuff.

Thank you to my family and my husband who have always been super supportive of my macabre tales.

And finally, thank you, dear reader, for taking a chance on my debut collection. I truly hope you survived the night and that you will tell others about the experience.

Milton Keynes UK
Ingram Content Group UK Ltd.
UKHW040856181023
430840UK00001B/12

9 798223 635123